THE CAPITAL MURDER

THE CAPITAL MURDER

James Z. Alner

COACHWHIP PUBLICATIONS
Greenville, Ohio

The Capital Murder, by James Z. Alner
© 2018 Coachwhip Publications
Introduction and Afterword © 2018 Curtis Evans

Published 1932
No claims made on public domain material.
Cover image: *Bothrops* (1867) by Leopold Joseph Fitzinger

CoachwhipBooks.com

ISBN 1-61646-424-0
ISBN-13 978-1-61646-424-0

INTRODUCTION

THE CAPITAL MURDER, BY JAMES Z. ALNER
(JAMES ALNER TOBEY)

Curtis Evans

Take it from Alfred A. Knopf or leave it; but he has published a book by an author whose name he doesn't even know. It is a detective story, called "The Capital Murder," and the name given is James Z. Alner, freely acknowledged to be just a nom de plume.

The only address accompanying the manuscript was New York General Delivery. And checks are cleared by this "Mr. Alner" through the Chase National Bank. The contract was signed by mail and all communication has been through the good offices of the U. S. Postmasters General and his able staff.

The leading character in the story is an epidemiologist, which gives rise to the theory that the author is a scientist. However, he might be a stone mason or an actor at leisure or even the long-absent Judge Crater, for all Mr. Knopf knows. It is very mysterious and puzzling and has aroused the interest of the Knopf office no end. However, it is very likely that when a statement of royalties falls due, Mr. Knopf will have little trouble in reaching the anonymous writer. That always brings them around, as fish food brings the goldfish and delphinium catches the worms.[1]

Remaining stubbornly unknown for 85 years was the true identity of the author of *The Capital Murder*, which, as shown in the above excerpt from a books column by one "Jerome Coignard" (this name itself probably is a pen name), was published in 1932 by the pseudonymous James Z. Alner. Longtime mystery fiction expert Allen J. Hubin has suggested that James Zalner (1887-1950), a Lithuanian immigrant who resided for decades in Binghamton, New York, might have been the man behind *The Capital Murder*, but here in the introduction to the first reprinting of the novel I can confidently assert that extant evidence points overwhelmingly toward Dr. James Alner Tobey as the gentleman in question.

James Alner Tobey was born on July 15, 1894 in Quincy, Massachusetts to Rufus Tolman Tobey, a jeweler and amateur horticulturist descended from generations of Maine farmers (including James Shapleigh, a first lieutenant in the Maine militia for whom James Tobey had been named and who served as the basis for his 1915 admission into the Sons of the American Revolution), and Mary Ann Sherry, daughter of English immigrant William Alner Sherry, a fresco painter and partner in the prominent Boston interior design firm Wallburg & Sherry. An energetic and industrious scholar, James Tobey was extensively educated at the Roxbury Latin School, the oldest school in continuous existence in North America; the Massachusetts Institute of Technology, where he served as both the vice president of the chess club and a lieutenant in the Cadet Corps; George Washington University Law School; and American University. During much of the First World War, he was employed with the Board of Health in West Orange, New Jersey.

In 1918 Tobey, while on leave in Manhattan from mosquito eradication work in Charleston, South Carolina, wed Lena May, daughter of a farmer from Catskill, New York. The couple, who would have two children together, resided in Washington, DC, before settling in the well-healed community of Rye, in Westchester County, New York, boyhood home of Founding Father John Jay. After the Second World War, Dr. Tobey and his wife moved for a time to affluent Newtown, Connecticut, made tragically infamous in 2012 by the Sandy Hook Elementary School shooting; there in 1955 the ever-prolific Dr. Tobey published yet another book, *The 250th Anniversary of Newtown,*

DR. JAMES A. TOBEY

Connecticut, 1705-1955. The couple would later return to Rye, where Dr. Tobey passed away at the age of 86 on November 23, 1980.

Though still a young man in the 1920s, Tobey by that decade had established himself as a prominent public health official in the northeastern United States, serving with numerous public and private health organizations and publishing myriad books and articles on the subject of wellness and disease eradication. Among his serious works are *Riders of the Plagues: The Story of the Conquest of Disease* (1930); the pioneering *Cancer: What Everyone Should Know About It* (1932), which includes a forward by H. L. Mencken, to whose magazine *The American Mercury* Tobey was a frequent contributor; and *Public Health Law* (1947), deemed by scholar Edward P. Richards the "last great public health law treatise."[2] His many health and medical articles spanned such topics as "Common Colds," "Cancer Quacks," "Facts about Milk," "Heart Disease," "White Bread Versus Brown," "The Control of Human Sterility," "The Modern Concept of Leprosy," "The Truth about Acidosis" and "The Army and Venereal Disease." Another piece provocatively asserted, "We Could Eat Acorns and Weeds." Clearly in many respects Dr. Tobey was a man ahead of his time.

Like other advanced Progressive thinkers of his day, Dr. Tobey in the 1920s and 1930s advocated, to quote from one of his monthly columns in the newsletter of the American Public Health Association, "the centralization of federal health work" into one vast Department of Health. This vision finally would be realized in 1953, when the United States Congress and the administration of the newly-elected President Eisenhower created a cabinet level Department of Health, Education and Welfare, since 1979 the Department of Health and Human Services.

Around the time of the writing of *The Capital Murder*, Tobey forcefully challenged Ray Lyman Wilbur—secretary of the interior under Republican president Herbert Hoover and later a prominent exponent of "rugged individualism" and critic of Democratic president Franklin Roosevelt's New Deal—when Wilber sanguinely pronounced, amid the agonizing throes of the Great Depression, that the health of the country's children would likely benefit from economic crisis, by inducing lax parents to tighten their belts and prioritize their children's care. "Anxiety, fear, discouragement and other effects of economic strain can and do lead to mental troubles, which may adversely influence the health and well-being of individuals," countered Dr. Tobey, reasonably enough.[3]

No doubt when the eminent Dr. Tobey in 1932 submitted the manuscript for *The Capital Murder* to the prestigious publishing firm Alfred A. Knopf, he believed he had a public reputation to protect and thus circumspectly sought to conceal his sole contribution to classic crime fiction in a cloak of protective anonymity. (Tobey dedicated the book to his father, hiding his father's name as well, behind the initials "R. T. T.") To be sure, Knopf's stable of mystery writers at the time included the estimable hard-boiled icons Dashiell Hammett and Raoul Whitfield and the popular English writer J. S. Fletcher, viewed by many Americans at the time (however improbable this may seem to us today) as the most distinguished mystery writer from the British Isles since Arthur Conan Doyle, creator of Sherlock Holmes; yet Knopf's stable also harbored admittedly lesser detective fiction lights, ones entirely faded today, such as Stanley Hart Page and Maurice C. Johnson, which likely emboldened Dr. Tobey to make his lone mystery writing venture. Certainly Dr. Tobey would have been far from alone among highly educated and professionally accomplished persons at the time in having both the yen for reading detective fiction and the desire and the will to try his own hand at it; for this was the era when the detective story was considered "the normal recreation of noble minds," in the words, we are told, of English barrister and author Philip Guedalla.

*****

James Tobey's sole published detective story, *The Capital Murder*, is set in—it should not surprise readers of this introduction to learn—Washington, DC, capital of the United States of America, where James Tobey resided in the 1920s, when he attended George Washington University Law School and American University and later served as administrative secretary of the National Health Council, a nonprofit association of health organizations founded in 1922. The novel concerns the strange demise of a beautiful, enigmatic blonde,

Beatrice Sigurda, late of the Argentine. With two tiny puncture marks in her neck and a "look of inexplicable horror" on her face, she is found quite eerily dead while seated fully clothed on the "rich red divan" in the "luxurious sitting room" of her house on Q Street, located just a few blocks from the Serpentine Club in N Street, where regularly gather five distinguished men—Commissioner Henry Selden, of the Public Service Commission of the District of Columbia, Lieutenant Runy O'Mara, of the United States Navy, Doctor Basil Ragland, an eminent psychiatrist, Lance Starr-Smith, a famous architect, and Trevor Stoke, an epidemiologist with the federal health service—to discuss murder and other fine arts. Also in the company of the

accomplished men is "Jim," an utter nonentity conveniently on hand to chronicle the tale as Trevor Stoke's "Watson."

Although all of these men play a role in the investigation and elucidation of the case, the star detective, as it were, is Trevor Stoke, of whom Jim worshipfully writes:

> No serious outbreak of disease could occur anywhere in the country without Stoke, who would appear calmly on the scene sooner or later. If the epidemic involved interstate affairs, the Government sent him in; if it was purely a local matter, the state health authorities invariably invited his services. Typhoid, cholera, typhus, septic sore throat, and other maladies yielded to his uncanny ability to run down the true causes of outbreaks. . . . He developed into the greatest of sanitary detectives.
>
> Stoke was no sallow scientist, but a virile individual. His war record had brought him a medal or two for bravery under fire when he was supposed to be behind the lines in his laboratory, and his civilian career had shown him to be resourceful and courageous. Although well built, he was of medium size and rather ordinary in appearance, neither handsome nor homely, but simply an alert, normal person who enjoyed life and worked hard for an indifferent salary.

It likely will have occurred to readers that this is something of a fulsomely flattering self-portrait rendered by Dr. Tobey, but then if Dorothy L. Sayers could place herself into her Lord Peter Wimsey detective saga as clever mystery novelist Harriet Vane, why should Dr. Tobey not have been able to play detective as Trevor Stoke? And, truth be told, the fiendish murder of Beatrice Sigurda proves a most appropriate case for an epidemiologist sleuth. As some readers of vintage mystery no doubt will discern, *The Capital Murder* slightly anticipates a celebrated slaying in a debut detective novel by a vastly better-known mystery writer from the 1930s, but I will say no more on this particular subject in order to avoid spoilers.

In his only known detective novel Dr. Tobey evinces familiarity with detective fiction of the classic era, referencing not only the great Sherlock Holmes, of course, but Dupin, Lecoq, Max Carrados, Reggie Fortune, Peter Wimsey, Anthony Gethryn, and Philo Vance. Trevor Stoke's self-effacing chronicler, Jim, is, to be sure, every bit as forgettable as Philo Vance's wallflower amanuensis, Van; and it is amusing indeed when, at the climax of the novel, the cornered culprit snarls to Trevor Stoke, "Yes, I killed . . . Beatrice Sigurda . . . and now I'm going to kill you, you and that nincompoop toady of yours!" Seldom has even a lowly Watson been afforded so little respect.

Not amusing at all (though it is revealing of the times), is the casual racial and ethnic prejudice expressed by several characters in the novel, including Jim himself (see the afterword); yet readers who enjoy Dr. Tobey's essay in fictional foul play, of which the "method used by the murderer of Beatrice Sigurda" was praised as "ingenious" by the *New York Times Book Review*, will regret that Jim never actually chronicled Trevor Stoke's *second* case, concerning the matter of the US congressman's corpse "found crammed in a locker of a leading golf club in the District of Columbia." Intrepid Trevor Stoke canceled his impending errand to battle a plague of hookworms in the Virgin Islands in order to solve this baffling case, which concerns yet another dastardly crime masterminded by a member of the most diabolically lethal species of them all: *man!*

Footnotes:

[1] Jerome Coignard, "Of the Making of Books," *Brooklyn Daily Eagle*, May 22, 1932. The Jimmy Hoffa of the Thirties, Judge Joseph Force Crater was a New York State Supreme Court Justice with suspected Tammany Hall connections who vanished on August 6, 1930. He was declared legally dead nearly a decade later, on June 6, 1939.

[2] See "Historic Public Health Law Books" at http://biotech.law.lsu.edu/index.htm.

[3] "Child Health in the Depression," *New York Times*, 1 December 1932.

THE CAPITAL MURDER

To
R. T. T.

CHAPTER I
FIVE MEN AROUND A TABLE

When the strange death of Beatrice Sigurda was announced, five men were gathered about a table in a garden. Midnight had come and gone. Earlier that evening this moonlit garden had been the scene of life and gayety, but now it was dark and somber, lonesome and almost deserted.

Four of these men were listening intently to the fifth, who was standing by the table, leaning a little forward with his hands upon it. Over him a Japanese lantern moved lazily in the sultry air and cast weird shadows across his face, accentuating the gravity of his demeanor.

"Gentlemen," he was saying, "as a climax to the events of this evening we have murder itself. I have just been notified that the dead body of a woman, a woman known to all of you, has been found in a house on Q Street not a quarter of a mile from this club."

The commissioner paused, but none of the men spoke.

"While we have been discussing crime in this garden and hearing strange noises and seeing strange things, a crime is committed in our immediate vicinity. At midnight the corpse of Beatrice Sigurda was discovered under conditions that are extremely suspicious. It seems unquestionably to be murder."

Again he paused. Reality had intruded upon the unreal. As Commissioner Selden had so aptly declared, this was the climax to a series of startling episodes on that fateful June night. What had begun as an evening of festival and entertainment had ended in tragedy. Between its beginning and end there had transpired many events directly concerned with the crime itself.

Time and place contributed to the sensational aspects of this macabre announcement, but no more so than the five men who received it. They were unusual men, individuals of distinctive and vivid characteristics. Each was destined to play an important part in the solution of this perplexing mystery, which came to be known throughout the country as "the Capital murder." The leading role fell, however, to my distinguished friend Trevor Stoke. It was he, you may remember if you followed the case, who was actually responsible for clearing up this peculiar crime, even though Detective Yates received most of the public credit for it.

A challenge earlier in the evening really started Trevor Stoke on his celebrated career as a detective, although he had been a species of sleuth for many years. Stoke was an epidemiologist with our federal health service; in other words, a national authority on epidemics and their varied causes.

No serious outbreak of disease could occur anywhere in the country without Stoke, who would appear calmly on the scene sooner or later. If the epidemic involved interstate affairs, the Government sent him; if it was purely a local matter, the state health authorities invariably invited his services. Typhoid, cholera, typhus, septic sore throat, and other maladies yielded to his uncanny ability to run down the true causes of the outbreaks.

Activities such as these constitute detective work of a high order, but never before had Stoke been called upon to investigate a deliberate homicide. That his training for this unusual task had been efficient was soon demonstrated by his methods and results. He developed into the greatest of sanitary detectives.

Stoke was no sallow scientist, but a virile individual. His war record had brought him a medal or two for bravery under fire when he was supposed to be behind the lines in his laboratory, and his civilian career had shown him to be resourceful and courageous. Although well built, he was of medium size and rather ordinary in appearance, neither handsome nor homely, but simply an alert, normal person who enjoyed life and worked hard for an indifferent salary.

Among Stoke's diversions was the Serpentine Club, in the garden of which we were gathered on that June night six years ago. He liked the old red brick building on N Street where Secretary Seward had once lived, but most of all he liked the quaint garden which distinguished this one bohemian resort in the entire District of Columbia.

This garden was extensive for a dwelling in the heart of such a city as the nation's capital. Its area was sufficient to accommodate a hundred or more persons at one time, as it did on those evenings when the customary monthly entertainments were held. The members and guests sat at tables under the acanthus trees or near the poplars which lined the high brick walls with which the garden was surrounded on three sides.

In this sedate retreat, away from the noise and confusion of the city, one could read in peace, or sup in cool shade, or drowse in the enervating atmosphere of midsummer along the Potomac, or indulge in stimulating conversation, somewhat different from the crass oratory in vogue on Capitol Hill at the other end of the city. Domino-players were at a minimum in this club.

The table occupied by the five men who had lingered late in the garden on this particular night was situated near one of the brick walls which separated the garden from an alley. Close to the table was an unpainted wooden door which gave every evidence of rare use. No one was ever seen to enter or go out by it. For all practical purposes it was part of the vine-covered wall. But not on this evening.

Several groups had remained in the garden after the entertainment, which as usual among such an unusual membership was bizarre, aesthetic, and dull by turns. Eventually all had departed except these five men, these five who were so different and yet who found so much in common.

Besides Stoke, who seemed relatively inconspicuous in this coterie, there was Henry Selden, then one of the three commissioners of the District of Columbia, Dr. Basil Ragland, the eminent psychiatrist, Lieutenant Runy O'Mara of the United States Navy, and Lance Starr-Smith, the famous architect. To be strictly accurate, there were six. I was the sixth. My sole function, however, was that of a listener and later a chronicler of the stirring adventures that ensued.

Of these five men, Lance Starr-Smith was the most striking in appearance and personality. He was tall and muscular and his visage was adorned by a luxurious black beard, not one of those piquant Vandykes, but a well-rounded one, positively vibrant in its general quality. To his intimates, who were few, the dignified architect was known as Bushy. Not many persons were able to penetrate beneath the austere reserve with which he usually surrounded himself; few desired to do so, in fact, for he had an incisive tongue and a cynical disposition. Despite this discomforting drawback, if it was one, he was brilliant, interesting, and at times entertaining.

All of these men were directly interested and even involved in the science of criminology. Mr. Selden, for example, had jurisdiction over the metropolitan police department, among other city divisions. Dr. Ragland had long been an authority on the medico-legal aspects of poisons, although in recent years he had specialized in mental diseases. The debonair Runy O'Mara had seen service in the intelligence department of the Navy before his mechanical-engineering genius had brought about his transfer to the Bureau of Aeronautics and the control of one of the drafting-rooms. Starr-Smith had designed the new District jail and was said to have delved deeply into the study of crime.

No wonder, then, that this notable quintet had been drawn together as if by an invisible magnet. Perhaps fate had a share in it, perhaps something more tangible.

From ghosts to criminals is an easy transition. The conversation that evening had started on the subject of the supernatural. Starr-Smith, who seemed pensive at first and devoted to star-gazing, had suddenly come to life and regaled us in his pleasantly resonant voice with a gruesome narrative of a nocturnal visitor of revenant characteristics who had come to him at his former studio in the historic old Octagon House on Eighteenth Street.

Talk was not the only event in the garden that night, but only the prelude to things more dramatic.

"What a gorgeous night for a murder!" Runy had remarked, cocking an eye at the moon.

Mr. Selden gazed at his ebullient young friend with frank disapproval. The commissioner was old enough to be Runy's father and was conscious of the fact. He was the typical successful business man in public life, with close-cropped mustache and iron-gray hair, a member of every important civic and commercial organization in the city, genial, officious.

"Murder," he declared, "does not occur in such an orderly community as this."

"Do you really suffer such a delusion?" asked Starr-Smith with what might be suspected as a polite sneer.

"There are, unfortunately, criminals in every community," said Dr. Ragland, "just as there are many other diseased persons. The criminal," he continued, "is invariably ill, mentally if not physically, emotionally without question."

"But, doctor," interposed Runy, "some of these playful gents who poison their sweethearts with exotic chemicals, as they all do, and who otherwise disport themselves must be fairly intelligent. Some of them must, in fact, be positive geniuses. Many crimes are planned and executed with real finesse, obviously by men of talent, if not of scruples."

"Quite true," replied Stoke, "but the possession of intelligence does not necessarily mean that a man is not also mentally deranged. Many a brilliant mind houses a brain with paranoid tendencies. An intellectual person may be unbalanced, no matter how clever. Isn't that so, doctor?"

"Correct," answered Dr. Ragland sagely; "emotional instability and intelligence are separable elements, even though they may overlap a little."

How little did we realize that this theory was soon to be put to the test!

"Many criminals," continued the doctor, "are persons of brilliant mentalities, but in practically all of them there is an insane trend, using the word in its legal rather than its medical sense."

"Why, then," demanded Mr. Selden, "can't all crimes be solved by you psychological duffers—pardon me, scientists?"

"They can be," was the reply.

"But," objected Stoke, "first you have to corral all of the suspects and subject each to a scientific quiz. In order to get your suspects, you have to analyze the facts and circumstances, which requires an expert study of the environment. You would apply the same technique used in ferreting out the cause of an epidemic."

"Like hell you would," was Runy's scornful comment.

"And what do you consider the infallible method?" asked Starr-Smith with a slightly unpleasant inflection on the "you."

"Applied science, particularly mathematics and engineering," answered the militant Celt; "what criminology needs to take it out of the rut is the proper use of physics and chemistry, not such a deluded science as biology, as Stoke in his childish innocence would have us believe."

"A doctorate in philosophy never helped anyone solve a crime," asserted Mr. Selden, "all that is needed is practical experience, the kind displayed by the trained professional detective."

"I suppose you are referring, even if vaguely, to your stalwart police," remarked Starr-Smith, ironical once more.

"I am," replied the commissioner. "Crime is actually detected by those who have made a life study and business of it, not by amateurs, all mystery stories to the contrary. I doubt," he continued, turning to Runy, "if any of the successful detectives ever heard of calculus and such higher mathematics."

"Most of them can't even add and subtract," countered Runy.

"If your detectives knew more about the motivation of human conduct, as explained by the psychiatrist, they would be better equipped," asserted Dr. Ragland.

"They use common sense, which is even better," was the reply.

Starr-Smith had been listening to this repartee with an amused smile. Finally he spoke.

"As is not unusual," he said, "each of you gentlemen sees the problem solely in the light of his own interests and attainments. There is some truth in what each of you says so vehemently, but an astute criminal would be more than a match for any one of these theories. The crude performer of homicide may be emotionally unstable, but not every murderer—"

He paused abruptly, turning his head to look at the unused door beside him.

This door was about six feet from our table. Stoke sat with his back to it. I was at one side of him, Runy on the other. Next to Runy was the architect; Dr. Ragland and Mr. Selden were facing the door.

In the moment of silence that followed this pause we heard several distinct raps upon the door. It sounded as if someone was knocking against it with a metallic instrument.

"What in the devil is that?" said Dr. Ragland.

"Who is it at this time of night?" asked Runy.

As Starr-Smith shrugged his shoulders disdainfully, as if to deprecate the excitement, Stoke rose and stepped toward the door.

"Let us see," he said.

As he reached for the rusty knob, there came a low thud as if a knife might have been driven into the wood.

Over the wall came the sound of a voice. It was plaintive, agitated, the voice of a person in great distress.

"*Madre de Dios*," it wailed.

Then silence.

CHAPTER II
DAGGER IN THE DOOR

As this agonizing cry died away in the stillness of the night, Mr. Selden took command of the situation. At once he was the public official.

"See who is there," he said crisply; "someone must need help."

Pushing our chairs back in our excitement, we had all risen, all, that is, except Starr-Smith, who remained seated, languidly lighting a cigarette.

Despite Stoke's frantic attempts to open the door, it resisted his efforts. As Runy placed a chair against the wall and was about to climb over, there came the sound of splintering wood. With a violent effort Stoke had torn the door from its half-rotten hinges and flung it open.

From the garden the light streamed into the alley. It was empty.

"I can't see a damn thing anywhere," Runy called from the top of the wall.

"There is nothing to see, there is no one here," said Stoke, who was now out in the alley.

That part of the alley near the door had been in the shadow, as the dim light from a street lamp, round the corner of an intersecting alley, did not illuminate it. The remainder of the alley was fairly light, however, either from the moon or from the street lamps at either end. The light was sufficient to reveal its emptiness.

Stoke and I reconnoitered in one direction while Runy and Mr. Selden went stealthily in the other. Dr. Ragland and Starr-Smith remained in the doorway, the latter nonchalant, the former nervously dangling the black ribbon of his glasses.

"There is nothing," Stoke repeated when he had returned and we were all gathered once more about the table.

"Yes, there is something," said Dr. Ragland suddenly in an awed voice.

He pointed to the door.

Protruding from its upper portion was the handle of a knife. This part of the door was shielded from the light by the branches of one of the trees, and none of us had noticed the gleam of the blade, to which our attention was now so dramatically directed.

Stoke, who was nearest, pulled it out with a slight effort. He placed on the table before us a peculiarly shaped dagger.

"So our nocturnal visitor left a little memento," commented Starr-Smith with his first real show of interest.

"By rights it ought to be dripping with gore," remarked Runy somewhat flippantly.

"This may turn out to be a serious matter," Mr. Selden reproved him.

The weapon was a short dagger with a flat blade, slightly curved at the end. It was not a poniard or a dirk, but more like a hunting-knife, except that the hilt was carved to resemble the scales on the back of a reptile. The head was smooth and worn, but it looked as if a crude workman had endeavored to carve a snake's head and fangs.

"I should turn this thing over to the police at once," said the commissioner musingly; "they can find out for us what it is all about."

"Your faith in the police is positively naïve," retorted Dr. Ragland. "Sit down, Henry, and let us consider this thing for a minute or two."

"Here is a swell chance for us to test our theories regarding crime," said Runy blithely. "Personally, I think the whole thing is a joke."

"That voice, that weird cry, did not sound very jocular," said Dr. Ragland with a shudder. "Shut that door, someone."

"Well, then," demanded Runy, "what is the psychological explanation for it?"

The doctor did not deign to reply.

"What do you deduce by your own remarkable system?" Starr-Smith asked Runy, who rose promptly to meet the challenge.

He picked up the dagger and turned it over a few times. Then he examined the still open door, while the rest of us regarded him with amusement, mixed with what remained of our consternation.

"Unfortunately I haven't my microscope nor my trusty calipers with me," began the lieutenant, "but I will now state positively that this stiletto was wielded by an agitated foreigner of medium height and good muscles, who got the knife from a drawer where it had lain unused for six months. He was barefooted and was probably a Spaniard."

"Marvelous," said Starr-Smith, while Mr. Selden looked at Runy quizzically.

"Now it is the biologist's turn," Runy went on complacently. Stoke smiled good-naturedly.

"The remarkable analytical powers displayed by our nautical friend must be quite apparent," he commenced. "The position of the dagger in the door gives an indication of the intruder's height, and the force with which it was driven in shows that he was stocky. The rust on the blade confirms our companion's impression that the implement has not been employed for some time. The lack of footsteps would lead one to believe that our guest, a man, was probably barefooted. The words he spoke were Spanish."

"You are explaining very nicely," said Dr. Ragland, "but you are adding nothing."

"I will add this, then," returned Stoke; "the user of this dagger was a South American."

"Wonderful!" commented Starr-Smith.

"And how do you know, or did you guess, that?" asked Runy.

"I have seen daggers like this before on my travels," was the quiet reply.

"Enough of this palaver," broke in Mr. Selden impatiently; "we are wasting time. The police ought to have been notified of this episode long ago."

"Don't get excited, Henry," pleaded Dr. Ragland, who, like all specialists in the treatment of nervous diseases, was himself high-strung and excitable; "the man has vanished. We made a thorough search of the neighborhood and found nothing."

In my mind's eye was a picture of the doctor and his tall companion standing in the doorway while we searched. "Tell your honorable police in the morning," concluded the physician.

"Yes, morning will be more than ample time for them," added Starr-Smith with more than a trace of sarcasm.

"The police," stated Mr. Selden with a tone of finality, "will produce an explanation of this without much delay."

"But supposing they don't?" queried Runy.

"That, of course, is inconceivable," murmured the architect, while Mr. Selden glared at him.

"You do not seem to show the proper amount of respect for the sagacity of the established guardians of the law," remarked Dr. Ragland.

"I have the utmost respect for them," protested Starr-Smith, "but I recognize their limitations."

Mr. Selden seemed to be restraining himself with difficulty.

"The proposition that I was about to advance when we were interrupted," continued the architect, "was that the police are often hopelessly outclassed when it comes to dealing with a master criminal."

"There is no such thing," growled Mr. Selden.

"Consider the innumerable unsolved crimes," the architect went on suavely. "I do not mean the reported crimes that are not solved, which are numerous enough, but the unreported, the unknown ones. Many apparently natural deaths are actually homicides, but they are accepted for what they appear to be. The perpetrator of crimes such as these is the real master. Nor are such clever, unsuspected crimes the work of demented persons."

"Nonsense," said Dr. Ragland.

"Some criminals may be mentally disordered," went on the speaker, "but the same is true of the average run of law-abiding citizens. A few criminals are not only well-balanced, but brilliant. They leave no facts for the engineers and the epidemiologists to find."

"Bunk," said Runy.

"And do you think," inquired Trevor Stoke, "that such master minds, assuming there are any, really escape detection?"

"Not always, of course not," was the answer; "they engage in a dexterous and sometimes, no doubt, pleasant battle of wits with their pursuers. They may even leave a deliberate clue here or there to add zest to the chase. The best man wins, to be sure, but the best man is as frequently the criminal as the police."

"Bosh," said Mr. Selden.

"An interesting, but rather erroneous, theory," murmured Stoke.

"And God help the rest of us, if true!" interjected Runy.

"It is a false theory," exclaimed the commissioner vehemently; "the criminal practically always loses in the end. I will admit that some crimes are not solved for long periods of time, and a few are never solved, but the great majority are cleared up expeditiously and successfully."

"Perhaps you are prejudiced, Henry," said Dr. Ragland.

"Do you mean to imply," demanded the commissioner of Starr-Smith, "that a highly intelligent person could plan what was virtually a perfect crime, assuming that an intelligent person would be guilty of such folly, and get away with it?"

"Not always or as a regular thing," replied the architect with a bit of asperity, "especially in such a well-ordered community as this, but the exceptional man could, has, does. There is no one here or anywhere else who could stop him or detect him."

"You forget that he is one man against society as a whole, one puny brain against many," suggested Stoke.

"One able brain is worth many mediocre ones," was the reply.

"What you claim is really a challenge to all our theories," said Dr. Ragland. "I am convinced that a knowledge of practical psychiatry is essential to solve a crime, any crime; Runy in his innocence puts entire faith in the physical sciences; Stoke wants to treat crime like a community disease; and, worst of all, Selden labors under the delusion that the higher form of that peculiar genus the professional detective is the last word. Now, you admit that there is something in all these theories, provided they are properly correlated, but you still think that a superior criminal could beat the whole combination, no matter how skillfully mobilized."

"I am positive that it can be done," answered Starr-Smith curtly.

"That is absurd," was the doctor's comment amidst general agreement.

"The murderer—" began the architect. Again he paused abruptly, listening.

Far in the distance came a faint wailing sound. It resembled a woman's scream, prolonged in terrible agony, and far away.

"What is that?" whispered Dr. Ragland. His face was pale.

No one spoke as we all listened for a repetition of that horrible sound. Again it came, but nearer and more distinct.

"It's a banshee," said Runy with a laugh. "Why, that's nothing but one of the commissioner's black wagons, probably out after some errant colored gentry."

"Runy is right," agreed the commissioner; "it is the patrol wagon in a near-by street. I would know that siren anywhere."

"Ghosts and murderers play subtle tricks on the nerves at midnight," said Starr-Smith, puffing nonchalantly on his cigarette.

"That reminds me," said Mr. Selden, starting to rise, "I must turn our trophy over to the police. This has been an interesting, even if profitless, conversation. I will bid you all good-night."

"Be sure and let us know what the gendarmes find out," Runy reminded him.

As the commissioner nodded curtly, Sam, the club's colored factotum, emerged hurriedly from the club-house and hastened toward us.

"Colonel Selden," he announced with typical Ethiopian unctuousness, "there am a most important and urgent communication for you-all."

The commissioner again bade us good-night and departed.

Since the rest of us were in no mood to break up the party, we lingered on and soon got round to a rabid discussion of the abilities of famous detectives, both real and fictional. Although Runy and Dr. Ragland expressed admiration for the methods of some of the detective heroes of fiction, Starr-Smith was decidedly cynical about them, and in this he was upheld, to my surprise, by Stoke.

"Most of your story-book criminologists are really shallow in their achievements," declared the architect. "Sherlock Holmes could not possibly have existed outside of fiction. His methods are preposterous. They may make good reading, yes, but his analyses are so obviously doctored and made to order that they are ridiculous when considered critically. Even Edgar Allan Poe's Dupin is a disappointment. He is nothing but a long-winded, prolix conversationalist, who does not even visit the scene of the crime, but sits at home and guesses— that is the word—at its cause, without adequate facts upon which to guess. Lecoq was a bungler. Some of the moderns are actually more clever than these classical examples of the amateur or story-book detective, but most of them are patterned after Holmes and the rest."

"Look here, my dissertating friend," broke in Runy, "why don't you write the real masterpiece?"

For once Starr-Smith was not cynical.

"Perhaps I shall," he replied.

"Someone is coming," said Dr. Ragland.

It was Mr. Selden. He was hurrying toward us as if in some trepidation.

"I thought you had gone home," Dr. Ragland greeted him.

It was then that he made his dramatic announcement.

"Gentlemen," said the commissioner ominously, "while we have been discussing crime in this garden and hearing strange noises and seeing strange things, a crime is committed in our immediate vicinity. At midnight the corpse of Beatrice Sigurda was discovered under conditions that are extremely suspicious. It seems unquestionably to be murder."

We were to see and hear even stranger things before this crime was solved.

CHAPTER III
THE HOUSE ON Q STREET

"It seems to be murder," the commissioner had said. Reality had intruded suddenly upon a highly theoretical discussion of crime.

For a moment no one spoke. Then, as Runy O'Mara emitted a low whistle of surprise, Starr-Smith, who seemed at that instant to be the most composed of the group, broke the silence.

"What leads you to believe that the woman has been murdered?" he inquired.

"The evidence reported to me by one of my most reliable detectives points to extremely suspicious circumstances," answered Selden. His joviality was gone now and he was the astute public official faced by a civic problem of unusual significance.

"Beatrice Sigurda, a comparatively young woman in the best of health, has been found by her servants sitting upright on a divan, fully clothed, in a lighted room. She is dead."

"What caused her death?" asked the architect.

"That fact is not wholly clear—yet," replied Mr. Selden.

"Is that all you have to go on?" was Dr. Ragland's query. "Endocarditis or any one of several other heart afflictions could explain that."

"I don't think it will explain this case," was the grim answer.

"Why, were there any signs of violence, or any weapons around?"

"No, but this officer of mine who is now on the scene has reported some gruesome details," answered the commissioner.

"Well, tell us, will you?" exclaimed Runy excitedly. "Here we have been sitting informing each other how to solve crimes, when one is committed just round the corner. A friend of ours, at least of mine, is the victim. Go on, tell us."

Selden turned deliberately to Runy and looked at him with a peculiar expression.

"How well did you know her?" he asked bluntly.

"Come, come, Henry," interposed Dr. Ragland, "please don't be so professional. Next you will be casting suspicion on our young friend, who, like all of us, has been sitting here all evening, wasting his time, no doubt, when he might have been out with some of the butterflies of the same type as the late Miss Sigurda."

"Runy has been out of trouble, anyway," said Selden pleasantly. "Of course, I wasn't being suspicious, but sooner or later we may want to collect all the facts we can about this person's life and her friends."

"I am at your service at any time, Mr. Selden," Runy spoke up.

"So are we all," said Stoke.

"We may be rank amateurs, Henry," broke in Dr. Ragland, "but at that we might be able to contribute something to the solution of this affair, if, as you seem to think, it really is a crime. You have not yet elucidated that point, though. What's this?"

The doctor paused as Sam came up and ostentatiously handed him an envelope.

"Hurry-up message for you, suh," he said, and lingered, with the darky's curiosity to see what it was all about. He sensed something extraordinary by the attitudes of all of us.

Dr. Ragland fumbled nervously at the envelope, tore it open, and read it hastily.

"The devil!" he ejaculated, then continued more urbanely: "It is really nothing. One of my most affluent female patients is having a tantrum at this ungodly hour of the night, and young Rollin, who called me as a consultant some time ago, insists that I rush over. And the place is in Georgetown." He sighed. "I am afraid the murder will have to get along without me," he continued, but made no immediate move to leave for his urgent call.

"Well, it can't get along without me," said the commissioner, "and I must be going. This is a serious matter," he added gravely.

"When did this homicide occur?" asked Starr-Smith abruptly. "Before the doctor's digression, I believe he had called attention to the fact that we had all been here all evening, at least since nine or thereabouts. Have you evidence that it really took place while we have been here?"

"Yes," said Selden, pausing, "Miss Sigurda was alive and well at half past ten. She was found dead at twelve thirty, or about three quarters of an hour ago."

"Whew!" whistled Runy again. "Say," he blurted, "you asked me how well I knew this dame. I danced with her two days ago at that soirée on Sixteenth Street, as I have quite a few times before, but I only knew her socially. I didn't know her any better than you did, commissioner. I saw you feeding her tea one afternoon over at the Siamese Legation."

"I presume most of us were socially acquainted with Miss Sigurda," answered Mr. Selden rather stiffly.

"No doubt," commented Starr-Smith.

"I never had that pleasure," remarked Stoke, whose role in the proceedings so far had been chiefly as a listener.

"You laboratory hounds miss a lot," countered Runy.

"Again, I regret that I must leave, even if I miss the repartee," said Selden with some asperity, as he moved toward the club-house.

"I guess the party is over, anyway," said Runy, as we all started toward the door through which we had to pass to reach the street. In the hallway I overheard Selden speak to Dr. Ragland.

"Look here, doc," he was saying, "there is more to this than is apparent. We could use your professional advice if you care to come over."

For a moment the physician hesitated.

"Not tonight, Henry," he said at last. "Rollin declares my patient really needs me, which means that she does. Though young, Dr. Rollin is a fairly sensible fellow and a comer, so I think I had better run over. Besides, Todd, the medical examiner, is a competent man. He could find angina in your fair one as well as I."

"He won't find angina," said Selden, "but he is a good toxicologist, which is what we need. It is poison he will probably have to trace."

"Oh, so that's it. Look here, Selden, why don't you take this young fellow Stoke along with you? I know it is unusual in a way, but then, he is a federal employee, you remember, and he is also a somewhat unusual person, as keen an analyst as I ever met."

"I am not very enthusiastic about amateur detectives," objected the commissioner. "They do fine work in storybooks, and they talk well in gardens, but this is a job for a trained man. Steve Yates is over there now. It was what he told me that convinced me this is no ordinary, simple death. It is murder, Basil."

"All right, you know best. Good night and good luck," and the doctor went out and got into his car. "Keep me informed," he called as he drove off.

"I, too, will say good-night," remarked Starr-Smith at the street door. "I would offer my valuable services, but they would probably be futile. If a crime has really been committed, as you insist, no doubt your highly efficient police will solve it with their usual expeditiousness."

There was a distinct trace of sarcasm in his tone, but his manner was so often cynical that Selden ignored it. I watched the tall form of the architect as he strolled nonchalantly away, cane in hand, toward Pennsylvania Avenue, in a direction opposite to that toward which the commissioner was already turning. Runy had remained somewhere in the club-house.

"By the way, Mr. Selden," remarked Stoke, "I happen to know a short cut over to the Sigurda house, if you want to save time."

"What?" said Selden.

Stoke quickly explained that his familiarity with the neighborhood was due to frequent visits to the home of Professor Kent, whose residence adjoined that of Miss Sigurda.

"I never met the lady," he added, "but I have seen her and I am acquainted with the streets, alleys, and back yards of her environment. I have, in fact, risked being shot by that queer gardener of hers by sneaking into Kent's house by the back way."

"Come on, then," invited the commissioner, "you might be of some help. We will take you along as a body-guard," he added, turning to me.

Thus began as exciting a series of adventures as have occurred to any couple of ordinary citizens, only one of whom was accustomed to coping with the inscrutable forces of nature. For me it was a new experience, one which I never regretted despite the frequent dangers we encountered.

As we walked quickly through the deserted streets and into an alley whither Stoke piloted us, Mr. Selden seemed preoccupied and he said nothing. This section of the city was quiet at that time of night, for it was away from the center. It was a district lined with old-fashioned brick residences built in unbroken rows. I had expected that the commissioner would impart some information about this alleged crime, but he said nothing until we reached Q Street and stood before the Sigurda house, which, as a matter of fact, was hardly three or four blocks from the Serpentine Club. As we turned the corner of one of the cross-streets, after emerging from one of the alleys through which Stoke had conducted us past the high brick wall in the rear of the house itself, I caught a glimpse of a blue-coat lounging on the steps. He watched us alertly and with some apparent suspicion, but, recognizing the commissioner at once, straightened up and saluted.

"Is Detective Yates inside?" asked Selden brusquely.

"Yes sir, he and the sergeant are right inside," answered the policeman.

Selden pushed open the door. A man in plain clothes barred our way. He stepped aside quickly, however, and indicated a door leading from the hall.

"Mr. Yates is in there, with a material witness," he announced rather importantly.

"Tell him I'm here," ordered the commissioner.

The officer vanished. In a moment a thickset individual emerged briskly. He wore a black fedora hat and had the stump of a cigar in his mouth. I never saw a person who so completely exemplified the professional detective. His feet were large and flat, and all I could think of was the typical gum-shoe man. When I came to know Detective Yates more intimately, I learned to admire him and his methods, but my first impression could have been better. His first impression of us was apparently none too favorable, either. He shook hands with the commissioner ceremoniously, shot a sharp glance at Stoke and me, and then greeted us perfunctorily as Selden introduced us.

"I've got the maid in there now," he stated, "while Riordan is watching the gardener out in the kitchen. I've been questioning that bird, too, and I think he knows more than he lets on. A foreigner he is, and putting on the no-speak-English stuff. The maid is a nigger and a smart one, but seems to be telling a straight story."

"Give us the facts again," asked Selden.

The detective quickly sketched the events as he had ascertained them. Miss Sigurda had attended a social function in the afternoon, a tea at a house on New Hampshire Avenue. She had gone in her car, being driven, as usual, by her gardener, who acted also as her chauffeur. She had returned about five thirty and had retired to her room to dress for a dinner engagement. At seven a man had called for her in a yellow roadster and after half an hour or so the couple had driven away together. At about nine thirty they had returned and had gone directly to the sitting-room on the second floor.

Half or three quarters of an hour later, the maid, who was in her room at the head of the stairs on the third floor, had heard a man's voice in the hall of the second floor saying good-night, and immediately thereafter the front door closed. The maid went to the sitting-room at ten, knocked, entered, saw Miss Sigurda writing, and was told that she was not needed again that night. She went to the kitchen on the first floor, said a few words to the gardener, who was sitting on the door-step, then retired to her room. At half past ten or quarter of eleven she distinctly heard a scream from the sitting-room. She paid no especial attention to the fact, as Miss Sigurda often indulged in high-pitched laughter which resembled a scream.

The persistent ringing of the telephone at midnight awoke the maid. The telephone stand was in the hall on the second floor, with an extension in Miss Sigurda's bedroom and another in the hall of the first floor. When she lifted the receiver, a man's voice excitedly asked for Beatrice. The maid explained that she was apparently asleep. The man shouted that he must speak to her at once. The maid noticed a light shining through the transparent transom above the sitting-room door. She tried the door, but it was locked, and so she endeavored to open the bedroom door, but it likewise was securely fastened. There was no response to her knocking.

"The maid began to get scared then," continued Yates, "but she goes back to the phone and tells the guy her mistress is sound asleep, and he says: 'My God, it's happened,' and hangs up. Then the maid lets out a yell and rushes down and pounds on the gardener's door in the basement."

The chauffeur-gardener was somewhat perturbed at being thus raucously awakened, but came upstairs and tried the door. Silence, an eerie stillness from within. The gardener returned to the basement to get a tool to force the door, but noticed a light streaming from the sitting-room window. There was a ladder in the garden and so he and the now thoroughly nervous maid placed the ladder against the wall and he climbed it.

What he saw resulted in a hurried telephone call for the police.

The desk sergeant summoned Yates, who arrived just as the patrol pulled up at the door.

"That's the story, chief," said the detective, shifting his cigar. "These gentlemen understand that what they hear is confidential," he added, gazing at us with some suspicion and, I thought, with a trace of resentment.

"Yes, yes," answered Selden impatiently, "they aren't reporters, but, er, assistants of mine. Technical assistants. Where's Todd? Has he been here yet?"

"Why, no, Doc's office said another doc called him out to Tenley-town about half an hour before I phoned him, but they would send for him and he ought to be here any minute. Funny hours these docs have—worse than mine," and the detective sighed, but there was nevertheless zest in his demeanor. He was at the beginning of a game.

"Where did this midnight telephone call come from?" inquired Stoke quietly.

The detective looked Stoke up and down quizzically, then turned to the commissioner.

"Did I get you that these gentlemen are in your office or something?"

"Mr. Stoke is a government official," replied Selden. "You may speak freely. He may be able to help us. The other gentleman is also all right," he conceded.

"That phone call came from a pay station in a drug-store run by a Greek in Georgetown. McNab is on his way now to get Nick out of bed and find out what he can about the guy that did the phoning."

I marveled at the thoroughness with which the detective had gone about the whole matter and I could see that Selden was impressed, too, though Stoke showed no signs of amazement.

"Where was the gardener all night?" he asked.

"He says," and the detective emphasized the word, "he was in bed, but it was blame funny that he had all his clothes on when he comes out of his room right after this maid calls him."

At this moment the front door opened and a large, rather florid man entered. He carried a black satchel. I thought he was probably a finger-print expert or something of that nature.

"The medical examiner," murmured Stoke in my ear.

"Howdy, doc," exclaimed Yates, "been having breakfast?"

The physician scowled and then smiled genially.

"Greeting, Sherlock. Good evening, Mr. Selden. How are you, Mr. Stoke?" and he nodded affably toward me, though I meant nothing to him. "I've been off on as—" he visibly curbed a profane adjective while in the commissioner's presence, "a wild goose chase as it has ever been my hard luck to run up against. Here I get a hurry call to go out to Tenleytown to look at a coon who has been stabbed to death and find what? A trivial flesh wound in a buck who, mind you, didn't even get it in the District of Columbia. The whole festival took place across the line in Maryland. What a life!"

"Hard luck, doc," commented Yates, "but you need the exercise and we will make up for the disappointment right here and right now."

"By the way, doctor," interposed Stoke suavely, "who summoned you on this wasteful expedition?"

"The call came from a good enough source," answered the medical examiner; "it was Dr. Rollin who phoned me. These kids get excited about nothing. When he has practiced as long as I have, he will get down to earth. Wait till I get hold of him at the next Medical Society meeting."

Stoke made no further comment and asked no more questions.

"Is the *corpus delicti* all set?" said the doctor. "If so, let's go. Lead on, Lecoq."

Yates pointed up the stairs.

"The body is in the middle sitting-room. Come on, doc."

"We might as well all go up," said Selden.

The detective hesitated.

"Just as you say, commissioner," he assented. "Of course, these gentlemen realize we want as little disturbance as possible. Things have to stay right where they are."

"Certainly, certainly," answered Selden.

We went up the stairs, the detective leading the way, the medical examiner following jauntily, though rather ponderously, for he was a trifle rotund. Before the closed door the detective paused.

"If you gents are not used to this kind of a mess," he said, "some of you may get a shock."

He opened the door.

CHAPTER IV
THE ROOM ON THE SECOND FLOOR

The detective had quietly opened the massive oak door leading into the luxurious sitting-room of the late Miss Sigurda, and stepped in, followed by Commissioner Selden, Dr. Todd, Trevor Stoke, and myself. Hardly beyond the threshold we paused. The room was illuminated by a cluster of lights in the ceiling at the center and by two floor-lamps, one directly opposite us beside a handsome desk of dark wood. The other lamp was at the right of the door by which we had entered, and stood near one end of a rich red divan. On this divan was the body of Beatrice Sigurda.

She was seated with her back to the lamp, her face toward a partially open window. The face was in the full light of the lamp, though the body was leaning slightly forward. The features were swollen and of a livid hue, while a look of inexplicable horror was depicted on the handsome face. The right arm was bent upward and the fingers partly clenched, as if the dead woman had clutched at something. The left arm rested on the divan, the fingers also tightly clenched.

The room had about it a pungent odor, as if something had been burning. Immediately the thought flashed through my mind that the woman must have been shot and the smell of the powder remained. After all, I had some detective instinct, or believed that I had. My reveries were interrupted by the voice of Detective Yates:

"There she lies, doc," he was saying, not flippantly, but in a business-like manner. "It's your turn now."

The medical examiner pushed his hat up and advanced, bag in hand. Before he could start his examination, Mr. Selden spoke sharply.

"Have you taken pictures yet, Yates?"

"The faint aroma of the flashlight powder is your answer," said Stoke quietly before the detective could answer. As my illusions about a pistol-shot vanished, I observed Yates glance keenly at Stoke and I think there was an almost imperceptible trace of admiration.

"Sure, all the details have been attended to. The pictures have even been developed and came out O.K., so we didn't need to repeat. Every angle of the whole room is in the records."

"Good work," remarked Selden, as Stoke also nodded approval. "Go on, doctor, see what *you* can find."

The physician obviously knew his gruesome profession, for his examination was meticulous. His work was interspersed with some running comments, from which it developed that there was no sign of any wound, either by fire-arm or knife.

"What's this?" he exclaimed suddenly, and pointed to the neck of the body. On the discolored surface were two tiny punctures, not a quarter of an inch apart.

The doctor studied them through a magnifying glass for several minutes. When he rose, he was obviously perplexed.

"What do you make of it?" asked Yates.

"Death must have occurred between three and four hours ago, or about eleven thirty," he announced, looking at his watch.

"From what cause?" inquired Mr. Selden.

"That I cannot say as yet," replied the doctor. "We will have to perform an autopsy as soon as possible. If I had been here sooner, I might have had a better idea."

"How about strangulation?" asked Mr. Selden.

"No, I am sure that can be ruled out," was the doctor's answer. "There are no abrasions from hands or fingers on the throat. The discoloration is from something else."

"A hypodermic, possibly," said Stoke.

"Possibly," and this time the doctor looked curiously at Trevor Stoke. "In fact, poison seems to be the most plausible explanation. That and an intense fright, which may have had a bad effect on the heart, if the heart was already bad."

"These punctures, though, are on the right side toward the wall," commented Selden, "and the body is or was back against the cushions, with the feet partly drawn up on the sofa. A person would have had to lean across her to do that trick."

"What is behind that curtain?" said Stoke quietly, pointing to the wall behind the divan.

"What curtain?" demanded Yates.

"It is obvious that the wall behind the divan is covered with a piece of tapestry," replied Stoke.

For answer the detective strode to the wall and placed his hand on it, with the result that there was a perceptible give to what was apparently a highly decorative solid wall of the house. He ran his hand to the side, inserted his forefinger, and pulled aside a heavy curtain, revealing a door.

"Well, I'll be damned," he ejaculated. Then he dropped the curtain, examining it minutely and leaning across the body to do so.

"It don't look like any slits where a needle or anything has been through this," he said at last, "but let's get this corpse to the morgue as soon as possible."

The detective went to the door and called, and in a few minutes two policemen appeared with a stretcher, upon which the body of Beatrice Sigurda was placed, covered, and taken to the waiting patrol wagon. Dr. Todd also took leave, shaking hands all round.

"Let's know what you find, doc," was the detective's final godspeed.

While the police were about their business, Stoke was strolling nonchalantly round the room, while I remained beside Mr. Selden near the door. Stoke touched nothing, but he seemed to find much of interest, despite his detached air. He looked out of the open window at the foot of the divan, gazed at the pictures on the walls, stopped for some moments by the desk, which stood open, and then wandered to the door which apparently opened into a chamber at the front of the house. His glance roved over the various chairs and other articles of furniture and over the heavy oriental rug. Whether he saw anything of importance or not I don't know, as he gave no indication of surprise or interest and said nothing when he rejoined us. By that time the detective was back in the room, headed for the mysterious door.

"You will probably find it locked," said Stoke.

The detective said nothing, but tried the knob.

"Yes, it is locked," he reported, rather belligerently. "Now, where in the devil does that door go to?"

"I noticed another door at the head of the stairs as we came up," remarked Stoke. "There must be a rear chamber, and perhaps this door communicates with it."

We went out and Yates tried the door indicated. It was locked. He took something from his pocket and with a few deft movements had the door open. The room was dark, but instantly the gleam from a flashlight held by Yates was illuminating all parts of it. Then he entered.

"Do you mind if I turn on the lights?" asked Stoke. "It may help."

"Go ahead," growled Yates.

As Stoke stood in the doorway, he reached just to its right and the lights flashed on. The room was an empty chamber, with a bed, fully made, on one side, and chairs and other articles of furniture. To the left was a tall dressing-table, with a full-length mirror.

"The door should be behind that table," said Stoke, moving toward it.

"Don't touch a thing," snapped the detective, dropping to his knees and examining the floor closely.

"The door is there; any fool could see it below that table; but this table hasn't been moved for weeks," he continued, as he rose.

"This is probably a guest chamber that has not been used recently," remarked Selden.

Stoke shrugged his shoulders.

"Possibly Mr. Yates already has reason to think otherwise," he remarked.

The detective was now standing near one of the rear windows. Beside him was a wash-bowl with running water. When he came toward us, he said nothing, however, but led the way back to the sitting-room.

"Were there any clues at all in here?" asked Commissioner Selden, looking around. The detective was gazing again at the locked door, as if there might be something baffling, frustrating, about it. Finally he turned away, stepped closer to the divan, and removed two of the pillows which had been near the middle of it. Their removal disclosed a brown paper bag.

"Only this, and it don't tell much," he answered.

"Was it empty?" asked Stoke.

"Empty as a dime-novel detective's head," was the reply, "but," Yates added in a tone as if to convey the impression that he meant no aspersions on any of us interlopers, "it had a kind of funny smell."

"What kind of an aroma?" persisted Stoke. "Like bananas?"

The detective laughed.

"It does not seem likely that a woman of Miss Sigurda's refinement would have a bag of bananas in her effete living-quarters," chided Mr. Selden.

"How would you describe this odor, then?" asked Stoke turning to Yates.

"It was more like the smell of a zoo than anything else," the latter answered. "Here," he said, "have a whiff yourself, there's some of it left."

Stoke took the bag and looked it over. It was a plain brown paper affair such as might be obtained in any grocery store, except that it was of tougher material than the average. I judged that it would hold about a peck. Stoke placed it near his nostrils, then moved directly under the light and looked intently inside. Then he held the bag up to the light.

"Did you notice these discoloration?" he asked of Yates.

"Yes, but what do they tell you?" retorted the detective. I began to sense that he resented the presence of my friend, though Stoke's manner had been courteous and deferential all evening.

"Of course, they do not reveal much yet," he said pleasantly, "but after a little expert attention by some of the cognoscenti of your detective bureau, they might be quite informative. And then again, they might not," he mused.

"Everything will get complete attention," assured the commissioner, as Stoke handed the bag to the detective. "What else, if anything, Mr. Yates?"

"There was a letter on the desk," announced Yates, taking an envelope from his pocket-book. "It wasn't addressed to anyone."

He handed the letter to the commissioner, who read it and passed it to Stoke, while the detective watched with a cynical smile. Although I was omitted in this ceremony, I saw this epistle later. It was written on delicately scented note-paper and read as follows:

Dear Rog,

I wanted so much to acquiesce in your plans, but there is a reason why I could not. I cannot tell you all now, but there is a power in my life that is greater than myself. You and I together might prove stronger, but alone I am helpless. Alone. Alone.

B.

"Where was this peculiar epistle?" Again it was Stoke who inquired.

"Folded up in this very envelope, off to one side of the desk, as if someone had written it, stuck it in the envelope, see, and then kinda thrown it aside."

"In despair," commented Stoke, approvingly.

An officer appeared at the head of the stairs.

"The finger-print fellas are here," he announced.

"Send them up," ordered Yates curtly. "Well, gentlemen, let's go down and let Simpson and his helper come up and see what they can do."

As we descended, Stoke murmured to me: "These professional detectives are markedly efficient. They think of everything. If exactitude will solve crimes, this one ought to be solvable. If," he added, "it is a crime, as it certainly seems to be."

Hardly had we reached the bottom of the stairs when the telephone rang. The auburn-haired policeman who had been in evidence as announcer, and who seemed much excited by the whole affair, promptly answered.

"Mr. Selden wanted on the telephone," he proclaimed.

Selden held a monosyllabic conversation, consisting mostly in such phrases as "Is that so?" Whoever was on the other end of the wire was doing most of the talking. Eventually Selden remarked that he would try to find out, asked his loquacious friend to hold the line a moment, and turned to us.

"Do either of you gentlemen remember where Dr. Ragland went?" he asked. "It's Todd," he explained, "and he wants to get hold of Dr. Ragland for a consultation on the autopsy."

"It was somewhere in Georgetown," said Stoke. I could add nothing.

Selden conveyed this information to the medical examiner, advised that a message be left at his house, and apparently was informed that that had been done; then, after a few more remarks, he hung up.

"Todd is positive it is poison," he told us, "but he is unable to tell what kind, and he is one of the best toxicologists in the country. Before Ragland turned to psychiatry, he dabbled a good deal in the physiological effect of poisons, wrote papers on it and all that sort of thing, and knows a lot about the subject, so Todd wants his help, as he has several times in past years."

"There is no question, then, about this being a poisoning case?" remarked Stoke.

"None whatever," answered Selden; "I have full faith in Todd's opinion. Besides, what evidence there is points to that. And, speaking of evidence, here's Yates now."

The detective joined us, disappointment plain on his countenance.

"Hardly a finger-print worth a hoot," he confided.

"There isn't much to go on in this case, is there?" said the commissioner, with obvious perplexity.

"Less than that," murmured Stoke.

The commissioner looked at his watch. It was half past four.

"There does not seem to be much more that I can accomplish here," he remarked, "and I have a board meeting at ten tomorrow, so I am going home and get a little sleep. Yates can handle the situation."

He took out a card and wrote on it with his fountain pen, then handed it to Stoke.

"Your assistance has been very helpful so far," he commented, "though I don't think any of us have got tremendously along. This card will secure admittance for you if you care to drop in in the morning."

"I should be delighted to co-operate with Mr. Yates to the best of my ability," replied my friend. "I am sure that Mr. Yates has a difficult matter well in hand and has acted most efficiently. I am, of course, not a professional worker in this field, but I recognize technical ability when I see it."

His remarks were natural, with none of the unction of the studied flatterer. The detective held out his hand cordially.

"Well, good night, Mr. Stook," he said. "Glad to have had you here and hope to see you again. You and I can talk over some things later on."

Stoke and I stepped out and strolled toward the bachelor apartment on K Street which my friend occupied. He insisted that I accompany him and not attempt to go out to my own room in Chevy Chase.

"Staggering in at dawn would give you a bad, even if false, reputation," he commented.

When we were inside the apartment and Stoke had donned a faded dressing-gown, I sat limply in a morris chair, thoroughly fatigued after the unusual excitement of the night.

"All you need with that rig is a violin and some cocaine," I remarked, stifling a yawn, "and you would be Sherlock Holmes himself."

"Speaking of stimulants, let us indulge in some coffee," and in a moment he had the aromatic beverage under way in his electric percolator.

"What do you make of it?" I asked, as I sipped a cup of his delicious blend, which was not even dated.

Stoke lit a cigarette and pensively blew a wreath of smoke at the ceiling.

"What a feast this affair is going to be for the erudite examples of journalism here and elsewhere!" he said. "In another hour or two extras will be out with big black headlines, saying: 'Mysterious Death of Society Girl.' Her whole history, or as much of it as the newspapers can dig up, will be presented with the usual exaggerations. 'Beauty Foully Murdered,' 'Police Expect to Make Arrests Soon,' and all the rest of the bunk. It's that same history, though, that will interest me, and the question is where to get the authentic facts. Murders, like any other disaster, such as an epidemic, are solved not from the immediate facts, but from a string of them, which culminates in the event which brings the police and the detectives, with all their machinelike efficiency and usually their utter lack of any appreciation of the personal and human equations involved. This Yates, though, seems to be a fairly intelligent and not wholly unlikable person. He has been quite business-like."

"I suppose," I said dreamily, "that you already have a theory as to who or what kind of person did this." I was thinking of the many detective creations of fiction who visit the scene of the crime and after a few keen glances reconstruct the whole episode in their minds and by sheer intuitive power reason out the whole event or chain of events. "Who do you think—" I began.

"My dear man," cut in Stoke, "I have no more idea who or what was responsible for the death of Beatrice Sigurda, or how it came about, than you have, or Yates has, or anyone else except the murderer himself. And he isn't here to tell us."

CHAPTER V
A MORNING VISIT

A few moments later, or so it seemed, Stoke was shaking me. As I rolled over drowsily, he called out cheerily:

"Awake, arouse, to arms! Sustenance awaits and then work. Have you forgotten that I have a card of admission to a perplexing crime?"

His tone was light and cheerful, but beneath it was a somber note.

"What time is it?" I asked.

"Nine o'clock already and we should have been on the job long ago. We shall be a big disappointment to Detective Yates. He probably did not expect his protégés too early, but, then, sleuths do not wander in when the festivities are completely over. No doubt Mr. Yates remained on duty all night."

"Have you been to bed at all yourself?" I inquired suspiciously, "or have you been occupied in considering this matter? If so, what is your theory?"

Stoke laughed.

"I have been sound asleep since five a.m. when we turned in. Thinking about the affair put me to sleep, in fact, and, unlike my usual experiences when you visit me, I was disturbed by none of those sonorous sounds which frequently emanate from your direction when you are in the arms of Morpheus."

"But," I insisted, "have you no ideas about this affair? I thought you technicians usually got a pretty clear conception of who might have done it after visiting the scene of the crime."

"Don't be absurd," rejoined Stoke. "You know I never investigated a crime before in my life, although an epidemic is usually due to someone's criminal negligence; and what few facts have come to light in this particular murder do not reveal much as yet."

"There is no question but that it is murder, is there?" I continued.

"No," answered Stoke, "murder by poison and fright combined. But enough, enough, into the shower with you and let's go."

I sighed and rose reluctantly. By the time I had completed my ablutions, a pleasant breakfast was ready, cooked and served by Stoke himself. Obscure scientists lack valets, butlers, and similar retainers. As I attacked the grapefruit and it retaliated by squirting in my eye, Stoke placed a morning paper before me. The headlines already told the story of the mysterious death of Beatrice Sigurda. Poison was suspected, declaimed the paper. By good fortune, Commissioner Selden had been nearby and had personally assumed charge of the case, assisted by Detective Stephen Yates, well-known criminologist. There was no mention of Stoke or anyone else.

As soon as we had finished our repast, we were on our way. Near the house on Q Street a group of the morbidly curious, always attracted to the scene of a crime by some sadistic impulse, were idling, though two stalwart policemen kept onlookers away from the front door. Both officers were new men who had not been on duty when we had left the house several hours previously.

Stoke stepped up to one of the policemen, who eyed him officiously, as was to be expected, since he had a traffic emblem on his arm.

"Good morning, officer," began Stoke politely. "Is Mr. Yates inside?"

"Who wants to see him?" the man dodged.

"He is expecting Mr. Stoke," replied Mr. Stoke.

"He didn't say nothing to me about it," said the guard. "No one is allowed in that house. Move on, there."

The last order was addressed in a domineering tone to a number of onlookers who had gathered about. I suggested to Stoke that he show his card, but he ignored me, and we sauntered nonchalantly away. Stoke turned down the next street and into an alley, which led for a short distance past a number of small brick garages and on through to the next cross-street. About half-way down, this alley was joined by another at right angles which apparently went to the next street, though it turned slightly and it was not possible to see that street from where we stood. At the moment the alleys seemed deserted.

Stoke paused before a weather-beaten wooden door, set in a brick wall at least seven feet high.

"This is the rear of the Sigurda house," he told me in a low voice.

Glancing up and down, he cautiously tried the knob. The door was locked. I noticed that there was no garage.

Guided by Stoke, we moved back to the next door, which also was locked, as we discovered by turning the knob. As we lingered before it, this door suddenly opened and a man stood looking at us.

"Good morning, professor," said Stoke blandly, and stepped in. I followed, but as I did so, I glanced back and was surprised to see another man lounging in a recess formed by a door some little distance down the alley. He was watching me keenly from below a slouch hat pulled well down over his face. Then the door closed behind me and we were in the garden adjoining that of Miss Sigurda's house.

"This is Professor Kent," said Stoke, introducing me to the man who had admitted us. He was of middle age, with a bald head and a Vandyke beard. His eyes were keen and piercing.

"Were you expecting someone?" asked Stoke of his friend.

"Why, no," answered the latter, "I was getting a little fresh air when I saw my knob turn and I opened to see who it was. You certainly surprised me, though I am used to having you wander in at all hours. Have you heard about the tragedy next door?"

"Yes, quite an interesting case," replied Stoke.

"I was not surprised," remarked the professor calmly. "Beatrice was playing a dangerous game most of the time."

"Was she?" asked Stoke. "How?"

"Some of her male companions were received at the front door only, some came only by the alley, and a few had access through both entrances," was the professor's reply.

"Which was your entrance?" Stoke said jovially.

The professor laughed.

"Miss Sigurda and I were acquaintances, but whenever I called on her, there was nothing surreptitious about it, as you probably know. We have talked ethnology together on the front steps and in her kitchen. She probably didn't know it was that science, but I often got information about South American characteristics from her. The gardener is an interesting subject, too, a mestizo."

"I suppose the police are in the house this morning?" Stoke asked next.

"They have been there all night. I was working late on my report to the Smithsonian, already overdue, and I saw lights most of the night."

"See anything else suspicious?" inquired Stoke. "I understand the tragedy occurred early last evening, about half past eleven."

"Did it?" exclaimed the professor in surprise. "The papers did not mention the time. Now that I think of it, someone paid a call through the back way last night."

"When?"

"Oh, probably about half past ten."

"Did you see him?" asked Stoke with what seemed to me like a trace of excitement.

"No, it was dark and the alley is dim behind us. Besides, there is an arbor of wisteria along the center of the garden next door. It is very convenient for casual visitors, especially at night," remarked the professor.

"I suppose you were in your study on the second floor?" continued Stoke.

"Yes."

"Did you, by the way, hear any screaming or violent noises?" was Stoke's next question.

"No. Shortly after that I went to the front of the house for a pipe. Look here, Trevor, the intensity of your interrogations would lead one to surmise that you were the detective force," said Professor Kent, smiling.

"Speaking of detectives," answered Stoke, "have you told any of this to the police yet?"

"The police have not honored me by asking and I doubt if the facts would add anything," replied the professor.

"They are interesting, if not precisely enlightening," remarked Stoke. "By the way, did you also see this visitor depart?"

"No, I got so engrossed in writing about the Mayan ideology that I probably should not have noticed even if the garden door had been slammed, as it usually is not by the nocturnal visitors next door."

Stoke dropped the subject and for some time he and the professor carried on an animated conversation about archaeology and ethnology in Central and South America, a topic upon which Professor Kent was an authority, as he had been in charge of a number of expeditions in quest of Mayan ruins. Since neither he nor Stoke paid any attention to me, I strolled about the professor's garden. Near the high wall I heard voices on several occasions. I also noticed that the rear of the house beyond, the one adjoining the Sigurda residence on the farther side, was shuttered and obviously closed for the summer, as were one or two of the houses across the alley, which faced on the street in back.

Just as I was beginning to get impatient, Stoke joined me.

"Professor Kent has kindly invited us to lunch," he said.

"We shall enjoy it, I am sure," I answered.

"But you forget our engagement," said Stoke quickly, and before I could say anything further, we were out in the alley. I looked for the watcher I had noticed when we entered, but saw no one, except a burly policeman who was loitering in the alley. He looked at us, but said nothing and we went round to Q Street once more. It was now about noon. A few idlers still stood before the house, but the traffic officer we had accosted before was gone. In his place was the auburn-haired policeman whom we had seen in the house the previous night, or, to put it more accurately, morning.

"Howdy, officer?" said Stoke. "Mr. Yates still in?"

The policeman looked at us without interest and was about to be brusque, as is usual with policemen, when he displayed signs of recognition.

"Oh, it's you, Mr. Stopes," he said. "Sure, Mr. Yates has been there ever since you left. He didn't say nothing about your coming back, though," he added dubiously.

"The commissioner's card to the rescue," murmured Stoke to me, as he handed that open-sesame to the officer, who read it, returned it, and, with considerable deference, conducted us to the door and inside, where another officer was lounging in the hall.

"Riordan, tell Mr. Yates the commissioner's friends are here," said the auburn-haired officer as he returned to the sidewalk. Yates himself entered from the back of the house.

"Afternoon, Mr. Yates," Stoke greeted him; "we are just in time for lunch."

"Hope you brought some, then," said the detective, but he shook hands in a friendly way.

"So you know the old duffer next door," was his next remark. "Did you get anything out of him? I've been too busy here, but I had him on the list."

Stoke quickly informed Yates of the facts imparted by Professor Kent. The detective listened, but made no comment.

"Do you mind if I look at the sitting-room again?" asked Stoke.

"Go ahead," assented the detective; "I'll send Kelly after some sandwiches and then join you."

We went upstairs. The room was just as we had left it some hours before, except that there seemed to be more dirt here and there. The black smudges reminded me of a Pittsburgh hotel. When I called Stoke's attention to them, he simply grunted.

"The finger-print expert's left-overs," he informed me.

The first thing Stoke did was to go to the window. It was placed diagonally and looked across to the blank brick wall of Professor Kent's house. Just beyond the recess between the two houses stood a large tree. Its branches were, however, some distance away.

"No chance for any poison darts from an opposite window or from that tree," said a voice behind us. It was Yates, who had come in noiselessly.

"Not unless they could be shot in a curve," answered Stoke. "I'd like to get a good look at that garden, though."

"Come on into my room, then," invited the detective.

"Your room?" queried Stokes.

"Sure, the back chamber. I took a little snooze there after you gents left," answered the detective with a smile. From the rear window of this chamber a complete view of the garden was possible. Stoke looked out.

"That ladder looks interesting," he exclaimed, pointing to a wooden ladder leaning against the tree.

"Yeah," said the detective noncommittally.

"Come, now, Mr. Yates," said Stoke ingratiatingly, "the more I know, the more I may be able to help you."

For a moment a gleam came in the poker face of the detective.

"I'm not going to keep anything from you, see," he said. "Mr. Selden gave me orders to let you help all you want and can. Somebody came into that garden last night, as the fellah next door says. Well, he used that ladder. The gardener says he put it on the ground alongside of the wall the afternoon before. This morning it was standing by the tree. And that ain't all. See that pile of lime out there."

The detective pointed to some lime beside the path.

"The guy that came in walked across the grass, steps on the edge of that lime, and gets the ladder and goes up it. The marks are on the rungs."

"A clue at last," murmured Stoke.

"Maybe," said the detective cautiously, "but he had funny shoes on; hardly a mark on them. The impressions don't tell much."

"Where did he put the ladder?" asked Stoke.

"Right under the sitting-room window," answered the detective. "The marks are clear."

"Would it have been possible for the gardener to have done all that himself?"

"Sure, we don't know who it might have been. But I've looked at every shoe that fits him and there's no lime on any of them," answered the detective.

"But," expostulated Stoke, "the maid testified that the gardener got the ladder and climbed up to the window when she could get no response at the door of the sitting-room."

The detective scratched his head.

"That's so," he admitted, "but he says the ladder wasn't where he left it that afternoon. Someone had used it some time."

"We'll have to ask him a few more searching questions," suggested Stoke.

"He's a hard witness," commented the detective; "claims he don't know much English, and none of us knows his lingo. I'll third-degree him if necessary and he'll tell or he'll sweat blood."

"Let me try him later," suggested Stoke. "I am reasonably proficient in Spanish, which I presume is his language."

We were interrupted by the auburn-haired policeman.

"The grub is downstairs," he announced, "and the maid is making you some coffee. Say," he blurted, addressing Stoke, "I'm sorry I didn't know you at first when you came along, but there's been a lot of nuts trying to crash this place today. There was a young guy in a naval uniform gave me a great blarney, said he was Irish like me, was a friend of Mr. Selden's, and knew the girl. Then there was a tall guy with black whiskers, polite but sarcastic like. They didn't get by me, though. Orders is orders."

"All right, Kelly, keep them all out, and now beat it," said Yates tersely, and Officer Kelly departed.

We descended to the dining-room and seated ourselves about the table where Miss Sigurda had entertained many a distinguished guest. For a while we ate in silence, as both Stoke and the detective seemed wrapped in thought. Finally the detective wiped his lips, produced a cigar, stuck it in his mouth, and chewed it savagely.

"There's damn little to go on in this case," he stated.

"Less than that," agreed Stoke, "but the facts are coming out gradually. Have you any other information of significance?"

"There's hardly anyone to suspect," continued the detective.

"Is there anyone?" asked Stoke.

"Yes," answered Yates, getting confidential, "the person who is most suspicious in this whole ghastly business is right here in this house right now."

I could not suppress an involuntary shudder, but Stoke merely puffed calmly at his cigarette.

"You are theatrical, not to say mysterious, Mr. Yates," he commented.

"I am going to have him in the parlor and let you question him," went on the detective. "You see what you can get out of him. I've pumped him in seven different ways without being violent. Now let's see where you can get."

There was a trace of challenge in the detective's words. Silently we got up and went to the front room. The detective placed a chair near the window in a good light. Stoke took a seat near the center of the room. The detective went to the door and beckoned to one of his cohorts.

"Bring in Mr. San Remo, that Indian gardener fellow," he said.

CHAPTER VI
SAN REMO AND OTHERS EXPLAIN

When Officer Riordan returned he was accompanied by a short, thick-set man, whose skin was brown, and whose black eyes gazed at us keenly. He held a cap in his hand which he turned and twisted nervously. The detective looked at him in a hostile manner, but Stoke's glance was interested, if non-committal.

"Your name?" began Stoke.

"Miguel San Remo," was the answer, surly, but distinct.

"Miguel San Remo," repeated Stoke; "and where are you from, Miguel?"

"*Aqui*, here," was the reply.

"No, I mean what country do you come from?" continued Stoke.

"No understand," answered the gardener.

Detective Yates snorted and was about to blurt something, but Stoke, smiling, raised his hand, and the detective subsided. Stoke looked pensively at the table, then suddenly he shot his next question at the obviously unwilling witness.

"*Habla usted español?*"

"*Si, señor*," came the answer quickly, and then a look of hesitation appeared upon the man's face.

"You gentlemen will pardon me if I now communicate with our friend here in impure Castilian," he remarked.

"Go ahead," growled Yates; "I don't savvy it, but we have guys on the force that do. Ask him for the details of the night of the murder. Trace every second of his movements. Go over it two or three times. Catch him in a corner. Go to it, Mr. Stoke."

I was watching the man narrowly and I thought I detected something about his demeanor that suggested that he had a good notion of what Yates had suggested. I surmised, in fact, that Señor San Remo understood more English than he was willing to admit.

For about ten minutes Stoke asked questions rapidly in Spanish, and the gardener answered them, at first abruptly and shortly, but soon excitedly and at greater length. He gesticulated and became quite voluble. Yates never took his eyes from the gardener's countenance and chewed vigorously on his half-smoked cigar. I caught words and phrases now and then, but the pace was too fast for my one year of college Spanish, which was the kind used in Madrid and presumably not in South America, anyway.

Finally Stoke paused and turned to Yates with a smile.

"Did you get anything?" inquired the detective.

"Yes, a little," answered Stoke.

"Well, I dunno what you were saying," continued Yates, "but you sure went at it like a professional, Mr. Stoke. What's the good word?"

"In the first place," replied Stoke, "our amigo here is an Argentinean, as was, in fact, his mistress, though of course of different caste. He has been in her service for eight years, it seems, having joined her in the old country. Miss Sigurda owned a plantation there. He has described the life in some detail, who her friends were, and other interesting facts."

"That's all very good," said Yates impatiently, "but what about what happened here last night?"

"Oh, I haven't got to that yet," replied Stoke urbanely, as he turned again to the crafty gardener.

The Spanish conversation continued for another ten minutes, the half-breed now less loquacious, but by no means reticent. Finally there was another pause.

"What does he say about the ladder?" demanded Yates.

"Oh, the ladder, yes, yes. I hadn't inquired about that yet," was Stoke's answer, to the evident disgust of Mr. Stephen Yates. He put several more questions. Then he turned to the detective.

"Señor San Remo might wait outside now, while I report progress," he suggested.

The detective instructed his uniformed assistant to take the gardener to the kitchen to await a call. When they had departed, he looked at Stoke expectantly.

"Here are the facts as revealed by our Argentine friend," reported Stoke. "In the afternoon he drove Miss Sigurda to a large white house on New Hampshire Avenue, where he waited for her in the car, returning about half past five and leaving her at the door, which he saw her enter. He then took the car to the public garage on Fifteenth Street where it is kept, returning to the house through the alley and the garden gate. He worked in the garden for a while. He says the ladder was on the ground by the wall, which answers one of your questions. He then ate his evening meal in the kitchen and afterwards walked to the basement door at the front of the house and stood there smoking, when a yellow car approached. In it was a man whom he identifies only as 'the doctor,' saying he does not know his name. He says, however, that he has an office on Vermont Avenue, where, as you are aware, innumerable doctors have their offices. After sitting on the steps for some time, an hour or so, he went to his room at the rear of the house, remained there half an hour, then went into the garden. He saw no one. The ladder was still beside the wall. He did notice a light in Kent's study next door. Kent was there and had a light; so his story checks to that extent. The maid came down and spoke to him, and next, he says, he went to bed. That must have been about ten. He claims to have heard nothing thereafter until awakened by a pounding on his door late at night."

"If anyone came into the house from the garden, he would have had to go through the passage by San Remo's room," broke in Yates. "Didn't he hear anyone?"

"He says not and he also states that he never listened, because people sometimes did come in that way," Stoke went on.

"Didn't he ever see any of those people?" asked Yates pointedly.

"He declares not," answered Stoke, "but in that regard the inference is proper that he is lying."

"I'll break every bone in his nigger body if I have to do it to make him tell," ejaculated the detective. "Someone who had a key and who knew this place came in here last night. Maybe," and he leaned over confidentially, "he will come again. Murderers are drawn back sometimes."

"I doubt if this one favors the house again," countered Stoke. "This is no ordinary crude killer. This one does his work with a certain finesse."

"Well, go on," suggested the detective.

"When he was rudely aroused by the excited maid, he says he dressed hurriedly, then went upstairs and tried the door to the sitting-room, which was locked; so he returned to the garden to get an implement of some kind from the tool-house in order to pry open the door. Then he noticed the ladder, no longer lying against the wall, but standing against the big tree. He also saw a light from his mistress's window, so he placed the ladder against the wall, climbed it, and looked in. There he saw the body of Miss Sigurda, so he descended as quickly as he could, told the maid, who shook all over, so he says, but who telephoned to the police."

"That don't add anything to what I already know," declared the detective.

"And you got your information from whom?" asked Stoke.

"From the maid," replied Yates, perplexed. "At that, their stories agree. Those two either are in cahoots or maybe that's what did happen."

"This gardener," continued Stoke, "is much more intelligent than he seems. Some of his story rings true, and all of it appears plausible. But," and he paused pensively, "much could have happened that has not yet been elucidated."

"I think I'll lock that guy up as a material witness," declared Yates.

"If you will pardon the suggestion," remarked Stoke, "I should leave him here for a while, apparently disregarded, but meticulously watched. What he does may reveal something."

Little did we then realize that this advice was to be productive of a most dramatic aftermath.

"Well, we don't seem to be getting very far," asserted Yates.

"It does seem a bit disappointing," acknowledged Stoke, "but I did acquire some useful information about the past history of the fair deceased."

"It's last night's history that interests me," answered the detective.

I could readily see that Stoke had fallen somewhat in his estimation. He had begun to think that this quiet, though obviously discerning, young man was of no more help than any interpreter might have been. He called to Riordan.

"Fetch that colored wench," he ordered.

In a few minutes the maid was ushered in. She was a young, dark-complexioned, rather trim black woman, neatly dressed.

"Tell us your name again," commanded Yates, who apparently intended to conduct this inquisition himself.

"Pansy Thedford," answered the girl brazenly.

"What happened here last night," demanded Yates.

"I done told you all that once before. What do you keep after me for?" she answered vehemently. "I'm going to get my lawyer, I am."

Yates stood up. His look was forbidding and the colored woman cowered before it.

"You're going to answer my questions or go to jail," he said firmly.

"Honest, boss, I've told you the truth every time," she cried. "Yes-suh, yessuh, I'll answer your questions."

"How long were you employed by Miss Sigurda?" asked Stoke quietly.

"Two years, sir," she replied, turning to him.

"Did she employ you here or somewhere else?"

"Right here in Washington. I was just out of high school," was the answer.

For some time Stoke plied the girl with questions, while Yates listened with growing impatience. I could not see that any progress was being made, especially as Stoke kept asking about Miss Sigurda's friends and who was accustomed to visit her and when. The maid described a number of men, but disclaimed any knowledge of their names.

"Who was Miss Sigurda's doctor," asked Stoke suddenly.

"A gentleman over on Vermont Avenue."

"His name?" demanded Stoke.

"I don't know. I never heard it," was the evasive reply.

"You lie and you know it," exploded Yates, but the maid refused to change her answers after further intense questioning.

"Take her out," snapped Yates at last.

When the woman had gone, he glared at us.

"I agree with your thoughts," remarked Stoke, with his customary suavity; "we must trace this doctor who seemed so familiar with the departed on the night that she did the departing."

Yates was about to make some vehement assertion when Riordan appeared in the doorway, deferential as usual in the presence of his superior. Like all traffic minions he could be bumptious, officious, crabbed, arrogant, and belligerent to some poor, unwitting minor offender against a more or less unreasonable traffic regulation, but in the august environment of the mighty he was all servility.

"There's a naval officer out here who insists on seeing you, Mr. Yates," he announced; "says he has something very important to impart, as he puts it, to you. Won't go away. Can't get rid of him," he added apologetically.

Yates deliberately pushed his hat over one eye, expectorated, or, perhaps I should say, spat, disdainfully, and said:

"I'll be a cock-eyed runt if I want to see any fussing naval officers right now, even if they are admirals. Where is this guy?"

"Right here, chief," came a pleasant voice. "I took the liberty of following this handsome and efficient officer right in. Pardon the intrusion, but I have a clue, a real clue, for you in this Sigurda case."

Before us stood Runy O'Mara, smiling his irresistible smile.

"Hello, Stoke," he called, and hastily added, turning to Yates: "Detective, you and I are old friends. Don't you remember the time an over-zealous cop—ahem, officer— arrested me under the mistaken impression I was driving a trifle fast, and I got my friend Joe Grauss, the fourth assistant commissioner of deeds, to call Pete Yates, your second cousin, who induced you to suggest to the traffic bureau that the charge be forgotten? That was only last December."

"Nothing like that could happen in the District of Columbia," countered Yates, but he seemed amused.

"I could just as easily have discussed the matter with Commissioner Selden, Henry Selden, whom I know rather intimately," continued Runy, "but why bother a busy man with such trifles?"

"Quite correct," answered Stoke, "don't bother busy people with trifles."

"I am here on no trifle," replied Runy, archly, "but on a matter of importance. Yes, I will take a chair, ignoring the lack of an invitation to do so. Gather round, gentlemen, and let me explain and your time will not be wasted. I know who came to this house to visit Miss Sigurda last night."

"The devil you say!" blurted Yates, waving Riordan away, pushing his hat to the back of his head, and sitting down. We all gathered about Runy with an attitude of expectation.

"Who was it?" asked Stoke.

"Let me tell it in my own way, will you?" was the reply. "Who was it called Dr. Ragland, eminent as a student of poisoning as well as of neurology, away last night? Who was it sent a call to Dr. Todd, the medical examiner, so that by the time he got a chance to do a post-mortem, the poison had so diffused itself that it could not be recognized? Who was it made a telephone call to this house at midnight?"

"Well, who was it?" demanded Yates.

"It was the same man who drove up to this house at about seven in a yellow roadster, took Miss Sigurda to dine at the Sevilla restaurant and brought her back in that same yellow Fiat roadster some two hours later, though the couple had left the Sevilla three quarters of an hour before they reached the house, a ten-minute ride from downtown F Street."

"Who was it?" insisted Yates.

"Don't *you* know?" asked Runy, turning to Stoke. "Here you are emulating all the celebrated amateur sleuths in captivity. Don't you know?"

"I don't know," confided Stoke, "but," he added, "I can hazard a fairly scientific guess."

"Well, guess away," returned Runy.

"Enough of this palaver," interposed Yates; "who was it? Cut out the comedy. This is no pink tea."

"It was Doctor Roger Rollin," said Stoke quietly.

"Bravo, bravo," said Runy, "yes, it was. I should suggest, Mr. Yates, that you and your associate sleuth have earnest converse with the young physician, who has offices in the building at the corner of Vermont Avenue and K Street. You will find him right now, or could have ten minutes ago, in room 432, with a pretty nurse in the outer office, and probably with a homely female patient in the inner sanctum."

"Bravo in turn to you, Runy," praised Stoke. "And would you condescend to explain how you garnered all this interesting information?"

"Sure, tell us," advised Yates.

Runy smiled blandly.

"Not having been invited to participate in the investigations, I camped in the commissioner's car parked outside the Serpentine Club and had a lovely snooze. Mr. Selden was a bit startled, also somewhat irate, when he started the car about four a.m. and woke me up in the back seat, and I spoke to him from the darkness. However, just at the moment, Old Bushy came sauntering along and joined the party."

"You mean Starr-Smith?" asked Stoke.

"Right, and between us we assuaged the exasperated commissioner, rode out to Cleveland Park with him, and by skillful cross-examination got all, or most, of the facts out of that reluctant person. After a cup of coffee in his living-room Starr-Smith and I walked downtown, discussing matters *en route*. Then I got busy following up some of the suggestions. First I visited the Greek out in Georgetown, who had already been chivvied by one of Mr. Yates's minions, and discovered that the midnight phone call was made by a gent who left a yellow roadster in front of the door. I also got a description of the man. By that time it was morning and I wandered over to the headquarters of the Medical Society and by some astute questioning ascertained what docs came to the place in yellow roadsters. One of three or four who did so was Rollin. Then to visit a large number of people who knew the late Mademoiselle Sigurda. After a lot of fruitless questioning I found a young lady friend of mine who saw the couple enter the Sevilla. A check-up at the Sevilla, which cost me a nice gratuity to a couple of waiters. Shall I submit an expense account, Mr. Yates?"

"Such zeal is worth the opportunity to spend one's own cash," remarked Stoke. "But proceed with the revelations."

"By that time lunch was ready at the club, where Starr-Smith joined me again and we had another conference. Incidentally, I tried once to beat my way into the house here, but the red-headed cop hadn't slept well or something and I couldn't get by his eagle eye. This afternoon I visited the yellow car, talked to more people all around, and finally paid a professional call on the doc himself. He was very evasive while he felt my pulse, and all I got out of him was a couple of c.c. pills, which any naval surgeon could have given me. Another item for the expense account."

"Good work, anyway, lieutenant," said Yates. "Do you know Dr. Rollin?" he asked Stoke, who acknowledged that he had met the gentleman once or twice.

"Phone him, please, and we will honor the guy with our presence," said the detective ominously.

CHAPTER VII
WE CALL ON THE DOCTOR

"It might be better to take the doctor unawares," suggested Stoke in reply to Detective Yates's request that an immediate appointment be made by telephone with the suspected Dr. Rollin.

Yates chewed on his cigar stub in cogitation.

"Perhaps you're right," he admitted. "Let's go."

As we rose to leave, Runy acted somewhat embarrassed.

"I don't want to butt in on your party," he announced with an air that plainly indicated that nothing would give him greater pleasure than to join us.

"I am sure Mr. Yates will be glad to have you come along," said Stoke, "especially since you have seen the gentleman recently and can identify him if necessary."

Yates nodded assent and we departed. It was only a few blocks from the house on Q Street to Vermont Avenue, where the building containing Dr. Rollin's office was situated. The lobby had an antiseptic smell, such as is encountered in hospitals and some doctors' offices. We took the elevator and rose to the fourth floor past various sanctums occupied by dentists and physicians. A few steps down the corridor and round a corner and we came to two doors. One was marked: "Dr. Roger Rollin. Private." The other bore the legend: "Roger Rollin, M.D. Office Hours by Appointment. Entrance."

"Considerable swank for a beginner," commented Stoke. "A couple of years ago and he was only an interne."

Yates was about to enter, followed by Runy and me, when Stoke laid his hand on the detective's arm and drew him back.

"If I may suggest," he murmured, "you and Lieutenant O'Mara might remain outside for a few moments while I make arrangements to see this disciple of Æsculapius."

A look of surprise came over the detective's face, then a flash of anger.

"Say, what's the idea?" he said. "I'm handling this case."

"Yes, of course, of course," replied Stoke, "but there is a good reason for this procedure. The moment I am in the august presence of the desired, I will open that door marked 'Private' and usher you in. Runy stays with you because he can recognize your man."

A light seemed to dawn on the detective.

"I get you. Go ahead."

Stoke and I went in through the door marked "Entrance" and came into a rather small ante-room. A young woman in a white uniform, who was sitting at a desk, looked up as we entered. I was immediately struck by her resemblance to Beatrice Sigurda, though no doubt it was merely a coincidence.

"Is the doctor in?" inquired Stoke politely.

"Did you have an appointment?" said the girl in a sweetly officious manner, without, I noticed, answering the question.

"No," answered Stoke, "but I wanted to see him on professional business."

"The doctor doesn't need any supplies now," she remarked suspiciously.

Stoke laughed.

"I am not a salesman or detail man," he assured her, "but am connected with the Government."

"Oh, did you want to see him about his liquor permits?" was the next naïve inquiry.

"No, no," said Stoke a little impatiently, "about another matter, a medical matter. Will you please tell Dr. Rollin that Mr. Stoke of the Public Health Service is here and would like to see him at once?"

As I watched the girl, I thought I detected a sharp look come into her eyes as Stoke mentioned his name.

"Wait a minute," she said, and disappeared through a door.

We waited more than a minute. Then there were sounds of a commotion in the hall outside, and the door was flung open. In the entrance appeared Detective Yates, holding firmly to the arm of a young man dressed in a natty blue suit, who was protesting vigorously about something. He wore a hat and carried a black satchel. Stoke moved quickly to the door and spoke hurriedly to Yates in a low tone. Immediately Yates and his charge retreated and Stoke closed the door. Hardly a moment later the office assistant appeared in the other door. Stoke stood looking at her nonchalantly.

"I am sorry, Mr. Stoke," she said with a winning smile, "but the doctor had to go out on an emergency call, a matter of life and death, so he cannot see you right now."

"Will he be back soon?" asked Stoke.

"I am afraid not for some time. Couldn't you drop in tomorrow or some other day? I am sure the doctor will be delighted to see you then."

"He'll see me now," remarked Stoke with grim significance, and strode to the outer door. Some distance down the hall was a little group, which I discerned as Yates, Runy, and the expostulating gentleman whom the detective still held firmly by the arm. Stoke beckoned and Yates and the protesting doctor entered.

"Take him into the private office," suggested Stoke. "Runy can entertain this blushing Florence Nightingale, who will, furthermore, remain right here until wanted."

When we were inside and Stoke had closed the door between the ante-room and the office, Yates released his prisoner and took a position before the other door leading to the hall.

"What is the meaning of this intrusion, this outrageous intrusion?" demanded the doctor, for it was unquestionably he.

"Say, you," said Yates truculently, "this is no intrusion. I've got a John Doe warrant right here in my pocket and I have a mind to lock you up. What do you mean by trying to run out when the police come to see you?"

"The police!" gasped the doctor, whose belligerency seemed to vanish at these words.

"Yes, the police," answered Yates, sticking his jaw forward, like an umpire addressing a protesting ball-player, "and, what's more, we're going to ask you some questions and you're going to answer them, see, or it'll be the worse for you."

The doctor seated himself at his desk and toyed with a paper-cutter. When he looked up, he was still pale, though calm and apparently collected, but he would probably have enjoyed hurling the paper-cutter at all of us.

"I have done absolutely nothing to bring the police to my office," he remarked. "What is it you want of me? And how do you happen to be involved in this matter, Mr. Stoke?" he inquired coldly.

"As an officially designated assistant, Dr. Rollin," answered Stoke blandly; "I am merely helping this gentleman to gather some salient and pertinent facts about a recent episode which seems suspiciously like a homicide. Since you are, or were, a friend of the deceased, we felt that you would not object to aiding us with any information about the situation that might be helpful."

"What do you refer to?" asked the doctor rather huskily.

"To the death of Beatrice Sigurda, of course," replied Stoke.

The doctor stared at Stoke. His face was ashen.

"I know nothing, absolutely nothing about it," he declared.

"You were a friend of the lady, were you not?" asked Stoke.

"Why should I answer that or any other question?" demanded the doctor.

Mr. Yates strode forward. He placed his hand in his pocket and produced some metallic contrivances. They were handcuffs.

"If that's what you think, you can come along with me," he said.

Stoke waved back the irate detective.

"Come, come, now, doctor," he admonished gently, "no one is accusing you of any complicity in this affair. We are merely trying to find out a few simple facts about the events of the evening. Since you were the lady's physician and, in fact, were known to have visited her the same night on which her death occurred, you can readily see why we are interested in asking you a few innocuous questions. You have nothing to lose by being frank with us."

The doctor's color had returned somewhat and he seemed less upset.

"I don't want to conceal anything that I may know," he told Stoke, "but I don't like this man's attitude."

Before Yates could burst forth with a slightly rabid reply, Stoke continued:

"In his zeal to get to the bottom of this distressing affair and perform his duty as an official of the police department, this gentleman often has disagreeable tasks to undertake. He is only doing what he considers proper from the standpoint of public welfare."

"That's right," grunted Yates.

"Now, doctor," went on Stoke, "you did visit Miss Sigurda last night, didn't you? How did you find her?"

"She was physically all right, but mentally depressed," replied the doctor. "Yes," he continued, more at his ease, "I not only called on her last night, but took her to dinner and brought her home."

"And you dined where?"

"At the Sevilla on F near Fourteenth Street."

"How long had you known Miss Sigurda?" was Stoke's next question.

"Practically ever since she came to Washington," replied Dr. Rollin, "which is a little over two years. I was introduced to her by a common friend, and since she needed medical attention, I became her physician and have acted as such ever since."

"What were the nature of her ailments?" inquired Stoke.

The doctor bristled somewhat.

"That is a professional matter which I am not required to reveal."

"Quite true," assented Stoke; "I merely was interested in knowing whether she displayed any mental disorders of significance. I believe you are well known as a specialist in mental afflictions, are you not, doctor?"

The young physician was obviously pleased. He stroked his rather meager black mustache complacently. I, who knew Stoke so well, had recognized the faint irony in his tone, but the physician was oblivious of it.

"Why, yes," he admitted, "most of her troubles were mental, except, of course, the usual run of respiratory infections, gastro-intestinal disturbances, and other minor maladies."

"Would you have classed her as schizophrenic?" went on Stoke.

"No, not as bad as that," answered the doctor; "she was occasionally addicted to neurasthenia, but without paranoia."

"Suicidal?" asked Stoke suddenly.

"No," said the doctor, and then hesitated, as if an idea had come to him. "Come to think of it, she did sometimes show emotional conflicts, confusional psychoses, and other symptoms which might have led to suicide. Was there any indication that she might have caused her own death?"

"I don't believe that point is clear yet," answered Stoke evasively. "Did Miss Sigurda have many intimate friends?" he went on.

"No, she didn't," was the reply; "she knew or was acquainted socially with about everybody in town, and she was on the go all the time, but few persons knew her intimately. She was a seclusive type and, between you and me, had something of an inferiority complex, which she compensated for by the kind of exhibitionism which makes some people ardent society participators. I often accompanied her to various social functions, as she seemed to like my company."

"Very illuminating," commented Stoke. "Your description of Miss Sigurda is extremely helpful in aiding us to estimate her character."

Detective Yates spat noisily in a shiny cuspidor near the doctor's desk, but said nothing. Dr. Rollin was smiling pleasantly.

"By the way, doctor," pursued Stoke in an offhand way, "won't you continue to enlighten us by telling us where you went after leaving Miss Sigurda's house last night? What time was it when you left?"

The doctor hesitated again—seemed rather reticent, in fact—but answered after a moment's reflection:

"I took leave about ten or ten thirty, I think, and came to the office for my instruments, then drove to see a patient in Georgetown."

"Who was the patient?" asked Stoke in such an inoffensive manner that the doctor replied immediately:

"A Mrs. Clarence Carpenter."

Yates made a note.

"Did you make any telephone calls while in the office?" continued Stoke.

The doctor was showing less assurance in his replies.

"Why, yes, I believe I did, but I forget whom I called."

Stoke did not follow up this line, but I noticed Yates jotting something more down in his note-book.

"And where did you go from Mrs. Carpenter's?" he inquired.

"I remained there for some time, as she was in a state of elation; in fact, she was so bad that I called a confrere in consultation."

"Who?" asked Stoke.

"Dr. Basil Ragland," replied the doctor with no hesitation, "and I waited until he arrived. We discussed the case, instructed the attendant, which consumed altogether a couple of hours of my time. Then I went home to bed. You see, Mr. Detective," exclaimed the doctor triumphantly, turning to Yates, "I have a perfect alibi for the evening. Your suspicions, if you had any concerning me, were utterly unfounded."

"That remains to be seen," said Yates. "You might tell us why you started to run away when we first came to see you this afternoon."

"Oh, that is easily explained," replied the doctor. "You do me an injustice to call it running away. I didn't get the name mentioned to me by my office girl, or at least attached no importance to the one she mentioned. She probably got it wrong, anyway. I had a most important call to make and started away. When you, if you will pardon me, so rudely intercepted me, naturally I knew nothing of who you were or the significance of the occasion and I was excited."

"You were that, all right," agreed Yates.

"Did you ever attend Miss Sigurda's gardener professionally?" asked Stoke suddenly.

"Yes, once or twice. A queer specimen, too," said Dr. Rollin, "with a much higher I.Q. than his appearance would lead you to believe. Beatrice—that is, Miss Sigurda—called him Miguel and he was utterly devoted to her. Do you suspect him?"

Stoke ignored the question.

"Did you ever administer opiates to Miss Sigurda?" he asked.

Again the doctor hesitated.

"Once or twice," he admitted cautiously.

"In what manner?"

"Orally—that is, by mouth—always," answered the doctor.

"Never hypodermically?"

"Never."

Stoke seemed to muse for a moment.

"I think that's about all, unless Mr. Yates has something on his mind. You are positive, are you, doctor, that you have omitted no details of your own movements on the night of the death?"

The physician seemed to ponder before he replied. "I can think of nothing else of importance."

Stoke rose. For once Yates seemed to be satisfied, or at least not to desire to continue the inquisition. He fumbled with his note-book, which seemed to be full.

"Sorry to have caused you all the trouble, doctor, but you won't regret having been frank with us. Say, could you give me a piece of paper? This pad of mine is all filled."

"Certainly, certainly," said the doctor eagerly, reaching in his desk and handing Yates several sheets from a prescription pad.

"Much obliged," Yates acknowledged, as he added them to his own pad and returned it to his pocket. "Well, let's leave the doc in peace," he remarked, turning to Stoke.

As we moved toward the door, Dr. Rollin rose.

"If you don't mind my making a suggestion, gentlemen," he said deferentially, and paused.

"Sure, go ahead," prompted Yates.

"You might do some intensive interrogation of that professor who lives next door to Miss Sigurda. I know for a fact that Beat—Miss Sigurda, did not like him and had repulsed his advances. He used to go over there at all hours and she threatened to call the police once and have him thrown out if he didn't leave immediately, or so she told me. I did not know him at all, never met him, in fact—that is, not formally—but he is an old bachelor, and apparently something of a nymphomaniac, or so I have heard. It may be nothing, of course, but if I were you, I would look into it. Come to think of it, I believe he spent some time in South America several years ago. Yes, by all means, follow up that whole possibility."

"Thank you very much for the suggestion," said Stoke before Yates could comment. "By the way, doctor, did you ever have occasion to call on Miss Sigurda through the garden entrance?"

"No indeed, I always used the front door, as I naturally would," replied the doctor indignantly.

We went out, Runy joining us.

CHAPTER VIII
A COUNCIL OF WAR

As we emerged from the elevator on the ground floor of the professional building after our interview with the evasive Doctor Rollin, Detective Yates strode, not walked, to a telephone booth. Before it he paused for a moment, pushed his hat a little more over one eye, gazed at us truculently, and blurted:

"In my twenty-two years and five months as beat-walker, desk sergeant, and detective I have met any God's quantity of lying guys and I know the breed. See? Well, that quack is one of them, or I'm a plumber."

"You are not a plumber," said Stoke. "Furthermore, if I were you, I should put the estimable doctor under surveillance for a while."

"Just what I'm going to do," replied Yates. "Wait here a moment while I telephone and get one of the boys on the job."

He phoned quickly, after cussing the operator for some little delay in getting his number.

"It's police headquarters I'm calling, you young sap," I heard him say.

When he emerged, red-faced, from the booth, he came up to Stoke and drew him aside. The two conversed in a mysterious manner for a few moments. Then they rejoined Runy and me.

"I'll stick round here for a while," said Yates, "but you gents needn't wait. I'll see you tomorrow morning, then," he continued, addressing Stoke.

"Well, *au revoir*, captain," contributed Runy, as we departed; "hope you don't have to feel the doc's pulse again."

Yates grinned.

"So long, admiral," he countered, "keep up the good work and we'll give you a real job on the force some day. Also a better uniform."

We sauntered down the street past the University Club and the ponderous building occupied by the Veterans' Bureau. Stoke seemed pensive and we did not interrupt his cogitations. Suddenly he stopped.

"In an hour or more we dine," he announced. "Let us feast together at the Serpentine Club, perhaps in company with Mr. Selden, if we can pry him away from his attractive family. Call him up, will you, Jim, and lure him over? And, Runy, you come with us and not with the attractive family while Selden's protecting influence is absent. In the meantime," he continued, "I have some business to attend to, so I will join you later."

As he turned to leave us, while Runy was stopping to buy all the evening papers, he grasped my arm and spoke to me in a low voice.

"Be prepared for a little adventuring tonight. You and I are going to do some midnight prowling. Get in a catnap now if you can. Go over to my place or grab a hammock at the club."

Runy and I strolled along through Lafayette Square, the air fragrant with perfume of the midsummer flowers which decorate this famous park. Stoke disappeared up Sixteenth Street, past old St. John's Church. As the debonair lieutenant and I wandered along, a rakish gray roadster containing a most attractive young female in a red hat stopped opposite and a horn was honked vigorously. With a hurried apology, Runy darted through the traffic and joined the young lady and with a parting wave to me was whisked away. Alone I meandered to the club.

After telephoning to Mr. Selden, who was still in his office at the Municipal Building and apparently rather reluctant to leave it, though he finally consented to join us, I sought a quiet spot for a siesta. Strangely enough, the billiard-room was vacant and so I stretched out on the cushioned seat which runs across the side of the room. I was awakened some time later by a crash beside me and leaped to my feet. A billiard-ball had bounced off one of the tables and apparently missed my head by inches.

"A thousand apologies," exclaimed a voice.

Standing nonchalantly before me was the tall form of Starr-Smith, billiard-cue in hand.

"I was about to arouse you, my dear Watson," he continued pleasantly, "as your companions in criminal investigating are assembling, but I assure you the means I took were purely accidental. Hoping that you might talk in your slumber and reveal some interesting developments in our *cause célèbre*, I was amusing myself knocking the balls about while you slept, when one escaped."

"Stoke and Runy and Selden and I are dining together," I said. "You had better join us."

"Thank you," he replied, "Stoke has already asked me, and he has likewise induced Dr. Ragland to come over and make a quorum. No doubt we shall solve the crime tonight by means of erudite deductions, brilliant analytical conclusions, and other absentee intelligence." He was getting cynical again.

At seven thirty the same five men who had been around the table in the garden of the Serpentine Club on the night of the crime were sitting together again in a quiet corner, as Sam hovered solicitously about with his menus.

"I rather expected a convocation of the crime club tonight," remarked Starr-Smith.

No one spoke.

"How am that murder case?" inquired Sam unctuously, with the familiarity of the privileged colored retainer.

"Do you know, Samuel," exclaimed Runy, who had somehow managed to break loose from his fair companion of the gray roadster, "do you know," he continued blandly, "the deed was done by a green sea serpent, sent to the house by parcel post?"

"Is that so?" asked Sam, the whites of his eyes showing.

"The matter is hardly one for levity," said Mr. Selden reprovingly. "I came here at some inconvenience to talk business, serious business, with you gentlemen, and, with all due respect to our jovial young friend, I don't want to waste my time."

"The irrepressible Mr. O'Mara has displayed some real detective prowess, despite his jocund tongue, I understand," said Starr-Smith.

Runy, now serious, briefly recounted his findings with respect to the yellow car and the movements of Dr. Rollin. "Furthermore," continued Runy, "that blonde cutie in the doc's office is in cahoots with him on a lot of things. I spent some time alone with her, you remember, while Stoke and the sarge were interrogating the doctor himself. The poor young thing needed sympathy and I was kind and gentle, as befitted my altruistic nature."

"Yes, yes, go on, Don Juan," broke in Dr. Ragland, and even Selden laughed.

"Well, it seems that she phoned to you on behalf of her boss," explained Runy, turning to the physician. "She also revealed that he knew Miss Sigurda much more intimately than he was willing to admit. In fact, I suspect blondy of a slightly more than trivial jealous disposition."

"It looks to me," observed Dr. Ragland, "as if my young medical colleague might be classed as a suspect in this case."

"What little there is to go on so far," assented Selden, "points more in his direction than toward anyone else. Todd and Ragland are agreed that death was caused by an obscure but powerful poison, possibly administered hypodermically. It was the kind of thing a medical man would be qualified to do. This particular man knew her well—intimately, in fact. He was with her on the night of her death. He sent messages to the two physicians in the whole District of Columbia who would have been most competent to detect the exact nature of the poison if they had been able to analyze it soon enough, and as a consequence of those more or less fictitious calls neither Todd nor Ragland was available. Finally, his demeanor when questioned was far from frank, was it, Mr. Stoke?"

"Far," replied Stoke.

"Besides," broke in Starr-Smith pensively, "he tried to throw suspicion on another person."

"We have got to find a motive, though," exclaimed Runy. "When all is said and done, these facts are extremely circumstantial, and there isn't much real evidence. If you will pardon the question, doctor," he continued, turning to Dr. Ragland, "did you find anything about Miss Sigurda that might have suggested a motive, a reason for getting rid of her at this time?"

"Casanova speaking again," said the architect, with his customary trace of sarcasm. "His suggestions are positively seductive."

"Oh, now, I understand," replied the doctor. "To answer the question bluntly, Miss Sigurda was not in the physical condition which has inspired a good many murders, not to mention such other crimes as abortion. No, you will have to look elsewhere for your motive."

"Consider all of the persons who are at all suspicious in this case," continued Selden; "they are very few. First the maid, second the gardener, third this Dr. Rollin."

"You can practically rule out the maid," said Dr. Ragland; "the psychology does not fit. This crime was carefully planned. A Negro does not do that. When a Negro commits murder, as unfortunately does happen, it is either in a drunken frenzy or in an impulsive brawl. A mulatto might plan a homicide, but more likely against one of his own race, if he did it at all. No, I doubt that the maid was the actual culprit, though there might be complicity."

"The facts, which are even more important than all this psychological theory, do not point toward the maid, either," interjected Runy.

"Now, on the other hand," Selden pursued, "Basil's theories would not hold good against this gardener, a half-breed mixture of degenerate conquistador and Argentinian Indian. Revenge for some old wrong, or some other reason, would have induced him to do it."

"Would a more or less illiterate peon have been likely to have employed a hypodermic, assuming one was used?" asked Starr-Smith rather scornfully.

"What proof have we that it was used?" countered Selden. "The only marks of violence were two strange punctures on the dead woman's neck. Many things could have made wounds like that."

"Someone could have entered the house or could have been in the house," explained Dr. Ragland, "crept up to that unoccupied room, opened that door behind the curtain, which was less than a foot from the head of the unsuspecting beauty, and blown a poisoned dart at her. It couldn't have been done from the window."

"The body might have been moved," suggested Runy.

"There were no incriminating finger-prints on it," said Mr. Selden. "The evidence seems to be that it was not moved, but that she died where she was found. Yates has already obtained Dr. Rollin's finger-prints. They are also in the room, but not in the right places."

"Then how do you explain the dust behind that door and its obviously unused condition?" demanded Runy.

"That might be camouflaged, though it hardly seems likely," admitted the commissioner.

"Could someone, a person intimate with Miss Sigurda, a person she accepted as a friend or more than that, have been sitting on that divan with her, one arm about her?" began Runy.

"There you go again," laughed Dr. Ragland.

"I'm serious," protested Runy. "It would have been comparatively easy for him to have reached for a hypodermic needle—perhaps he had it cached behind that curtain—and given her a jab with it."

"There were two jabs," said Stoke.

Runy scratched his head, perplexed. Starr-Smith laughed cynically.

"Then how explain the letter found on the desk? What bearing, if any, does that have?" inquired Selden. "It was addressed: 'Dear Rog.'"

"Dr. Rollin's first name is Roger, is it not?" suggested the architect.

"Yes, but what of it?" demanded Dr. Ragland. "If you will pardon my harping on the psychological aspects of the case, all that letter shows is that Miss Sigurda was depressed. She mentions a power that threatened her. She was frightened about something. She may have feared some calamity. Does anyone know when that letter was written, anyway?"

"The handwriting expert says it was probably written that same day," remarked Selden.

"He must be an astute observer," sniffed Runy. "And how did he arrive at that remarkable conclusion?"

"I am not familiar with the technical details of the gentleman's craft," answered the commissioner, rather brusquely.

"Inasmuch as the fair Beatrice spent part of the evening with her physician friend, it seems probable that she wrote the billet-doux to him after he had departed, if it is to him," was Dr. Ragland's comment.

"Will someone now please explain the telephone call in the middle of the night, made from a fruit-store in Georgetown by a man who left a yellow roadster outside and who exclaimed, according to the maid: 'My God, it's happened,' or words to that effect?" Selden went on.

"If Rollin killed the girl, why would he dash out to Georgetown afterwards and then phone to his victim?" asked Runy.

"You forget that he had a patient there," said Dr. Ragland, "but I can't forget it, having been called there myself."

"Can't you psycho-analyze the motive behind that phone call, Basil?" asked Mr. Selden.

"No, I can't, and won't, psycho-analyze it," replied the eminent neurologist. "What do you take me for, anyway, one of these itinerant phrenologists? Psycho-analysis is more often quackery than not. But I can give you a strictly scientific explanation, based on good psychiatry. A certain type of person who has committed a crime, perhaps for the first time, or, say, has attempted to commit a crime, will often have an irresistible impulse to check up on his efforts to ascertain whether he really accomplished what he set out to do. That might explain this particular call. Then again it might not."

For another hour or more the discussion continued. Although the facts and theories of the case were rather thoroughly mulled over, I could not see that any startling progress was made. The consensus of opinion seemed to be that the most important next step was to trace the exact movements of Dr. Rollin between ten o'clock and midnight of the night on which the crime occurred. At ten he had taken leave of Miss Sigurda and, according to his own story, had gone to his office and then to Georgetown, a matter of twenty minutes' drive in an automobile. At midnight he had made a telephone call to Miss Sigurda, who was already dead and had been for a half-hour or more. Somewhat later Dr. Ragland had seen him at the house of Mrs. Carpenter in Georgetown. Where was he during the two hours between ten and twelve? All agreed that his story lacked authenticity and that he needed a real alibi to avoid trouble.

"It seems to simmer down to our doctor as chief suspect, with one or two other possibilities," commented Mr. Selden.

"I wouldn't entirely overlook the next-door neighbor, though, even if it was the doctor who mentioned that possibility," remarked Starr-Smith, stifling a yawn. "Where was he all during the festivities? Mr. O'Mara or some equally competent sleuth might look into that."

"The assignment is refused," said Runy. "Stoke knows the old duffer and can easily find out. I will trail the doc, if it's all the same to my many colleagues."

Starr-Smith yawned again, somewhat more obtrusively. He seemed bored.

"What was it Shakespeare opined about sleep knitting up the raveled sleeve of care?" he said. "If you gentlemen have no further brilliant suggestions, I think I will go home and retire and obtain some scientific somnolence. No doubt most of you other gentlemen are ready to do likewise."

"Stoke and I," I began, on the verge of blurting out something about our proposed midnight meanderings, when I felt a warning pressure on my arm, "are—er—certainly ready to make up some of our lost sleep."

"Let's hope you comparatively early birds dream of a solution to the mystery," suggested Runy.

"I am afraid some of you experts will have to uncover more trenchant facts before we can dream true, as Peter Ibbetson used to say," replied the architect, with his usual sardonic smile.

"By the way, Henry," said Dr. Ragland, "have you or your police solved the mystery of the dagger yet?"

"No," said Mr. Selden shortly, and rose to go.

It was about half past eleven and we all departed. I phoned to my landlady, a solicitous elderly widow who took pleasure in worrying over my whereabouts, and assured her that I was all right, in good company, and wouldn't be home again that night. I think she had to get out of bed to receive my message, but it comforted her, nevertheless. Then I joined Stoke and we set off toward his domicile.

"You did not participate very loquaciously in the conference tonight," I remarked to him.

"I learned more by listening," he answered laconically.

"Are you still more or less perplexed?" I asked.

"More or less," he admitted, "but somewhat less than yesterday. Did you notice one peculiar thing about this conversation tonight? No one thought to mention the paper bag found on Miss Sigurda's divan."

"What of it?" I inquired.

"That bag tells more than has been perceived as yet," was the enigmatic reply.

"Does it?" I remarked. "How does that blamed bag fit into the doctor's movements?"

"It doesn't," he answered.

"Well, anyway," was my comment, "it looks as if Yates will soon have the goods on Dr. Rollin. Don't you think the evidence points rather seriously toward him?"

"Either to him or to someone else who has not yet appeared in the picture," was all that Stoke would say.

CHAPTER IX
MIDNIGHT ADVENTURE

I watched Stokes' preparations for our pending prowl with increasing concern. First he replaced his white shirt with a khaki one, then donned some dark clothes in place of his light-colored Palm Beach suit, as dark clothes were, he explained, less conspicuous at night. In fact, they were not conspicuous at all. Fortunately, I was already clad in a blue tropical worsted, with shirt to match, as giddy, Stoke declared, as Runy on an amorous rampage.

Having dressed suitably for the occasion, Stoke took a powerful flashlight from a drawer and at the same time handed me a somewhat smaller one. His next move was more ominous. It was to slip an automatic revolver into his inside pocket. In answer to my involuntary shudder, he remarked enigmatically:

"There probably will be no need for the artillery, but it's an ideal night for another murder, or a duel, or some other kind of fireworks. Let's go."

He opened the door into the corridor and looked out. The hall was empty and most of the near-by rooms were dark. From one transom a light streamed, however, and as we passed that door, I heard muffled clinking noises and a voice which sounded suspiciously like: "I'll raise you a buck."

Stoke grinned, as he muttered: "We are gambling, too."

I wondered what he meant, and my awe was further enhanced as he led me down three flights of stairs, avoiding the automatic elevator, and then not out the front entrance, which seemed deserted, but down another flight and into the basement. After traversing a number of dark passages he opened a door with a rather sudden click and ushered me into a black hole, which I took to be the alley behind the apartment. For a man with a scientific training and a keen appreciation of culture, Stoke knew more about alleys and back streets than any person I had ever met.

No more eerie night than this could have existed for our nocturnal adventure, whatever it was to be. There was no moon, the sky was cloudy, and, except for the occasional street lights which pierced the umbrous gloom, all was as black as the proverbial ace of spades. As if this were not enough, a wind had come up and was rustling the trees with a weird sound. The night resembled the fall of the year more than June.

By devious ways we journeyed for several blocks, Stoke acting as pilot, of course. I followed him blindly, which is a literal description of my feeling except when we crossed one of the fairly well-lit main streets, as we did several times. I had no idea where we were, but was beginning to feel the excitement of the chase, when suddenly Stoke seized my arm.

"Listen," he said softly.

From behind a wall came a peculiar sound, rhythmical and not unmusical. It resembled the strumming of some strange stringed instrument. Far in the rear of the wall was a faint glow of light.

"What is it?" I murmured.

"Only our architectural friend soothing himself with the exotic strains of a Spanish serenade," answered Stoke.

"What, who?" I sputtered.

"That is Starr-Smith's studio," explained Stoke; "it isn't far, you know, from the Sigurda house."

"Are you planning to call at this ungodly hour?" I asked. "You know he said he was going home to sleep when we left him."

"He probably changed his mind," replied Stoke, "but we won't disturb him, as our destination is elsewhere. This is merely *en route.* *En avant.*"

We proceeded along the dark alley until we came to a right-angle turn, dimly lit by a distant street light, emerged, crossed a street at a dark spot between the scattered lamp-posts, and plunged into another alley. We traversed the length of it silently, Stoke guiding me round a corner at one place, where there seemed to be a jog. At the end of a block he slowed up, as we were approaching another street. He drew me into the shadow as I looked ahead and saw a pensive figure standing on the sidewalk. It was a policeman. He seemed to be doing nothing in particular, faintly humming a tune and idling on his beat.

Stoke retraced his steps, but kept straight ahead instead of making the right-angled turn. He was going slowly and cautiously now, and gradually came to a stop.

"The Sigurda mansion," he whispered.

Much to my surprise, we were directly in the rear of the house on Q Street. Stoke tried the garden door, but it was locked. Then he tried the door of the adjoining house, not that of Professor Kent, but the one on the other side, belonging to the house which had been vacant. It also resisted his efforts.

"The professor is evidently working in his study," he told me, "but we can safely risk detection from that source."

I wondered how he knew that and then became aware of a faint glow behind the portion of the brick wall in the rear of the professor's house, which was alongside of Miss Sigurda's residence. Stoke tinkered with the lock for a moment, making slight rasping noises with a wire and a skeleton key, and then gently pushed open the door. As he held it ajar, I could see a light in the professor's study, but no sign of him by it. We were about to enter when Stoke's grip tightened on my arm.

"Shh," he warned, and I knew he was listening intently. In that one instant it seemed to me that I heard an almost imperceptible noise beyond us in the alley, as if a door had been shut ever so carefully. And yet I could not be sure. The feeling that someone or something, possibly sinister, is near you or behind you in the dark is far from pleasant, and I was distinctly relieved when Stoke finally stepped into the professor's garden and closed the door securely behind us.

Once inside, Stoke became rather reckless with his flashlight, which had an adjustable beam. He was careful not to display it much above the ground, hemmed in as we were by high walls on all sides, but he made sure that the garden was empty. Beside the wall adjoining the Sigurda house was a bench. We climbed it, and Stoke straddled the wall.

"Follow me," he said, as he disappeared on the other side. In a second I was beside him at the foot of the wall, the soft ground preventing any noise as I jumped.

"No lights," he warned, as he led me back toward the gate and then turned into the arbor and silently traversed the length of it. The roundabout approach to the house amazed me, but Stoke was always doing strange things, so I simply followed, as usual. He tried the basement door. It was not locked. Cautiously he pushed it open and stood listening again. Once more his grip tightened on my arm and he softly closed the door. Someone was coming down the stairs which led from the upper part of the Sigurda house to the basement.

Quickly Stoke drew me along the side of the house to the recess between the Sigurda place and the professor's house next door. There we waited. I felt that something startling was about to happen. It did.

We heard the basement door open, with a slight creak, then close with a click. Faint footsteps coming directly toward us—no, toward the wall near us. Then a faint scratching sound. Suddenly I was aware that Stoke was no longer beside me and that I was alone. I am no coward, but I must admit that I could feel my heart thumping away.

All at once a beam of strong light shone from a place below the wall directly into the face of a man who was in the act of climbing that wall, climbing it in almost exactly the place where we had come over.

In the flash of light, which went out at once, I saw the features of Professor Kent, distorted with fear. Then I heard him fall on the other side.

Almost instantaneously there was a red glow on the opposite wall, by the vacant house, accompanied by a weird whistling sound, and a sharp contact against the wall near where the flashlight had shone out. Then again I was aware of a form beside me in the recess.

"Stand tight," murmured Stoke's voice, "the shooting has begun."

Silence, deep, mysterious, awesome.

It seemed hours that we waited. Actually it was ten or fifteen minutes. Then Stoke moved slowly through the dark toward that basement door, I following, wondering what next. At the door he paused and I paused. Then we went in. With the door closed behind us and the bolt slipped, I felt a little more secure. We were safe from the menace outside, but there might be danger lurking within. The look on Kent's face could have been due to the sudden and probably unexpected presence of an unknown man with a flashlight, or it might have been due to something in this cursed house.

A beam from Stoke's flashlight made the affair a trifle more cheerful. Beyond us to one side was a door, shut. "The gardener's room," whispered Stoke.

Noiselessly we crept by it. Beside us were recesses that seemed like wood-bins or workshops or storage spaces. At the end of a corridor-like passage were the stairs leading to the ground floor. We made for them and were about to go up when Stoke held me back.

Again we strained our ears. A sound as if something were crawling or creeping toward us. It stopped, then started again. It was with difficulty that I refrained from letting out a yell. My nerves were getting frayed.

The beam from Stoke's flashlight illumined the ceiling.

All we could see were two or three pipes, probably steam pipes from the furnace. No sign of a living creature. The pipes were, moreover, close to the ceiling, and no human being could have been concealed there. The light roved over the bins and closets. Nothing, and no place where a man could hide. And yet that sound, malevolent, mysterious?

We went upstairs. Silence, and the musty smell of a closed house. In the front hall Stoke paused and listened again. Somewhere, far above, were more strange sounds. To me it seemed as if someone were opening a skylight. I visualized a duel on the stairs, and since I was unarmed, the prospect was hardly pleasing.

"Open the street door," whispered Stoke, "and look around for Yates. Tell him everything and leave it to him."

"All right," I assented; "and you?"

"I'm going upstairs," he replied.

If I had been armed, I should have accompanied him, but I realized that a man without a gun would be only an encumbrance; so out I went. The last thing I saw as I softly closed the door, latch unlocked, was the shadowy form of Stoke vanishing in the darkness toward the second floor.

I did not have to search far for my thickset friend the detective. He was standing at the corner in rapt conversation with the nonchalant policeman, now quite animated.

"So it's you, huh?" he remarked in a matter-of-fact tone. "What's up?"

"Stoke is in the Sigurda house," I blurted, "and there's someone upstairs. Someone shot at him in the garden, with a gun with a silencer on it, I think. Professor Kent was in there, but climbed the wall. Come on."

"Whew!" ejaculated Yates.

Instead of coming, he blew a whistle, and, as if by magic, three men in plain clothes appeared, from where I was too flustered to notice. The detective gave them hurried orders and they disappeared again. Then he and I and the uniformed policeman made for the house.

"Stay here," commanded Yates to the officer as we reached the steps.

I pushed on the door. Instead of giving, as I expected, it was locked. Yet I was positive that I had unlatched the spring lock when I came out. In an instant, however, Yates had a key out and the door open.

We entered and stood in the hall listening. It seemed as if all I had done that evening was listen, strained and intent. Not a sound, only silence, deep as a tomb.

"Come on," whispered Yates in my ear, and I followed him up the stairs.

On the landing he paused again. We were about to continue on up when there was a sudden dazzling blaze of light. For a moment I could see nothing, but as I emerged from the blinking state, I realized that someone had turned on the lights in the house.

"Did you do that?" demanded Yates.

"No," I answered.

"Well, who in hell did, then?" he said.

From downstairs came a voice.

"Who up there?"

It was San Remo, the gardener. He was dressed in a shirt and trousers. His feet were bare.

"Go back to bed, you," called Yates, "and leave the lights on." And without more delay he rushed up the stairs, I following. We reached the third floor without seeing or hearing anyone. The hall was not illuminated, but was dimly lit by the lights below. Before us we saw a ladder leading to a skylight, open. Gingerly Yates climbed it. Just as he was cautiously protruding his head, the beam of a flashlight caught him squarely in the eye.

"Don't shoot," said a voice, which to my relief I recognized as Stoke's. "Come on up."

Yates ascended. I climbed the ladder and joined the two of them in the darkness.

"There was someone on this roof and he tried to enter the house, but he heard me and decamped," explained Stoke. "What's more," he continued, "I think he went into the vacant house next door through a similar skylight."

"I have a couple of men in the alley," said Yates, "and they will get him if he goes out that way."

"How about the front door?" asked Stoke.

Yates made no reply, but strode to the front of the building and leaned over the parapet.

"Joe," he yelled, "don't let nobody out of the houses on either side." Then he went to the rear and peered into the darkness. As a signal, apparently, he waved his flashlight. From the alley below came an answering flash.

"Mike," he yelled, "come up here."

In five minutes one of his entourage appeared through the skylight.

"Stay here," was Yates's order, and he and I and Stoke descended the ladder and regained the ground floor. The policeman still stood outside the door.

"Have you seen anyone?" asked Stoke.

"No, sir, not a blessed soul," answered the man.

"No one came out of the house next door?" was the next inquiry.

"Not while I've been here," was the reply.

"Let's adjourn to the garden," suggested Stoke. "I want that bullet, if we can find it."

As we retraced our way through the house and came to the basement, the door into the gardener's room was ajar. San Remo came to the door, rather wild-eyed. Stoke addressed him in Spanish, the gardener gesticulated, and they conversed for a few moments.

Outside, Stoke and Yates hunted around in the vicinity of the wall, but without results.

"We will find that piece of lead in the morning, then," said Stoke. "I don't think there is any likelihood of our visitor returning tonight."

"Let's hope he does," growled Yates; "he'll get a warm reception."

"He shot at me with a gun equipped with an automatic silencer," Stoke told the detective. "Such devices are rare. A few inquiries among the artillery-venders may produce results."

Yates nodded.

"Say, what was that dago telling you?" he asked.

"He wanted to know what we were doing here when he had been told no one would be here tonight. He declares he heard nothing until just before he turned on the lights."

"Our next job," said Yates ominously, "is to find out what that professor who lives next door was doing over here in the middle of the night."

"Whatever he was doing, I don't think he was enjoying himself particularly," said Stoke. "Did you notice the terrified look on his face?"

"It was horrible," I said.

"Well, he couldn't have been here for any good reason," exclaimed the detective. "I am beginning to think we have a real case for suspicion in that old bird. These guys with pointed whiskers are always worth looking after."

"Leave him more or less to me," Stoke suggested. "I happen to know him fairly well and can probably find out all about his nocturnal meanderings."

Yates grunted what was probably an assent.

"This gardener," remarked Stoke, "may hold one key to this whole situation. We must quiz him again, and soon."

"I suspect him of having a finger in the pie, too," agreed the detective.

"San Remo," said Stoke musingly, "made one significant remark just now when I was conversing with him."

"Spill it," was the suggestion.

"He complained of dead rats around the place."

"Dead rats?" and the bushy eyebrows of Detective Stephen Yates were actually elevated. "Dead rats?" he repeated. "What the hell?"

"Poisoned, perhaps," Stoke told him blandly.

"Oh!" said Mr. Yates.

CHAPTER X
THE SECOND TRAGEDY

From the sound of his voice, the idea of poisoned rats must have puzzled the detective. For once I think his usual self-assurance had left him. I could almost hear him scratching his head in bewilderment. The excitement and strain of the evening had made my ears unusually keen. As we stood there in the dark in the garden my senses also made me aware of stealthy footsteps in the alley approaching the garden door.

"Someone is coming," I whispered.

"I hear him," replied Yates in a placid tone. He did not even lower his voice.

The door opened and was closed. A light flashed. "What next?" I thought, my frayed nerves being dangerously close to the breaking-point. The light shone up the path through the arbor as its bearer hurried in our direction.

"What luck?" asked Yates, as I was preparing to beat a judicious retreat.

"He got away," answered a gruff and rather surly voice, "and what's more, none of us so much as seen the. . . ." The last few words were picturesque in their characterizations. They were also just a trifle profane—just a trifle.

"Collect your men," ordered Yates, "and go through that house next door. Shoot if you have to."

The steps retreated. A low whistle sounded outside the garden wall. Then stillness.

"Let's go in," suggested Yates indifferently.

As we retraced our way past the door of the gardener's room, Stoke paused, then went on.

"I must interrogate that mestizo again at once," he told Yates, "but tomorrow morning will probably do. He is really more of a suspicious character than any of those others who apparently deserve suspicion in connection with this case."

"Yes, wait until tomorrow," concurred Yates. "I will keep an eye on him in the meantime. I expect I'll be here the rest of tonight. You gents needn't stay any longer, though. Better go home and get a coupla winks. Say, want an escort?"

"No, thanks," replied Stoke, "I have my escort in my pocket."

"Got a permit?" asked the detective jovially.

"One signed by Selden himself," answered Stoke.

"Why didn't you shoot back when the guy in the dark popped at you?"

"I did think of returning the compliment," answered Stoke, "but he probably ducked immediately, and it would have made a deuce of a racket and turned the whole neighborhood out, for my gun, un-like his, has no silencer. There would have been lots of confusion and much publicity. What probably happened is that our unknown antag-onist followed us into the back alley and went into the yard next door as we came in here. He stood on something beside the wall. Inciden-tally, he may have left footprints. When I flashed my light in Kent's face, he took a shot in my direction. Fortunately for me, he missed, and probably he realized that the chances of bagging his quarry were slight. Then he calmly got down off his perch, pocketed his gun, and went home. He is probably enjoying a peaceful slumber right now."

"Who else but the murderer would have done a trick like that?" demanded Yates.

"Well, you had a gang of police gentlemen around," replied Stoke with a smile, as he stood under the hall light.

"You know none of them has a silencer on his gat," expostulated the detective, "nor would they shoot at a light."

"Well, anyway, Professor Kent didn't do it, even if I caught him in the act of making a strange and inexplicable visit to the house next door," suggested Stoke.

"He was lucky not to get the bullet in himself," said Yates.

"How do we know that he didn't?" declared Stoke, with sudden energy. "I heard him land on the other side, but don't remember hearing anything more. I did notice that bullet hit the wall, though. Be sure and find it for me as soon as daylight comes, will you?"

We returned to the garden, pulled a bench to the wall, and searched the ground on the other side with our flashlights. There was no sign of a body. Furthermore, the light in Kent's study was extinguished.

"I think we'll leave the way we came," remarked Stoke casually, and he led me to the garden gate. As far as I could determine in my rather agitated condition, we went back exactly the same way we came, except that we stopped nowhere and reached Stoke's residence without adventure.

My friend paused before his apartment and whistled softly. Pinned to the door was a note. He detached it, unlocked the door, switched on the lights, glanced keenly about, calmly sat down, and gazed at the envelope without opening it. I sank wearily into another chair and watched him with a somewhat limp interest.

"Here's a funny one," remarked Stoke at last. "This epistle is addressed in typewriting to 'Señor T. Stoke' and is marked 'Private.'"

"Why not read it?" I suggested faintly.

"A pregnant idea," replied Stoke cheerfully, opening the envelope, which was sealed. "It is in Spanish," he announced.

"What does it say?" I inquired eagerly, my lassitude overcome by this new strange development.

Stoke read, translating into English:

People who mind the business of others may meet the same fate as the one they found. There is a power in your life which is stronger than you.

"Evidently intended as a warning," mused Stoke. "Do you know, Z," he continued, "we are gradually accumulating some tangible clues." And with that he went to bed.

Morning came too soon, for my sleep had been fitful. When Stoke hauled me out of bed, he seemed in excellent spirits.

"I've got it," he announced when he had me sufficiently awake to know what he was saying.

"Got what?" I retorted; "the solution to the Sigurda murder?"

He laughed.

"No, not yet, only the bullet. I've been over to Q Street already, arrived there shortly after dawn. Yates and I and that eccentric gardener searched around that wall, and, strangely enough, it was San Remo who found it."

He showed me a piece of lead, a triumphant look on his face.

"That gardener is a more important link in this whole affair than anyone realizes," he told me. "The more I talk with him, the more I find out. This time I got out of him that he did hear someone come in through the garden on the night of the murder. He says he *thinks* it was someone who came often, but he is evasive as to whether he knows who that person is and dodges all attempts to get a description of this important individual. Kent, you will remember, told us that he saw someone come into the Sigurda garden at half past ten that night. San Remo is confused when I ask him if the visitor went past his room and replies merely that he came into the garden."

"What about Kent?" I asked. "Have you found out why he was over there last night?"

"Not yet, but soon. Get up now, Boswell, and accompany me on another inquisition."

I sighed and rose, washed, ate a pleasing breakfast, and was ready once more for the fray.

"Where are we going this morning?" I inquired, as Stoke put down the newspaper he had been reading while I masticated.

"Oh, hither and yon," was his airy reply, as he picked up a pipe from his smoking-table and put it in his pocket.

Explaining that he would like to retrace our steps of the night before, he led me out by the basement door and through the alleys, now flooded with daylight and occupied by occasional scavenger wagons and other signs of civilization, including parked Fords, some of which had spent the night where they were, and some, several weeks.

"In order to orient you, here is where we stopped and listened to the dulcet strains of Starr-Smith's guitar, if it was a guitar and if it was the bushy-faced assistant detective," Stoke told me.

As he spoke, the solid door leading into the garden of the architect's studio opened and the man himself stood before us, cane in hand, as if he were about to sally forth on some matutinal pilgrimage.

"This is indeed a pleasure," he said. "Now I shall get the latest news of our little affair, the details which the garrulous press have omitted. Any progress in the sleuthing since our *tête-a-tête?*"

"Events, if not results," replied Stoke. "But first you submit to a cross-examination. What kind of a god-forsaken instrument is it you play late at night in the solitude of your eerie sanctum?"

Starr-Smith laughed, showing his white teeth through his black beard. He seemed in high good humor, with less of the cynical attitude of bored superiority which usually characterized him.

"It might be a dulcimer, but it isn't, only a weird string instrument I picked up in the West Indies once, a citternino I think they call it. Were you prowling round last night, by any chance, that you had the pleasure of hearing me?"

In a few words Stoke told the architect how we had gone to the house on Q Street last night, passing by his door on the way, and how Professor Kent had been seen climbing the wall. He described the shot from the mysterious assailant, but said nothing about finding the bullet.

"What do you make of it?" he asked Starr-Smith.

The other thought for a few moments before he answered.

"It must be that the murderer or an accomplice is still in the city," he remarked. "It seems strange, however, that a clever man would return to a place which he must have surmised was carefully watched. The circumstances would seem to rule Kent out, unless," he paused, "it was his accomplice who did the peculiar shooting. I think I would check up on Dr. Rollin's movements last night, too."

"That is being done," said Stoke.

"It might be well, also, to find out what, if any, relationships there may be between the doctor and the professor," suggested Starr-Smith. "This whole thing has a sinister look to me. It will probably get worse before it gets better."

"Perhaps," said Stoke, as the other turned in the opposite direction. "By the way," he added, "I should like to drop in some time and see that ukulele of yours."

"Delighted to have you do so," replied Starr-Smith cordially, as he waved adieu.

"I actually think he can be quite human at times," I told Stoke, as I watched the tall figure depart down the alley.

My friend made no reply, but led me on until we had reached the rear of the Sigurda house. Instead of stopping, however, we proceeded round to the front of the house, where we encountered the red-haired policeman. He accosted Stoke at once and handed him an envelope. Stoke read it.

"Fine!" he exclaimed; "another of the assistants has produced the goods. We will postpone our session with San Remo for an hour or so. If anyone wants me," he told the officer, "I will be at the Serpentine Club."

Once more we migrated, reaching the club in a few minutes. There we found Runy O'Mara impatiently walloping the billiard-balls about. He hurried to meet us.

"So you got my message all right?" he asked.

"You certainly are a fast and furious worker," remarked Stoke with obvious admiration. "Here I give him a mission at seven a.m., waking him out of his beauty-sleep to do it," he told me, "and he produces results at ten."

We sought a quiet corner in the garden. Runy took a paper from his pocket.

"Compare that with yours," he said triumphantly, placing another beside it.

Looking over his shoulder I saw two copies of the typewritten warning which had been affixed to Stoke's door the previous night. Which was the one Stoke had removed I could not tell, as they seemed identical.

"A perfect match," commented Stoke. "This is my billet-doux," he said, picking up one. "See, Jim, it has the pinholes; otherwise they are virtually the same. Where did you get the other, Runy?"

"I wrote it myself," answered Runy dramatically.

"I surmised as much," said Stoke, "but on what typewriter?"

"On Florence's."

"Whose?" demanded Stoke.

"On the machine of the Florence Nightingale who works for Dr. Roger Rollin," was the startling reply. "Her nickname is Peggy, and her real one is Mercedes. Because of my previous acquaintanceship, developed since our initial visit in company with our excitable detective force, I made a little call shortly after you routed me out so rudely.

By assuring the janitor that I was Peggy's boy friend and that I had a surprise for her, I managed to induce him to let me in to leave it on her desk. It cost me a dollar as a bribe. The amount of money I have spent on this damn case is enormous. At that, he wouldn't leave me all the time I was there, but what was more natural that I should sit down at her typewriter and leave a little love-note? Having memorized that Spanish, I wrote a duplicate of your note, which I inadvertently forgot to leave, though the janitor thinks I did. Incidentally, that box of candy which I did leave, all done up in red ribbons, cost me another couple of bucks. Wait till Selden sees my expense account. The funny part is I just took a chance on that place, with no idea that it would prove such a successful find."

Runy was positively jubilant.

"The next question is who wrote the original note," suggested Stoke. "Your blonde female friend may have done so. On the other hand, the doctor, having access to the machine, may have written it himself. Have you any ideas on that score, Mr. Reggie Fortune, the great detective?"

"Florence—I mean Peggy—wrote it," retorted Runy coolly.

"Explain," commanded Stoke. "Aside from the fact that the psychology of the message might point to a female mentality, how do you know she did it?"

"As you are aware, Yates has had the doc shadowed ever since our visit, which took place only yesterday. I talked to the old bulldog while awaiting your august presence. The doc hasn't been near his office since he left it after we did yesterday. He couldn't have written that message, unless Peggy carried the typewriter to him wherever he was."

"And where was he?" asked Stoke.

"I didn't have time to ascertain that fact, but Yates can enlighten you," was the answer.

"I shall probably see the head sleuth in a little while," said Stoke. "In the meantime, Runy, why not cultivate your blonde friend a little more assiduously? This part of your job ought not to be so distasteful."

"Maybe not, if I keep out of sight," Runy remarked ruefully. "Suppose I take Peggy out somewhere, though, and meet Gladys, or Evelyn, or Marguerite, or one of my other particular friends?"

"I imagine you have overcome that difficulty before," suggested Stoke dryly.

"All right," acquiesced Runy, with a twinkle, "I will expose my innocent, virgin self to the wiles of this young siren, purely in the interests of science and justice. It will probably cost me more of my hard-earned funds. If Jim looked less glum, I would try to borrow five from him."

I was about to expostulate that I was financially unable to accommodate him, but he dismissed my protestations debonairly and departed.

"A born sleuth," commented Stoke as the lieutenant went on his jaunty way. "He combines a Colonel Gethryn with the Honorable Peter Wimsey."

Sam, the club factotum, breathless and excited, rushed up to us.

"A most emergent communication on the telephome," he panted, addressing Stoke, who rose to get the message.

"As soon as I finish, we will go over and have a heart-to-heart talk with San Remo," he told me. "We can't let him wait any longer. He has waited too long now."

Prophetic! In a few minutes Stoke returned. His face seemed grim. My friend was not one to display emotions, but I, who knew him so well, detected a change. To my inquiring glance he responded with a statement that made my blood run cold.

"San Remo was found dead a few minutes ago."

I was too amazed and horrified to say a word, so he continued, with a peculiar note in his voice:

"Strangely enough, it was Professor Kent who found him and telephoned to me. He called the policeman out front, who told him where I had gone. What a fool I was to wait! Let's go."

As we returned hurriedly toward the ill-fated Sigurda house on Q Street, Stoke's face was set and determined. At the door he paused, hand on knob. It shook just a trifle.

"Starr-Smith was right," he said, "this affair is getting worse before it gets better. Worse, much worse. And the end is not yet."

He said nothing further, but opened the door.

CHAPTER XI
THE PROFESSOR ELUCIDATES

The dead body of Miguel San Remo lay in the garden which he had tended so long and evidently so faithfully. The corpse was at the end of the wisteria arbor, nearest the house, as if he might have emerged from the basement and had run toward the garden door. The face was distorted and one hand tightly clutched his throat, as if he had been choking or gasping for breath.

The sight was not a pleasant one, and even Stephen Yates, who was more or less immune to tragedies, seemed shocked when he arrived in the garden a few minutes after us. Dr. Todd, the medical examiner, accompanied him. Even Todd was less nonchalant and less sacrilegious than usual in the presence of Death, that inexorable master of the fate of man.

Professor Kent met us at the Sigurda house. He was disheveled and rather wild-eyed, a high-strung scientist, as well he might be, in view of his own harrowing experiences during the past dozen hours or more.

Yates looked down at the prostrate form of the half-Indian, half-Spanish gardener, whose potential revelations had been so eagerly expected by Stoke.

"Looks like another clue has gone to hell," he said succinctly.

"Yes," agreed Stoke, "but, bad as this is, it may afford something to go on. What happened here, Kent?" he asked, turning to the professor. "You saw some of the circumstances, I believe."

The professor wiped the perspiration from his face.

"I was in my study when I heard a fiendish yell, a scream it was, and out staggers this man, holding his throat. He was making a rattling sound." The professor shuddered.

"What time was this?" asked Stoke.

"About quarter to ten this morning," was the reply.

San Remo must have met his fate immediately after we had left the vicinity, even while we were receiving Runy's report at the Serpentine Club.

"What then?" put in Yates.

"I rushed downstairs," continued Professor Kent, "through my own yard and into the garden next door."

"Was the alley door of the Sigurda house unlocked, then?" inquired Stoke.

"It was not only that, but open," answered Kent, "but I thought nothing of it until now that you mention it. Strange, wasn't it? When I reached the man, he was lying prone on the ground, writhing a little. His face was blue, actually blue. He murmured something, then seemed to lapse into unconsciousness. I rushed through the house to the front door and called the policeman outside, who came on the run. When we got back, the poor fellow was dead, or practically so. The officer sent me to get some water, but we couldn't force his lips open. He seemed paralyzed. After a few more ineffectual attempts to aid him, the policeman telephoned to headquarters. He told me you had gone to the Serpentine Club, so I called you there. What a revolting experience!"

"You say San Remo murmured something," insisted Stoke. "Did you catch what he said?"

"It was in Spanish, but I know the language," replied the professor. "What he said was disconnected and incoherent, but I clearly caught the words: 'The doctor, go quick.'"

"The doctor," exclaimed Yates significantly.

"He might have been calling for medical assistance," suggested Dr. Todd, somewhat sententiously.

"Humph!" was Yates's only comment. "See what you can find," he told the medical examiner almost brusquely.

The doctor knelt over the dead figure. After a brief examination he grasped the arm.

"Rigor mortis already," he murmured over his shoulder. With a strong effort he detached the hand from its rigid grasp on the throat.

"Look," he said.

We peered down. Clearly on the exposed skin were two red punctures, even more ruddy than the surrounding epidermis.

"Why, those lesions are similar to the ones found on Miss Sigurda herself," reported the doctor excitedly, "and the case is clearly poison of some sort. A quick-acting poison, too."

"You can do an autopsy right away this time," said the detective.

"Yes, and I will get Ragland to help me," responded the medical examiner, as he rose. "We'll find out just what was used on this bird, or I'll resign," he added vehemently.

"The wagon is here," Yates announced. "I told Joe to drive up the alley to avoid a scene."

Covered with a sheet, the body of San Remo departed from his garden.

"You saw no one enter or heard nothing else?" Stoke asked Kent after the gruesome burden had been removed.

"Not a thing," the professor replied. "I was in the bay window of my study from the time I finished my breakfast until this thing occurred, perhaps an hour altogether."

"And you noticed no one in the alley or the garden?"

"No one attracted my attention," was the reply.

"Let's adjourn the meeting to the professor's library, where he and probably the rest of us will be more composed," suggested Stoke, taking Kent's shaking arm in a friendly way.

We left the fateful garden, occupied only by one of Yates's men, who had arrived on the Black Maria and remained behind. Inside the professor's house we went upstairs to his study, a comfortable, well-lighted room, lined with bookcases. In the protruding window was a desk. On it was a pile of manuscript.

"My monograph on Mayan customs and civilization," explained Professor Kent, as Stoke sat down at the desk and glanced idly at the papers.

"By the way," said Stoke, turning to Yates, "what has become of Pansy, the maid?"

"Oh, we let her go to friends on U Street yesterday afternoon," replied the detective.

"Then she wasn't in the house during our visit last night," commented Stoke.

Professor Kent had become suddenly pale. He sat down in an arm-chair—rather, he slumped into it.

"Last night," he gasped, "I had another terrible experience."

"Yeah?" said Yates, as if in surprise.

"Elucidate, professor," said Stoke kindly; "we have all been having exciting adventures lately."

Professor Kent sat upright in his chair.

"I will tell all," he began, "even going back to the night of the murder." He moistened his lips.

"As I have told some of you previously," he went on in his precise way, "I was acquainted with my next-door neighbor and had visited her. I will go further and say that I knew her very well and visited her rather often. Although perhaps old enough to be her father, we found much in common, and I am not so old as not to have derived real pleasure from her company. Her mother, by the way, was German, which accounts for the blond hair, and her father was an Argentine gentleman. Miss Sigurda had traveled extensively and knew many of the places which interest me."

Yates seemed impatient, but Stoke nodded and apparently did not mind the introductory remarks.

"On the night of the tragedy I was working here on my manuscript, which, gentlemen, I assure you, is my only mistress, when I noticed a visitor enter the garden gate of the Sigurda mansion. He was a tall man, but I know nothing more about him, as it was too dark to recognize the man, and, besides, I caught only a few glimpses of him in the gloom. Almost immediately after he entered the basement door, it was opened again and left open, and the gardener came out. I saw him plainly in the light from the basement."

"In other words, then," interposed Stoke, "the visitor might have, or probably did, encounter San Remo as he entered?"

"They must have passed in the corridor," answered the professor.

"Well, San Remo won't tell us now, worse luck," commented Yates.

"And then what?" asked Stoke.

"Then I filled my pipe and went to the front of my house just in time to see a yellow car drive away."

"Did you notice who was driving it?" inquired Yates.

"No," replied the professor.

"Did you care?" asked Stoke abruptly.

The professor stared at his friend with a rather pained expression.

"I wouldn't say that I cared," he replied, "but I went down to my steps, smoked my pipe for a moment or two, and then did a very impulsive thing. I decided to call on Miss Sigurda."

"Knowing she had another visitor?" was Stoke's query.

"Yes, to be frank, gentlemen, I thought very highly of my neighbor. I admired her intellect, and while it was hardly my place to do so, I had expostulated with her regarding these surreptitious visitors who seemed to have *carte blanche* to sneak in so frequently by the back way. So, acting on impulse, and probably with poor judgment, I stepped across to her front door and, since it was not locked, entered."

"Were you in the habit of doing this?" asked Stoke.

"Lately, yes," was the answer. "Since we had been getting so well acquainted, I was rather informal in my calls."

"Did Miss Sigurda ever repay your visits?" was Stoke's next question.

"Why, Trevor," returned the professor, "you know she had been over here once or twice, as I told you she had just left one morning when you came in."

"I had forgotten," said Stoke lightly. "Proceed, at any rate, as the plot seems to thicken."

"I encountered no one downstairs, so went up to the second floor and knocked on the sitting-room door. To continue is very embarrassing to me, gentlemen, but Miss Sigurda partially opened the bedroom door beyond and looked out. When she recognized me, she opened the door more fully and invited me to enter. I assure you everything was entirely proper."

"Was she fully clothed?" This time it was Yates who shot the blunt question. The professor grew extremely red in the face.

"Yes, yes, of course," he replied; "she had on an evening dress as if she had been out somewhere."

"Was she alone?" It was Stoke's turn to speak.

"There was no one else in her bedroom. I sat down by the window and laid my pipe on her dresser, while she—I hesitate to give you the wrong impression, gentlemen—stood by me and stroked my head."

The professor was rather distinctly bald.

"We conversed about trifles and then I mentioned that I had noticed someone coming in through the rear door. She dismissed the matter lightly, saying it was probably a friend of Miguel's. I insisted and I regret to state, gentlemen, that before long our conversation had developed into a little quarrel. She told me virtually that what she did was none of my affair. I reminded her of some favors I had performed for her."

"Favors?" Stoke was alert.

"Do not misconstrue this, gentlemen," pleaded the professor, "but I had made two or three monetary loans to her. I got nothing in return but her friendship, a Platonic relationship, I swear, which I prized highly. At any rate, I finally demanded to know if anyone was in the adjoining sitting-room. In the dramatic manner of the Latin race, she stood before the closed door and refused to let me ascertain. I then took my leave, considerably piqued, and returned home."

"And your pipe?" prompted Stoke.

Once again the professor mopped his brow.

"In my agitated condition I left it on the dresser in Miss Sigurda's bedroom. The fact did not occur to me until after the tragedy. Then the thought came to me that if it were found, it might look like incriminating evidence. There was, however, no opportunity to reclaim it, as the police were in possession of the premises. I very nearly told you about it, Trevor, when you visited me the morning after the affair, and was going to ask you to get it, restore it to me, and say nothing."

"Instead, you went after it last night, no doubt?"

"Exactly. I watched the house and was certain no one remained there last night. It was rather late before I got up sufficient courage for the job. When I did, I went first to the door in the alley, but it was locked. Then I climbed the wall."

"How did you get into the house?" asked Stoke.

"There is a way to spring the lock on the basement door, if you know how," replied the professor.

"I found that, too," said Yates, triumphantly. The professor gazed at him with evident admiration, then continued:

"The plan of the house is familiar to me, as it is similar to mine, and I had been there many times. I went direct to the bedroom.

Fortunately the door was not locked and I had no need to use the skeleton key with which I had provided myself."

"And your pipe?"

"Was gone. I struck matches and hunted all over that room and the next, but there was no trace of it. This was shock enough, but I got a worse one as I started to leave that terrible place. I was creeping cautiously down the basement stairs when I distinctly heard the rear door shut, followed by a hiss as if someone were directly in front of me trying to attract my attention. I was literally petrified with fright and I stood there for a long time not daring to move one way or the other. There was no further sound, and so finally I decided the noise was a figment of my disordered mind. Then—" the professor paused, unable to control a shudder, "then as I approached the back door, moving warily, something clammy and disagreeable brushed against my face. I ducked involuntarily, threw myself to the floor, and again lay still. My heart was pounding violently. I knew the door was only a few feet away and finally I rushed toward it, threw it open, and made for the wall. As I climbed over, the final shock came, as someone turned a flashlight directly in my face. I fell heavily on the other side and must have been stunned for a moment. At last, shaking all over, I got up and somehow managed to regain my own house. The light had been extinguished in my study and I went to bed and never slept at all the remainder of the night. Then comes this morning with another tragedy." The professor slumped back in his chair.

"What did this pipe of yours look like?" demanded Yates.

"It was a curved brier with a 'K' cut slantwise on the side of the bowl," answered Professor Kent. "Many people would recognize it as mine. The very thought of it frightened me and I acted imprudently."

"You sure did," commented Yates. He glanced at his watch, just as the professor's elderly housekeeper appeared in the doorway.

"One of those policemen wants the detective," she announced petulantly, as if all this fuss were distasteful to her methodical and well-ordered regimen.

"It's probably Todd on the phone," he said as he departed. After he had gone, Stoke gazed at the professor sympathetically.

"You believe me, don't you, Trevor?" almost groaned the eminent scientist.

"I have no reason not to," was the answer, "but it would have been far better if you had revealed all of these facts before; not that they are of outstanding significance, but every item is of some importance and must be dovetailed into the whole if we are ever to get anywhere."

"What do you suppose became of that pipe?" asked the professor querulously. "I suppose the police have it."

"They haven't," said Stoke.

"Then someone else has, which makes it all the worse," complained Kent.

"Don't worry about it," suggested Stoke, "but tell me something concerning these loans you mentioned."

"When Miss Sigurda first came here," the professor explained, "she seemed to have plenty of funds and was lavish in her expenditures. I met her soon after she came, as Mr. Secook, who owns the house, is a good friend and he introduced us within a week after she had rented it from him This abundance of money continued until a year or so ago, when she seemed to have less, and then about six months ago Miss Sigurda approached me for a loan. I gave her, or rather lent her, two hundred and fifty dollars and on two subsequent occasions let her have five hundred each time, although I had to take it from my savings account, since my salary is not large, as you know."

"Did she give you a note?" asked Stoke.

"No, it was purely an oral affair. It was an accommodation rather than a business transaction. Of course, I expected her to pay back these loans and I even considered charging her the same interest as the bank paid on my savings account, although she offered me more."

The conversation was interrupted by the reappearance of the ancient housekeeper. No wonder the professor sought the company of his young and beautiful neighbor, I thought, as I listened to her rasping voice coldly informing us that "that detective" wanted us at once next door.

"By the way," said Stoke calmly, reaching in his pocket as we rose to go, "is this your pipe?" He held out a shabby brier.

"Yes, yes, where did you get it?" exclaimed Kent excitedly.

"From the place where you said it was," explained Stoke. "How such a keen person as Yates overlooked it is beyond my ken, if he did, but I recognized this brier as a familiar one. So I, perhaps wrongfully, appropriated it, expecting to get the explanation sooner or later."

"What are you going to do with it?" queried the professor.

Stoke smiled.

"That remains to be seen," he said cryptically, "but, as I told you before, don't worry about the matter."

And with that we walked out, leaving the prostrated professor, who did not seem inclined to follow Stoke's advice. A policeman stood watchfully before his door.

CHAPTER XII
A RAT STAGGERS

"The Professor," commented Stoke, "is apparently already under surveillance."

"These police work fast," I suggested.

"Fast and furious, and often erroneously," he answered.

Inside the Sigurda house we found Detective Yates comfortably ensconced in the reception room at the front of the first floor. In one of his bulky hands was the remnant of a sandwich, which he was masticating in a very audible manner, while in his other hand he held a sheaf of papers. His hat was pushed to the back of his head, and his feet were propped up on an upholstered stool. He seemed, in fact, stolid, comfortable, and busy.

Waved to a chair, Stoke sat down nonchalantly and lit a cigarette. Yates gazed at my friend quizzically.

"Smoke a pipe much?" was the rather unexpected beginning of his conversation.

"Evenings as a rule," replied Stoke. "And you?"

"I suppose you have quite a collection of dudeens," was Yates' remark, with what, to me, seemed like a faint suggestion of irony. "Me, I prefer cigars. You can chew them. Besides, they don't stink up your pocket. However, more of that later; I've got Todd's report on the post-mortem on that Indian."

The detective selected one of his papers.

"He says this San Remo's death was evidently caused in the same way as Miss Sigurda's. A quick-acting poison, administered by some person or persons unknown."

"The last observation is hardly revelatory," said Stoke. "Does he hazard an opinion as to the nature of the poison?"

"Todd and Ragland worked together on this one and have more to say than in the first case. Although the exact nature of the poison is still," here Yates consulted the notes, "obscure, all of the corrosives and metallic salts can be eliminated. While not an alkaloid, the poison is unquestionably of the organic type. The corpse displayed symptoms similar to those of strychnine poisoning, and yet," Yates read the notes again, "there are conditions in this case which differentiate it from strychnine. They say, though, there is an undeniable resemblance to the cause of death in the Sigurda case."

"It would seem, then," said Stoke, "that the same agency, and possibly the same person, was responsible in each case. Was there absolutely no sign of any suspicious individual in the environs immediately following this last death?"

"We hunted everywhere, and still are looking, but not a soul has been discovered," answered the detective somewhat dejectedly. "By the way," he added, "how much do you suppose that professor knows about poisons?"

"I cannot answer that definitely, of course," said Stoke, "but my guess would be that he doesn't know much about such matters. He is primarily an ethnologist; that is, a student of the origin, development, and peculiarities of human races. His specialty is the Mayas."

"Humph," grunted Yates, "that don't prevent him from studying poisons as a side line."

"Quite true," assented Stoke, "and he may have done so, but I doubt it."

"What did you make of his story?" asked the detective cautiously.

"I have known Professor Kent for several years," replied Stoke, "though not intimately. I first met him in the Yucatan, where I was doing some work on Brill's disease, or typhus fever, and he was poking round in native ruins, having been sent, I believe, by the Smithsonian Institution. My impression from my acquaintanceship, fortified by what we have just heard, is that a rather naïve middle-aged man, a bachelor who has been wedded all his life to his work, was subjected to the spell of a hot-blooded siren who did a little gold-digging on a susceptible subject."

"Kidded the old boy along and pulled his leg, eh?" Yates put it bluntly.

"Something of the sort, and the professor, as his recital showed, is in a position which is, to put it mildly, embarrassing."

"More than that," returned Yates ominously. "There is more for him to explain than he has. Kelly," he called.

The auburn-haired policeman entered immediately.

"Go over next door and get Mr. Kent and also that sour-faced old maid and bring them both over here. Tell them I want to ask a few more questions. Ask Barber to come in."

The officer saluted and went out. As a man in plain clothes appeared in the doorway, the detective rose and sauntered out into the hall, beckoning the assistant after him. When Yates returned, he was alone.

Taking some papers from his pocket, the detective selected another.

"I don't think I have had a chance to tell you what the finger-print examination of Miss Sigurda's bedroom and sitting-room showed," he remarked pleasantly. "There was the usual mixture, Sigurda's, of course, and the maid's all over the place; also one or two of the gardener's." He paused.

"Proceed," begged Stoke, "I can feel a climax coming."

"Right," said Yates heartily. "Other finger-prints found included a number of those of Dr. Roger Rollin."

"How," I inquired in amazement, "could you find that out, not having a specimen of the doctor's?"

As Yates surveyed me with a condescending smile, Stoke reminded me how the detective had secured a piece of notepaper, handed him by the doctor when we interviewed him in his office. Then a light dawned on my puzzled brain.

"But," I continued, "why not secure a specimen from the professor?"

"That," said Stoke urbanely, "is being attended to at present; in fact, probably has been by now."

Yates shot a peculiar glance at my friend.

"Mr. Stoke," he began rather ceremoniously, "you and me have been working together on this case right well so far. I'm not keeping anything from you, and I expect you to do the same by me."

"Agreed," assented Stoke. "We will get somewhere by frank and open co-operation. You might, however," he went on pleasantly, "have informed me if you were sending your assistant into Kent's house to hunt for something while you detained him and his housekeeper in this house, as they are now being detained."

"Well, I knew you would be wise to what's what, all right," Yates stated in a conciliatory tone. "Sure, Barber is going over the place now. He has a search-warrant. We always carry them."

"It will be interesting to see what he finds," commented Stoke.

"But you, now, Mr. Stoke," continued the detective ingratiatingly, "aren't you keeping something from me? How about the old codger's pipe, now?"

Stoke smiled, and took the professor's brier from his pocket.

"Right," he said. "When I visited the bedroom upstairs the first time, I spotted this pipe, which I recognized immediately as Kent's. On the impulse of the moment I slipped it into my pocket, took it home, put it absently with my own collection, and did not think of it again until this morning when we started for Kent's place. How did you know I had it?"

"A guess, more or less," laughed the detective. "I saw it lying there, but was called off before I grabbed it. When I went back after your visit, it was gone. You were the only one in there likely to cop it, as the boys have their orders to leave things alone. I should have mentioned it to you in the first place."

"If you had, we could have compared notes," said Stoke.

It was obvious to me that a certain attachment had grown up between these two entirely dissimilar persons, a mutual regard which this incident had not appreciably affected. Further reference to it was interrupted by the appearance of the plain-clothes man. In his hand was a parcel.

"Come in," ordered Yates. "Let Mr. Stoke and me see what you've got."

The assistant advanced and handed a shoe to his superior. "This one has traces of lime on it, see," he announced. We gathered about. The detective held a well-worn high shoe. It had a rubber sole upon which were unmistakable traces of lime.

"What do you think of that?" asked the detective, a trace of triumph in his tone.

"Where is that ladder?" was Stoke's calm reply.

"Come on," said Yates, leading my friend and me to the garden. As we passed the dining-room, he told Kelly to inform the professor that we should be with him in a minute. There was a slightly portentous note to his tone.

The ladder stood where we had last seen it.

"I have looked this thing over pretty carefully," explained Yates, "and noticed the first time I did that it had been used recently and that the person who did so stepped in the lime in that pile there," pointing to a heap of lime in the garden. "You remember what we brought out about this ladder when we, or rather you, questioned San Remo."

"Yes, he used it to climb to the window, or so he said," Stoke reminded us, "and he also mentioned its change of position, the inference being that someone else may have employed it previously that same night."

"None of San Remo's shoes fit any of the marks left on the rungs, though," Yates told us. "We went over them with magnifiers and microscopes and calipers and everything else."

The detective then pointed out certain distinctive marks on one of the rungs. A piece of the wood had splintered. From his pocket, he took a small envelope and from it a tiny piece of rubber, to which adhered a grain of lime. A close inspection of the shoe revealed a small cut on the sole about half-way between the toe and the instep. The piece of rubber fitted it perfectly. In addition, there was a worn trademark in the center of the rubber. On another rung was a clear imprint of two of the letters etched in lime.

"What you think of that?" demanded Yates triumphantly.

"Obviously, Professor Kent, or someone wearing his shoe, has used this ladder recently," answered Stoke. "The next step would seem to be to interrogate him about it."

We returned to the house and resumed our seats in the reception room. Before sending the officer for the professor, Yates asked Stoke to conduct the examination. When Kent appeared, he looked more shriveled and apprehensive than before. Even his Vandyke quivered.

"Professor," began Stoke kindly, "some facts have come to light that indicate that you have not told us the whole story of your adventures on the night Miss Sigurda was murdered."

The professor winced visibly at the last word.

"It would be best if you told everything," continued Stoke. Yates acted as if he wanted to threaten, but managed to restrain himself.

"I will, I will," exclaimed the professor wildly. "What a terrible position this is for an innocent man! I have told you the truth, gentlemen, but not the whole truth."

"Anything you say may be used against you," warned Yates officiously.

"Oh, my God!" cried the professor.

"It isn't as bad as that," Stoke reassured him. "That is the formal warning given to all material witnesses."

"But I really did not witness anything," expostulated the agitated professor.

"Go ahead, anyway," prompted Stoke, "the whole truth will be salutary."

"When I said I returned home after my little quarrel with Miss Sigurda," began the professor, "that was correct, but I did not return immediately. As I came out into the garden, I noticed a light from the window of her sitting-room. Much as it distresses me to admit it, I was piqued at Miss Sigurda's unreasonable attitude, especially by her refusal to inform me who was her visitor. I stood for a moment looking up at the window. Then as I turned to depart, I noticed a ladder in the garden."

"Where?" asked Stoke.

"Lying beside the wall next to my place," the professor went on. "Acting on some insane impulse, I got it, placed it very carefully against the wall below the window, and climbed up. I wanted to see who was in that room so that I could reproach Miss Sigurda. It was a foolish thing to do, a dishonorable thing, but I was not myself."

"And what did you see?" pursued Stoke.

"Nothing at all," was the answer. "The room was empty. Realizing then what an idiotic thing I had done, I descended and returned home as quickly as possible. I was, however, unable to work any more that night, and, as I told you, could not even sleep."

"Did you leave the ladder where you had put it?" went on Stoke.

"I am not sure what I did with it, but I think I replaced it carefully," replied the professor. "But, as I say, what happened after I descended is vague."

Yates stood up.

"Let's go out in the garden and maybe your memory will get better," he stated decisively.

The professor hesitated.

"Yes," agreed Stoke, "an adjournment to the garden might serve to resuscitate your waning recollections."

"All right," assented the professor with a sigh, "the less I see of that garden, the better I shall feel, but you know I don't want to keep anything from you. I place myself in your hands entirely."

To the garden we went, the professor pale and resigned, Yates staid and a little sinister, Stoke efficient but suave.

"Show us now just what your movements were," prodded Yates.

The professor dutifully went to the door, paused suddenly as if he heard something, brushed his hands across his face in a hopeless sort of gesture, then approached the wall where the ladder was now lying, and carried it to the wall. He scaled it easily, looked in the window, swayed a little, descended heavily, and started to carry the ladder away toward the big tree. Half-way he stopped quickly and let the ladder drop with a thud.

"My God, look!" he cried. His finger pointed toward the basement door, horror depicted on his face.

Emerging from the opening was a rat, covered with blood. The rodent staggered as if inebriated. Fascinated, we watched its irregular course across the garden walk. All at once it stopped, gave a convulsive shudder, and rolled over, the little beady eyes open and staring.

We approached warily, but the rat was undeniably dead.

"It has been fighting with something," said Yates in a horrified whisper. Struck by a sudden thought, he rushed into the basement, where we heard him pushing boxes and ash cans about. Stoke knelt down and examined the dead rat.

"Poor thing," murmured a voice behind us. It was the professor, whose mien, though still pale, was compassionate.

"Get me a piece of paper, will you, Jim," was Stoke's request to me. "We will wrap up Mr. *Mus rattus* and subject him to a laboratory examination."

When I returned from the alley with a piece of wrapping-paper, Stoke had apparently completed a hasty examination of the rodent, which was a comparatively small one. Yates had likewise finished his foraging expedition, empty-handed.

"I have witnessed the death struggles of a good many rats," commented Stoke, "but most of them died either of bubonic plague or of an organic poison such as phosphorus. I never before saw one display antics like this."

"Say," blurted Yates excitedly, "I have an idea. Do you suppose one of these rats around here got plague or something and went and bit this Sigurda woman and caused her death that way? Or," another brilliant thought came to him, "maybe the murderer brought a couple of rats in here in that paper bag and let one of them loose on her. What do you think, Mr. Stoke?"

My friend regarded the detective with gravity.

"There are several reasons why what you suggest is improbable. In the first place, bubonic plague is spread not directly by the rat, but by the rat flea, scientifically known as *Xenopsylla cheopis*, which carries the bacillus from the sick to the healthy rat or to man. Bubonic plague is, furthermore, unknown in this locality and at present is practically absent from this country; when it does occur or threaten, the danger is usually in the vicinity of a seaport, the infected animals coming by shipboard from the Orient, where the disease is more or less endemic.

"Another fact which militates against your theory is that rats usually shun direct contact with man and seldom attack unless cornered. A rat sick with plague often loses this fear, but the rodent is not dangerous as a combatant."

"Do you suppose those little marks on both victims could have been flea bites?" continued Yates.

"No," answered the epidemiologist, "they had none of the character. I have seen quite a few and would recognize them easily. They do not remain as such distinctive marks. Those were punctures, not bites, at least not insect bites."

"What in the devil were they, then?" demanded the detective in a perplexed tone.

"Time, and not a long time, either, will tell," Stoke assured him significantly. "Meanwhile I am going to rush over to the Hygienic Laboratory with this rat and run an autopsy on him myself. Dissecting rats used to be one of my fortes."

He wrapped up the corpse carefully. As he turned to go, he turned once again to the bewildered detective.

"The trail is getting hot," he said. "Your theory, with a slightly different application, may not be so far from the truth. Leave it to me, and in a day or two I think I can report to you definitely on the cause of death."

"Of the rat?" asked Yates.

"No, of Miss Sigurda and Señor San Remo," was the reply. "You had better get Kent into his house," he continued.

The professor had fainted.

CHAPTER XIII
PARTS OF THE MOSAIC

A passing taxi took Stoke and me and the dead rat to the Hygienic Laboratory, near the banks of the Potomac. At the building Stoke went first to the director, a tall, rather dour-faced but keen scientist, who readily gave the necessary permission for Stoke's anthropological studies on the rodent. He led us to a laboratory room not then in use and gave his colleague *carte blanche*. Stoke promptly appropriated a couple of gowns from a locker, donned one, bedecked me in the other, and we went to work with scalpels, microscope, and other paraphernalia.

In a few minutes the rat had been completely dissected, its various organs exposed, and parts deftly colored with appropriate chemicals and inserted under the eye of the microscope. There is no need for me to go into the anatomical details, which were mostly mysterious to me, anyway, but Stoke worked expertly and seemed to find much to interest him. I presume he may have learned as much from his rat as had Dr. Ragland and the medical examiner from their more difficult examinations of the bodies of the two human victims of these strange murders.

Finally he laid down the implements, glanced at his wrist watch, and spoke.

"Little by little," he said, "the parts of the puzzle fit together. Similar punctures on each victim. Many on this poor rat. The same poison undoubtedly. Obviously not a hypodermic. Who would inoculate a rat? There was no one there to do so, at least no human agency. The paper bag—and what it contained! What a fiendish scheme!"

"Your remarks are as obscure as they are terrifying," I chided him.

"The parts gradually fit into the pattern, like a mosaic," he continued, "but too many of them are still missing. What a diabolical thing this is. Only a superior mind could have conceived of such a tragedy."

"I wish you would stop talking riddles," I urged again. He seemed lost in thought and ignored me, though he glanced at his watch once more.

"Tonight we will try for the cause of the crime," he went on. "A dangerous game; yes, a dangerous game."

"Damn it, Stoke, what is it all about?" I blurted impatiently.

"It's about time for Runy's next report," was his only answer. "Don't get excited, Jim, old top, it will all come out in good time. The mosaic is filling in and our sailor friend may have a stone or two to add to the interesting design."

What remained of the corpse of the rat was placed in a jar of alcohol, labeled with indelible pencil, and locked up in a cabinet.

"In case we don't get what we shall be after tonight, this will be partial evidence," he told me cryptically.

Still dressed in the laboratory robe, he stepped into the office of the director, located in a corner on the street floor. The director was having a highly technical discussion with an assistant about the electronic effect of high hydrogen ion concentrations of tricresol esters of prophyl benzoic acid on the ileo-cæcal cavity, or something like that, but he waved his assistant out and glared at Stoke.

"You remind me of the way Sir Astley Cooper visited George V," he began.

"George IV," corrected Stoke.

"Well, George whoever it was," and the director grinned. "At any rate, the great surgeon was so indiscreet as to come to his royal patient in a blood-bespattered coat. He was received less warmly than I greet you."

Stoke glanced at the stains on his robe.

"Apologize for me to the owner of this laboratory garment and tell him in what a good cause it has been employed."

Then he and the director conversed for a while in low tones while I read all of the notices on the bulletin board in the hall. Some of them seemed to have originated in the Middle Ages. As I finished the last of them, the director and Stoke emerged, the latter having discarded the bloodstained gown.

The director, noted for his parsimonious, as well as his brilliant, traits, drove us in his own Ford to the Serpentine Club.

There was no sign of Runy and no message from him. No one had seen or heard anything of that errant knight.

Stoke looked at his watch again. It was half past four.

"You stay here, Jim," he said, "while I go over to the room and telephone to Yates. I don't want to be overheard. As soon as Runy comes in, bring him over there. If he isn't here by five thirty, phone me."

Telling the doorman where I could be found, I wandered into the billiard-room, hoping to get a rest. The room was, however, occupied. Starr-Smith was just in the act of making a difficult carom shot. He was alone, apparently being addicted to solitaire billiards. When he saw me, he calmly finished the shot, then laid down his cue and greeted me cordially, for him.

"How goes the detecting?" he inquired.

In a few words I recounted the events which had transpired since that morning when we had met him coming out of his studio. He seemed much interested and asked a number of astute questions. The rat episode intrigued him most of all.

"And what did Stoke find out as a result of his examination?" he inquired.

"That I don't know," was my reply, "but it seemed to satisfy him. He says the parts of the mosaic are beginning to fit together."

"He must be an optimist," was the architect's only comment, with what, to me, appeared like a relapse into his customary sarcasm.

Our conversation was interrupted by the entrance of the missing Runy. He came in debonairly enough, but his countenance was far from suave. It was, in fact, decorated with a black eye.

Starr-Smith gazed at him curiously, but said nothing.

"Where did you acquire the black peeper?" I asked.

"Oh, nothing, a little mishap," he answered airily, "Where's Stoke?"

I told him of Trevor's whereabouts, and, excusing ourselves, we started off, leaving our bewhiskered friend engrossed once more in the billiard-balls.

We found Stoke alone in his apartment with a flock of papers before him. On them he was scribbling assiduously, but he stopped at once and gazed at Runy quizzically.

"Like every thousand persons I have met the last hour, I see you have your eagle eye fixed on my decorated ocular orbit," began Runy jauntily. "Another item for the expense account in this hectic case."

"Explain," said Stoke.

Runy deposited himself in a chair and lit a cigarette with his usual nonchalance.

"Not only this," he said, pointing to his eye, "but I nearly had the other one scratched out by a ferocious female."

"You must have had an exciting day," remarked Stoke blandly. Although he did not show it, I knew he was excited himself and eager for Runy to begin his narrative. So was I.

"When I left you this morning," Runy commenced, "I dropped into the office for a while to kid the commandant along. The old boy is all excited about the case and I tell him just enough so he winks at my continued absence from my important duties. The boys in the drafting room know more about the work than I do, so it's all right. Well, then it was nearly noon, or would be soon, so I trotted over to Vermont Avenue to take someone to lunch. Guess who. Correct. None other than Florence Peggy Mercedes. It seems she is of Spanish descent, though I never met a blonde Spaniard before. The family comes from South America, just like some others we know, or knew. Under the mellow influence of some expensive food, she confided in me and told me many things, so that we got real familiar, in an entirely correct manner, of course. It seems, in fact, that Peggy was a sort of fifth cousin of Beatrice Sigurda, and it was she who got Peggy the job with the doctor. In spite of which, there was evidently no love lost between the two ladies. Both were obviously after the doctor. Now that one is out of the way, the other gets her innings."

"Are you insinuating that this girl might have had a motive for being interested in the demise of Miss Sigurda?" asked Stoke.

"Yes, but I am not suggesting that she did it, although she might well have been a willing assistant, suspecting or even knowing what was under way," was the startling reply. "Of course, none of this came out directly. I am merely putting two and two, or six and sex, together by means of what Ragland would denominate the psychological method."

"But the eye?" queried Stoke.

"Presently, presently," countered Runy; "we shall reach that in good time. Well, anyway, we got along beautifully together, when all of a sudden Peggy's whole attitude changes. Like a flash she got cold and unfriendly and began to talk incoherently. Called me saucy names, in fact, and stood up and made a scene."

"That's peculiar," commented Stoke. "Did you by chance say anything improper?"

"Not a word," expostulated Runy indignantly. "I treated her like the lady she isn't. The explanation is that her boss walked in."

"What, the doctor?" asked Stoke.

"The same and none other."

"Alone?"

"Yes," continued Runy, "and he walks over to our table just as Peg seemed about to slap me one and says in a loud and arrogant tone: 'What is the meaning of this, young man?' Before I could so much as murmur where he could go, that jezebel clings to him and declares I was annoying her. Whereupon the doc sort of draws himself up very dignified-like, puts his arm around the girl in a comforting, sympathetic, and familiar way, and suggests that I get out. Now, no man can tell me anything like that, so I asks him if he plans to pay the check. He wants to know what check? Then Peggy pipes up with some more abuse, the innocent young panther, and the head waiter comes over and joins in the argument. By this time I am angered, as it were, so I invite the quack to step outside like a man. He snorts. Finally I went out after an exchange of mutual insults, paying the check at the cashier's desk *en route*. I waited outside for half an hour or so, but my friend failed to appear, so I moseyed off on other business."

"But the eye, man, the eye?" persisted Stoke.

"We are approaching the eye by degrees," answered Runy. "I will skip an important part of my narrative. Thinking that possibly Peg was putting up a bluff for some purpose, perhaps not wanting to be caught in my pleasant company by the irritable boss, with whom she might be on you know what kind of terms, I sashayed over to the office on Vermont Avenue. While I was waiting for the elevator, in comes none other than Hippocrates himself, important as hell, with a little black bag. He eyes me in a hostile manner and says: 'Where in hell are you going?' I asked him whose business that was, and one word led to another. All of a sudden he walloped me in the eye, really a feeble blow, but sufficient to discolor it and spoil my good looks. Then he turned and ran for the stairs, I in pursuit. I grabbed him, spun him round, and let him have it on the chin. He went down like a log. While the elevator man and another guy who was in the lobby were trying to revive him, a sort of a commonplace-looking man whom I had observed back in the restaurant sidles up to me and says: 'You have a nice socking power, lieutenant, but you shouldn't have done that. Keep your temper if you want to be a good detective.' It seems he was the plain-clothes man, or one of them, detailed to watch the doc. He told me to wait awhile and then he and another fellow took the still unconscious doc up to his office. He came down after a while, wiping his mouth, into which I think he had poured some of the bonded medicine used to revive my friend. He said he left before he came to, though. So that, my dear Trevor, is how I acquired the eye."

"The officer was quite right, Runy," said Stoke solemnly, though with a very slight twinkle in his eye; "you should have controlled yourself. You may have jeopardized your usefulness."

"Well, anyway, I got a lot more than a black eye out of this fracas," went on the belligerent Irishman triumphantly. "I managed to get some facts as well."

"Facts, eh?" and Stoke raised his eyebrows in an exaggerated manner. "Explain, Mr. Fortune."

"It seems that Dr. Roger Rollin, M.D., F.A.C.P., was in an alley in the rear of the Sigurda mansion last night between twelve and one. What's more, he had a gun on his hip."

"What?" ejaculated Stoke.

"I got this from Osgood, the plain-clothes man. He was on the job last night and trailed the doc all evening. It was harmless enough until about eleven thirty, when he sallied forth and Osgood shadowed him through the dark—and he says, believe him, it was some dark—right into the alley, where he disappeared completely. Osgood never picked up the trail again, so he went over to the doc's house and saw him come in at one fifteen in the morning. Another bull relieved him then until noon today."

"But the gun?" inquired Stoke.

"Ozzie had his ear to the doc's living-room window, open but the shade down. He couldn't see anything, but heard him load it, says he could detect the sound anywhere. Then he brushed against the doc in a crowd as he crossed Pennsylvania Avenue at Eighteenth Street and says he felt the bulge."

"He has no idea, then, what type of fire-arm it was?" asked Stoke.

"No, I am sorry to say," answered Runy, "but, listen, Mr. Scotland Yard, let's have some more dope on the doctor's movements. We have been wondering, you know, where he was between ten o'clock and midnight on the night of the murder. That gap in his peregrinations has not yet been wholly filled."

"Fill it, then," suggested Stoke.

"I think I can do a partial job," replied Runy. "We have good evidence that Dr. Rollin did leave the house on Q Street at about quarter past ten. He says he went to his office. I have checked that and found that he did. What's more, Peggy was there to meet him and they left together about quarter of eleven. Five minutes later Dr. Rollin was seen alone at the corner of N Street and Seventeenth, not two blocks from Miss Sigurda's house, and going in that direction."

"Who saw him?" was Stoke's next question.

"A friend of mine who knows him professionally and who does not care to have her name involved in this affair," replied Runy archly, "but there is no question about the identification, I think. Besides, his car was observed still parked in MacPherson Square near his office at quarter to twelve, but it was gone a little later."

"And how do you know all this?"

"After a heck of a lot of scouting round and asking several thousand people at least a billion questions, I finally came across someone who tried to park in front of that yellow car after a theater party. She was going to St. Mark's for eats. She came out a few moments later to get a compact she left in the car, and the yellow bus had flitted."

"All this is helpful," said Stoke, "and I appreciate it, but it is still a little indefinite."

"Yes, but the net seems to me to be closing in," answered Runy. "You will recollect that Dr. Todd reported that the death of Miss Sigurda must have occurred about eleven thirty p.m. Observe how the movements of Dr. Rollin, which I have described, fit into this picture."

"Into the mosaic," murmured Stoke; "but forget your black eye, Runy, and subordinate your personal prejudices. Keep an open mind, my sleuthing companion."

"As open as a Congressman's mouth," he replied; "but the noose is drawing tighter."

"Yes," asked Stoke, "but on whom?"

CHAPTER XIV
DANGEROUS GAME

"Suspicions in this case seem to oscillate between these two people, the doctor and the professor," said Starr-Smith.

He had joined us—that is, Runy, Stoke, and me—in a secluded corner of the Serpentine Club, whither we had gone to dine. The architect had already finished his own meal when he approached and inquired politely if he might sit in on the conclave, as he called it. Stoke readily assented and the bearded gentleman sat down, pensively smoking a black cigar as we consumed our dessert and coffee. In reply to several pointed questions from him, Runy had recounted many of the events which had happened, and had filled in the gaps lacking in our colleague's information.

With his acute engineering mind, Runy, serious for once, had weighed the evidence. Prior to Starr-Smith's appearance Stoke had told the lieutenant of Kent's story and of various other developments. He omitted some details, but covered all of the salient features of what he called his mosaics.

"It looks to me," commented Lieutenant O'Mara, "as if there were two separate mosaics, one built up of the evidence concerning your professorial friend; the other, rather more complete, but not extensive enough, constructed from the facts pinned on this quarrelsome medico."

Stoke said nothing.

"Neither seems to be impelling," remarked Starr-Smith, puffing stoically on his cigar. "In fact, both mosaics may prove disappointing, despite the suspicious character of the events connected with each. What was it that Sherlock Holmes laid down as an infallible rule?"

he continued with a faint trace of mockery in his tone. "Eliminate the impossible and what remains, no matter how improbable, gives the real solution."

"It was Dupin and not his imitator, the great sleuth of Baker Street, who promulgated that rule," Stoke corrected him.

"Whoever was the brilliant originator," the architect went on, his sarcasm more obvious, "what next?"

"I assume I have my functions still cut out for me," Runy answered; "a little more detailed and complete information about the exact movements of both of these birds."

"Don't you think their movements were a little too obvious for a really acute murderer?" asked Starr-Smith. "The crime itself was no blundering stunt, but a thing of real finesse. Think of it," he went on enthusiastically, "almost a perfect piece of work, subtly done, not a real clue remaining, nothing tangible to go on."

"You seem to admire it," said Runy, coldly.

"I do and I admit it," retorted the architect seriously. "The deed, if you will pardon the florid phraseology, was exquisite, and, being so, there is all the more zest in unraveling the tangled skeins. Eh, Stoke?"

"Possibly," answered the epidemiologist shortly.

"What's up for tonight?" asked Runy.

"A complete nocturnal rest with peaceful slumber for you," said Stoke. "We must all conserve our energies and not wear ourselves out."

"Chasing rainbows won't advance the cause, of course," suggested Starr-Smith.

Mention of Stoke's plans for the night, so far as I was aware of them, was on the tip of my tongue when I caught a warning glance from him, almost imperceptible, but the type of thing which I recognized from my long association with him.

In a few moments Stoke and I had said good-night to the two others, Runy announcing that he thought he would saunter over to see an acquaintance.

"By all means catch up on your social obligations," Stoke told him with a twinkle in his eye, realizing full well what sex the "acquaintance" of the attractive young bachelor would be.

Back in Stoke's apartment at about seven o'clock, he motioned me to the cot in the corner.

"Snooze, old dear," he commanded. "I will rouse you in time to be queen of the May."

The opportunity was indeed appreciated.

It was dark outside when I was awakened by Stoke. It was dark, and the curtains were drawn, but the room was dimly illuminated by a small lamp on the table. When I was fully awake and my senses were keen again, Stoke did a rather ominous thing. From a cabinet he took a little vial and set it, together with a small black oblong case, on the table before us. The vial was filled with a deadly-looking straw-colored liquid.

"In case of necessity open this bottle by breaking the seal," Stoke warned me. "Fill the hypodermic needle," and with that he opened the case and showed me a physician's syringe, such as is employed for administering antitoxin, "and let me have the full contents subcutaneously in the arm. I will do as much for you."

When he explained the reason, my blood nearly congealed. But more of that later.

This time we proceeded directly to the house on Q Street, with no attempt at concealment. It was then close to midnight. Stoke had, I noticed, equipped himself with his flashlights. He had also slipped his automatic, loaded, into his pocket. In addition he had taken with him a wicked-looking knife, a woodsman's knife with a sharp and apparently very serviceable blade.

At the door of the Sigurda house he nodded to an officer on duty in the street, produced a key, and entered. Once inside, he even switched on the lights and left them on in the hall. Then he put on the basement light.

"Keep your ears open," he warned me, as we went downstairs.

Without hesitation Stoke proceeded directly to the room of the late San Remo, the gardener, opened the door, and, preceded by a beam from his flashlight, walked in. He soon found the switch, put on the light, and pulled down the curtain at the window, which looked out on the garden.

"Turn out the light," he said curtly, "the shade is too porous."

As I complied with the request, he moved to a bureau in one corner of the room, opened a drawer, and took from it an object which made a crackling sound. It was a paper bag quite similar to the one found in the divan in Miss Sigurda's room the morning after she had met her fate. Stoke placed the bag on the bureau directly upon a guitar-like musical instrument which I had noticed there in the interval when the light was turned on.

Then he led me back into the basement, a black hole which extended the length of the house. The gardener's room occupied the space on one side at the rear end, with its window looking out upon the garden. Next to it was a small bathroom, then several closets apparently used for storage space. A hallway ran the length of the basement, from the door at the rear, along past the room and the closets, to a space under the front of the house, which was taken up by the furnace, a coal-bin, and some wash-tubs. Alongside this passageway were bins filled with a heterogeneous collection of barrels, pieces of wood, parts of packing-boxes, and other objects. There was some semblance of order, but not much. About half-way between the door and the furnace-room the stairs from the first floor came down to join the passage.

"We need plenty of light for our search," said Stoke, as he hunted for the various cellar lights and switched them on.

Even with four lamps burning in different parts of the passage and basement, the light was far from bright. Stoke was dissatisfied and he sent me upstairs to get a stronger light from one of the sockets in the dining-room. As I started down with it, I thought I saw a shadowy figure on the steps at the front outside, but, believing it to be the officer on duty there, paid no attention.

When I returned to the basement, Stoke was in the midst of the barrels in the bins, his flashlight darting here and there. Acting on his suggestion, I began operations in the furnace-room, and together we covered every inch of the cellar from one end to the other. We even looked in the furnace and in and around the wash-tubs.

The search was fruitless. We had spent at least an hour of the most careful hunting, but without result. For an instant Stoke seemed baffled. Then he gazed pensively at the ceiling, which was crossed and criss-crossed with pipes of varying dimensions and electric-light wires and cables.

The hunt began again along this ceiling. Again we scoured every recess. A bug couldn't have eluded us, but the object of our search did. Throughout the procedure Stoke never once abandoned his cautious attitude. He kept at a respectful distance, as if he expected that something might strike at him any moment. I did the same, as his instructions had been explicit.

"It isn't here," said Stoke finally. "Let's try the garden."

Leaving the lights on, we went outside, closing the door after us. In the darkness Stoke followed the wall round to the alley door, avoiding the arbor walk. Suddenly, as if on an impulse, he opened the door and stepped into the darkness of the alley outside, giving a low whistle as he did so. Almost simultaneously, a light was flashed in his face from a distance of a yard or two. Stoke stepped back and held the door ajar, but so that it shielded him. Two low whistles sounded and this time Stoke's light illuminated for a fraction of a second the stalwart form of Detective Yates.

"No luck in the cellar," I heard him whisper. "I'm going to search the garden. Put a man next door, will you? I'd rather not be disturbed by any shooting tonight."

"I'll go myself," came a grunt in return. "Barber and one of the men are out back here. When I whistle, go to it."

Stoke closed the door and shot the bolt. In a few minutes there came a low whistle from the other side of the wall which separated the Sigurda garden from that of the unoccupied house next door. I could also see the reflection of a flashlight as it was used there.

Another exploration began. Stoke scrutinized the arbor with particular attention, but, not finding what he wanted, toured the garden itself. Despite this rigid inspection, which was, of course, hampered by the darkness and the necessity for the use of flashlights, we still failed to find our quarry. Perplexed, Stoke stopped beside the wall next to Kent's garden.

"Looking for something?" said a calm voice from the wall directly over us.

With a snap Stoke extinguished his light, and as he did so, another beam of light from the other side of the wall shot out, just in time to display the disappearing form of a man. From the other side came sounds of a struggle, then silence for a moment, followed by the shrill blast of a whistle. Next came hurried footsteps through the alley, the opening of Kent's alley door, and muffled voices. Stoke drew me into the dark recess where we had stood once before.

"Yates has him," he whispered.

My friend conducted me once more to the alley door and peered out. After waiting a few moments, we heard the door in the adjoining wall open and footsteps approach. Stoke whistled and received an answering signal. It was Yates again.

"What ho?" asked Stoke.

"It was that damn professor himself. He must have been watching you all the time. Barber grabbed him when he spoke. He's got him in the kitchen now."

"Suggest you see what you can get out of him in explanation," Stoke told the detective. "I'll be with you in a few minutes."

We retraced our steps to the house and put out the various lights upstairs and down. As we came by the gardener's room on our way out, Stoke paused and listened intently. As he put his hand on my arm, I felt a distinct quiver of excitement in his grasp.

"Lights," he said.

As I turned on the nearest basement light, he cautiously pushed open the door and flooded the room with the rays from his electric torch. Nothing unusual met our gaze.

"Look," said Stoke.

Following his direction, I looked at the bureau. Much to my surprise and horror, the paper bag was moving slightly. From the hollow part of San Remo's guitar was coming a glistening black form.

"Give me the stick, quick," commanded Stoke.

In a second I had handed him a short broom-handle, with which he had provided me earlier in the evening. On the end was a wire, fastened securely, and bent into a narrow U.

"Keep your light on it," said Stoke, "and get that serum ready."

His flashlight in one hand, the stick in the other, Stoke advanced into the room, while I watched, fascinated, though I must frankly admit that my hand shook as I tried to keep my own flashlight focused on that gruesome thing.

It was over in a few moments. With the aid of the specially prepared weapon and the huntsman's knife, Stoke had deftly and skillfully secured his quarry. When he was certain of its demise, he placed it in the paper bag. There was triumph, mixed with concern, when he finally turned to me.

"Take it easy, Jim," he said to me calmly. "This is all in the day's work. We've been through worse than this together and probably have more to come."

"I'm all right," I blurted, though I was, to put it mildly, somewhat flustered. Like most people, except Stoke, who was never upset, I felt weak after the strain and stress of the night's events.

"Luck was with us," he went on. "Another two minutes and we should have been out of here with empty hands. This means an easy day tomorrow, with the chance to catch up on lost sleep, and then tomorrow night we will conduct a psychological test that will tell us more than all the detectives in this or any other city."

"The hell you say," came a grieved voice from the doorway.

It was Yates. He had become impatient, or else concerned about the time we had taken to join him, and had come over to investigate.

"No aspersions, Yates," said Stoke quickly and pleasantly. "At least, if there are any, they apply to me as much as to you, if not more. Tomorrow we will demonstrate before an interested and enrapt audience—you know whom—just how Miss Sigurda met her death."

"The—hell—you—say!" was the awed reply.

In a few moments Stoke had outlined his plans to the eagerly responsive detective, whose admiration for the scheme was visible and audible. When he had finished, Stoke inquired about the commotion next door and what had come out of it.

"This professor guy is the funniest proposition I ever saw," said Yates. "You know how sort of excited and agitated he was, how he fainted and everything. Well, tonight he acts as if he never had a care in his life and was afraid of no one. Why, he is cool and calm and collected, even sarcastic like the fellow with the black whiskers who's been chasing around on this case with Mr. Selden. I never saw such a funny change come over a man."

"You may," said Stoke, "witness an even greater change in him tomorrow night."

CHAPTER XV
THE TEST

Dr. Basil Ragland, eminent psychiatrist, leaned back in his chair and looked solemnly across his massive oak desk at Trevor Stoke, epidemiologist and amateur detective. The physician removed his eye-glasses, tapped thoughtfully on his leather-fringed blotter, and gazed out of the window.

"Yes, I suppose it can be done," he said at last, "though the results may prove disappointing."

"This test," began Stoke, "should be strictly a psychiatric one, just as if the subjects were before you in the clinic. By observing every mental and emotional reaction of the two men, especially when the denouement occurs, could you not form an opinion of possible guilty reactions?"

"It might be an indication, provided the stage is properly set," conceded the doctor, "but whether it would have forensic value is another question."

"We need not worry about how much weight such an examination will carry in a court of law," Stoke reassured him. "This is chiefly for our own benefit, to aid me in fitting some more parts into the mosaic which I am laboriously building."

"Life itself is a mosaic," observed Dr. Ragland a little pensively, "and some of us fit rather badly into it. Whoever committed that atrocious crime must have been a paranoid, certainly a psychopathic personality, with possibly dementia præcox."

"I lean toward the psychopath, and a brilliant one, at that," commented Stoke.

He and the doctor conversed at some length regarding the arrangements for the test to be conducted that night, while I listened, gazing surreptitiously now and then about the luxurious office. It was furnished entirely with serviceable antiques. Beside the huge mahogany desk was a tall grandfather's clock and along the walls were old-fashioned bookcases, really Governor Winthrop desks, filled with volumes. Among them were first editions and modern medical text-books, curiously intermingled.

Finally Stoke and the doctor concluded their conference. "By the way," said my friend, "have you an authoritative work on ophiology in your library?"

"Why, yes," was the answer, as the doctor rose and silently traversed his thick Persian rug to one of the bookcases.

He looked over the books for a few moments and then turned to Stoke with a peculiar expression.

"The best of my volumes on the Ophidia is not here. Come to think of it, I loaned it to a colleague at least a month ago," he said.

"Do you recollect who was the careless borrower?" asked Stoke.

"By Jove, it was none other than young Rollin—himself," answered the doctor, meeting Stoke's significant glance.

"Did he give any reason for wanting to take that particular book?" resumed Stoke.

"No; as I remember it, he was perusing the titles while I was doing something at the desk; and as I rose to go out with him, he asked if he might take along that particular work. I assented and he took it and I thought nothing more about it. So many of my books disappear the same way that I am inured to it. I keep my most precious ones locked up in my own bedroom."

It was after three o'clock in the afternoon when we finally took leave of the doctor. We had spent the entire forenoon luxuriating in bed, although Stoke had been up rather early doing considerable telephoning. I had been too sleepy to catch any of the conversations.

On our return we stopped at the house on Q Street. Detective Yates greeted us rather effusively.

"Everything is all set for your show tonight," he confided. "I've got two men watching each of the culprits, and both have definite appointments with me at ten thirty p.m."

As I suspected, by "culprits" he was referring to Professor Kent and Dr. Rollin.

"Don't relax your custody over the paper bag," admonished Stoke.

"The diamonds are in the safe," the detective answered with a chuckle. "See you later," he called as we continued on our way.

Back in Stoke's apartment, which we had left about one o'clock in order to get lunch in a well-known cafeteria on Seventeenth Street, Stoke sat down quietly, lit a cigarette, and looked indolently about.

"There has been a visitor here during our absence," he announced placidly.

"What?" I said with a start.

"Oh, I am a good enough detective to notice definite, even if almost imperceptible, evidences," he told me. "Nothing much is disturbed, but someone has been searching for something, and recently, too."

"The question is: who was it and what did he want?" I suggested. "Also, how did he get in?"

"The what is probably easily answered," he said, "but the who and how are less simple. Our intruder may have been after an important paper bag and its contents. *Quién sabe?* Who knows?"

In accordance with Stoke's instructions, I spent the next hour making discreet interrogations as to what persons had been observed in the vicinity of the apartment, but my efforts were not crowned with any particular success. Apparently there had been a good many visitors, both male and female, despite the fact that the building was devoted to bachelor suites. During my absence Stoke was busy with his notes and the telephone.

At dinner-time we proceeded to the Serpentine Club as usual. Contrary to custom, however, there was no sign of Lieutenant O'Mara, although Starr-Smith was sauntering nonchalantly about. Acting on Stoke's cordial invitation, he joined us, after parking his cane in a convenient corner.

We talked about various topics, veering eventually to the Sigurda case, in which the bewhiskered architect continued to display his accustomed solicitude.

"If you would like to sit in on an interesting experiment tonight," said Stoke, "come over to the house on Q Street at half past ten

tonight. We are going to put the suspects through a modified third
degree."

"Delighted," replied Starr-Smith. "Nothing could arouse my sadistic impulses any better. I will be there."

"Your observations of the attitudes of the two men ought to be
very helpful," Stoke suggested.

"Yes, if they do anything worth observing," was the rather scornful
answer.

When, about two and a half hours later, Stoke and I arrived at
the house on Q Street, we found that several of the other actors in
the forthcoming drama had already arrived. Yates stood talking to
Dr. Roger Rollin, who seemed rather excited, and Dr. Basil Ragland,
who, though calm of visage, was nervously dangling the ribbon of his
eye-glasses. Mr. Selden was likewise there, impatient for the business
to begin.

"Where's Kent?" asked Stoke of the detective.

"Get the professor," nodded Yates to one of his assistants. In the
interval while we waited, Starr-Smith walked, or, I should say, meandered, in.

"So this is the place?" he said, looking idly about, as he greeted
Stoke. "I've endeavored to beat my way in several times, but the highly efficient police have invariably thwarted my desires."

With the arrival of Professor Kent, the party was apparently
complete.

"Come on, gents," announced Yates importantly, "let's go upstairs."

"Upstairs?" murmured Kent dully. He seemed more or less in a
daze.

"Certainly, let's go," said Dr. Rollin rather loudly; "on with the
dance." His attitude was one of elation, as the neurologists would say.

Mr. Selden led the way up the stairs, followed by Dr. Rollin and
Yates, Dr. Ragland and Professor Kent, and myself. In the rear came
Starr-Smith and Trevor Stoke.

The room on the second floor was exactly the same as we had
seen it on the morning after the murder, except that the gruesome
body was missing. As the party passed inside, I noticed that Professor

Kent was exceedingly pale, but otherwise calm. Dr. Rollin, on the other hand, seemed flushed and nervous and obviously trying to appear unconcerned. He looked ostentatiously about him. Dr. Ragland was watching both men keenly. Yates paid no attention to them, but watched Stoke, who strode to the center of the room, which was only moderately illuminated by two floor-lamps, one by the head of the divan, the other by the desk.

"Take this chair, professor," said Stoke, motioning Kent to the chair by the desk, which had been turned round so that its occupant would face the center of the room.

Kent sat down listlessly and folded his hands in his lap. He seemed only faintly interested in the proceedings.

"Now you sit here, won't you, Dr. Rollin?" and Stoke indicated the corner of the davenport nearest the window.

The doctor hesitated, seemed about to demur, then apparently thought better about it, and sat down with a shrug of the shoulders.

"Anywhere you say," he remarked; "one place is as good as any other in this farce."

Stoke ignored this slur. Dr. Ragland had already pulled up a chair near the center of the room, so placed that he could watch both of the others. Mr. Selden stood behind him.

"Bring the table, will you please?" said Stoke, turning to Yates.

The detective went to a corner of the room toward the door and brought a small mahogany table, which he placed in the center of the floor, somewhat to Dr. Ragland's right. Stoke took a position behind it and looked about, while Yates fell back to where I stood in the background.

"By the way, Mr. Starr-Smith, won't you take the vacant chair?" Stoke remarked as an afterthought.

"Certainly, anything to oblige," was the bland reply as the architect lounged over to a chair set directly between, but slightly in the rear of those occupied by the professor and Dr. Rollin. Despite his blasé manner, interest was distinctly evident beneath his composure.

Dr. Rollin was far from composed.

"Can't you speed up this foolishness?" he blurted petulantly. "I have some professional calls to make in a little while."

Kent looked up at this outburst, but his stolid expression remained unchanged. Yates's jaw protruded truculently, but he forbore to say what he would have liked to say.

As Stoke stood by the table and began to address the group in his well-modulated tones, the scene before me was indelibly impressed on my memory, as I stood in the dim background beside the detective, whose keen eyes watched every movement of the suspected men before him and noted mentally every flicker of an eyebrow. The lights had been so skillfully placed that only Kent and Rollin were fully within their rays, though Starr-Smith's countenance was also visible. The light also shone on the polished top of the mahogany table, behind which my friend stood. Dr. Ragland and Mr. Selden were in the shadows, though their presences were sufficiently evident.

"You gentlemen will pardon the theatricals," Stoke was saying, "but we wanted to reconstruct certain features of the crime which occurred three nights ago in this very room."

Dr. Rollin moved restlessly, his eyes on Stoke. Professor Kent was looking at the floor, and he seemed to sigh ever so slightly. Starr-Smith was watching him with interest. With the light glistening on his beard, and his keen eyes aglow, he appeared both distinguished and alert.

"In this very room," continued Stoke slowly and significantly, "Beatrice Sigurda was murdered at this very moment. She was sitting on that davenport under that light."

The doctor gave a perceptible shudder. Kent remained motionless.

"The agent of the crime was on that same davenport with her," Stoke went on in his quiet, but effective manner. Dr. Rollin stood up indignantly.

"Do you mean to stand there and say that I was sitting here with that woman?" he almost shouted.

"Sit down," growled Yates, but the doctor remained standing.

"I've had enough of this," he cried wildly. "I am innocent. I know nothing about this crime. It's a lie."

"Sit down and let me continue," said Stoke soothingly, as Starr-Smith gave the doctor a contemptuous glance. "I am accusing no one. There was no person on that divan except Miss Sigurda. She was alone. No, not alone, for under one of those pillows was an object, a live object of destruction. See," and pushing the table out of his way and toward the chairs of his listeners, he strode to the divan and threw aside one of the pillows.

Beneath it was the paper bag, or a paper bag similar to the one we had found the morning we had visited the room for the first time. Kent had looked up with some show of interest, but his expression was immobile. The doctor had covered his face with his hands.

"See," said Stoke, picking up the bag and maneuvering himself so that he was behind the table once more.

For a moment he stood holding the bag, while a deathly silence reigned in the room, interrupted only by the hoarse, agitated breathing of Dr. Rollin.

"Have you ever seen this bag?" demanded Stoke suddenly, holding it before Dr. Rollin. The architect beside him was leaning forward watching intently.

"No, no, no," the doctor ejaculated, "I never saw it. I know nothing about it."

"And you?" and Stoke turned to Professor Kent.

The professor moistened his lips. It was a moment or two before he spoke.

"It looks like bags I have seen," he answered in a monotonous tone, without expression.

Stoke drew back. I wondered why he was acting so dramatically, as my friend was never given to the theatrical. It was a new side of him to me.

"As I have said," he went on, "this bag contains the actual cause of the crime, the thing that brought about Miss Sigurda's death."

He almost hissed out the last word. Dr. Rollin was in a cold sweat, Kent indifferent.

"I will show it to you," declared Stoke.

With a deft movement he opened the neck of the bag and threw upon the mahogany table a shiny object.

It was a hideous black snake.

With an incoherent yell, Dr. Rollin had made for the door, but Yates was there before him to block the way. Behind him loomed another menacing figure in the doorway, one of the detective's assistants.

"Stand still, you yellow cur," commanded Yates, and the doctor collapsed limply in his arms.

The room had been in a turmoil for a moment. Starr-Smith had risen, but was watching the proceedings unmoved, a cynical expression on his face. Dr. Ragland had never ceased to keep his eyes on one or the other of the two men.

Only Kent seemed unaffected by the scene before him. He had remained seated and had folded his arms, gazing with fascination at the motionless reptile on the table not four feet from him.

"The snake is harmless now," Stoke reassured us. "It is quite dead, but it was very much alive three nights ago. It was also alive last night. Perhaps Jim and I are lucky to be here after our nocturnal adventure in quest of it."

"What breed is the thing, anyway?" asked Starr-Smith, who was examining the viper in a gingerly manner.

"It is the deadly fer-de-lance," replied Stoke, "and, strangely enough, it comes only from South America."

"Well, gents, the show is over," said Yates in a matter-of-fact way. "I guess we can all go home. Shall I lock anybody up?" he asked, turning to Stoke with what seemed to me like an expectant manner. I judged that the detective would be disappointed unless he put someone in jail as a result of the evening's gruesome entertainment.

"Have you anything to say now?" Stoke demanded sternly of Dr. Rollin, who was half reclining on the divan.

The doctor turned a haggard face toward his questioner.

"I am innocent. My God, I am innocent," he gasped.

"Take him out," ordered Stoke, "and send him home."

"O.K.," assented Yates, though in an aggrieved tone, as if he had been cheated of a much desired arrest.

"Have you anything to say?" Stoke turned to Kent.

"Nothing," the professor answered in the monotone he had used all evening. "I want to go home too."

"You are at liberty to do so," replied Stoke, "and I hope you will pardon the dramatics of the evening."

"Oh, that's all right," answered the professor in the same dull tone. "I suppose you had to do it."

He let Yates lead him out.

Stoke picked up the fer-de-lance with an indifferent attitude and replaced it in the paper bag, as we gathered about him.

"I trust that this rather ghastly performance has been worth while to your investigations, Mr. Stoke," said Commissioner Selden in his sedate manner.

"This has all been very interesting, but have you actually learned anything?" asked Starr-Smith with a return to his usual sardonic manner.

Stoke looked at Mr. Selden and then at Starr-Smith.

"I learned," he replied, "what I expected and hoped to learn."

CHAPTER XVI
FER-DE-LANCE

The house on Q street was almost empty. The actors and audience of the drama, or perhaps it was only a rehearsal, had departed. All except Stoke and Dr. Ragland. Mr. Selden had been the first to go, and Starr-Smith the last. Cynical to the end, the bearded architect had recovered his cane, donned his black felt hat, which he wore half a degree over one side, not enough to be jaunty, but at a rather disdainful angle. His parting shot had been almost venomous.

"Don't persist in the delusion that you have learned anything by scaring two innocent morons almost to distraction," he had commented. "Third-degree methods such as these are hardly worthy of a scientist, or even a pseudo-scientist."

Stoke only smiled blandly, ignoring the veiled insult. Dr. Ragland was more courteous.

"Come over to my sanctum," he invited us. "I will pour out a consoling libation while we discuss the results, if any, of this test."

For my part, I was eager to leave the ghastly scene of so many morbid occurrences. I think Stoke was also pleased to do so. The doctor had his car and we departed in it just as Yates returned from the professor's house in time to exchange a few words with Stoke.

In the doctor's luxurious office we sank restfully into the soft chairs, while the physician got out some "medicine." It was a pre-prohibition wine of a sparkling sort. As we sipped it pensively, the doctor seemed to ruminate.

"What do you make of the evening's festivities?" Stoke asked him, although I suspected that my friend had some ideas of his own on the subject.

"Neither of your two suspects acted as a guilty man ought to act," replied the eminent psychiatrist. "By that, I mean in this particular case. My medical colleague resembled a person who might have been in a brawl and committed involuntary manslaughter and was trying to repress the thoughts of it, but his type, plainly hyperthyroid, is not the kind that plans and executes a deliberate and rather clever murder. If he killed anyone, it would more likely be in a fit of jealous rage on a golf course or in a street car."

"Unless," suggested Stoke, "the man is a good actor."

"That is, of course, a possibility," admitted the doctor. "He has studied psychiatry, and if he is any good at all at it, he ought to know how various types of criminals react. His outburst appeared genuine to me, however, but, then, he may have been preparing for the ordeal."

"He seemed distressed and frightened," was Stoke's comment.

"The man is obviously a coward, whatever else he may be," continued the doctor. "When an individual with that sort of psychology does commit a crime, usually in a frenzy, his conscience never gives him a moment's peace. He becomes totally neurasthenic—may even end up with a suicide."

"I thought suicide required bravery," I broke in.

"No, suicide is a form of flight," answered the doctor. "The act is the culmination of unbearable depression, impelled by melancholia which persists. A brave man, as we commonly employ the term, never commits suicide."

"Does the clinic tonight rule out Dr. Rollin, then?" asked Stoke.

"The result of our experiment seems to make him an improbable cause of this crime, but I wouldn't say that it ruled him out entirely," was the reply.

"What about Professor Kent?" was the next question.

"Ah, there you have the veritable antithesis of the high-strung young doctor. The professor can be agitated, as you have witnessed in your past experiences with him. Tonight, however, he was apathetic. The professor is a typical seclusive personality. He is studious, devoted to his books and his researches. He is a bachelor, which in itself is a sign of queerness. Pardon me, there is still hope for you, Mr. Stoke."

"Never mind me," laughed Stoke, "go on with your interesting word-picture."

"This seclusive type may be dangerous," continued the doctor. "Often they are cold, calculating, and cruel. The professor had isolated himself from the world and his fellows, carefully repressing everything sensual. Then along comes this attractive woman and changes some aspects of his life. She arouses jealousy in him."

"And you think," broke in the doctor's principal listener, "that the change was too much for this anchorite, if he was one?"

"As a matter of fact, I don't," replied Dr. Ragland pleasantly; "although I have built up a case against Kent, I should really doubt if he is the type that would commit a crime of this kind. Strange as it may seem, I think he would be more likely to do something sudden and desperate, not unlike the action, hypothetical of course, of our other subject, Dr. Rollin."

"Well, then, if neither of these two suspects exactly fits in psychologically with the crime as actually committed, what kind of personality would do so?" was Stoke's next question.

"Before answering that," said the doctor, "tell me the circumstances of this crime as you visualize them as a result of your investigations."

Stoke hesitated.

"What you may reveal will, of course, be held in strict confidence," continued the doctor.

"The mosaic is far from complete," was Stoke's prompt answer, "but enough has been shown to give me a fairly good idea of what happened on that fateful night. You understand that what I say is more or less conjecture in many of its aspects."

"Yes, yes, but go on," exclaimed Dr. Ragland eagerly.

"The person who committed this crime, probably a man," began Stoke, "must have had an impelling motive. What that was I am not yet sure, but I think we shall have an idea soon. It may have been a discarded love-affair, coupled with a lack of finances on the part of Miss Sigurda. We are following up that line. At any rate, the murderer decided some time ago to do away with the beautiful Beatrice. The affair was carefully planned by an intellect that deserves admiration for its ability, if not for the lack of scruples displayed. Obviously the murderer was a psychopath, but, disordered mentally or not, the brain was an acute one."

"That can happen, certainly," the doctor assented.

"Somewhere this man got hold of a fer-de-lance, one of the most deadly reptiles existent. The snake, scientifically known as *Lachesis lanceolatus*, occurs only in Central and South America, and its deadliness may have been familiar to Miss Sigurda, a native of the Argentine. The murderer may, in fact, have sent to South America for this horrible thing. The Washington Zoo has never possessed one, incidentally, and most of its officials have probably never seen one. This specimen must have been imported."

"Why should anyone send to another hemisphere for an agent of destruction when there are so many available here?" asked Dr. Ragland with some perplexity.

"There was a reason, I am sure," replied Stoke, "and the fact also indicates the careful preparations. It is not so difficult for a skillful detective like Yates to trace the sale of poison or the acquisition or use of a weapon, but what detective would think of a South American fer-de-lance as a cause of death? It was only more or less by luck that I found the thing."

"And how did you?" the doctor asked.

"One of the characteristics of the fer-de-lance is that it lives on rats and other small animals. The dead rats around the house on Q Street gave me an idea, and that together with the punctures on both victims, as well as the symptoms of poisoning in them, all pointed to poisoning by snake bite. As you are well aware, the symptoms are swelling, pain, prostration, and eventually paralysis and lapse of consciousness. The nearer the bite to the brain, the worse it is. In each of these cases, the bite was in the neck. The fer-de-lance, like the bushmaster of the Amazon and the copperhead of this country, which it resembles somewhat, can cause death in a very short period, often in half an hour. While this specimen was a comparatively small one, only about three feet in length, in contrast to those six feet long which are frequently found in South America, it was sufficiently potent. I should not care to have been bitten by it. That is why I made Jim carry anti-venin vaccine when we went on the hunt for this most dangerous game."

How lucky we were to escape the same fate as that of Miss Sigurda and San Remo, I thought with a shudder, as I looked back on our night in the basement of that terrible house. I remembered that Stoke had said that this snake would probably give no warning if it attacked. The fer-de-lance has no rattles, though it is even more dangerous than a rattlesnake.

"But wouldn't it be rather perilous to convey a live viper of this nature about?" asked Dr. Ragland.

"Not if due care were exercised," answered Stoke. "This one may have been in a torpid condition when the murderer put it in that stout paper bag, an innocent enough looking receptacle. He probably entered the house about half past ten or earlier. He may, in fact, have been there when Kent says he visited Miss Sigurda. At any rate, he left this bag with its deadly burden under a pillow on the divan. The summer heat, not dissimilar on that night to a tropic jungle, finally stimulated the fer-de-lance to action. It emerged from the bag as Miss Sigurda sat there placidly reading. It crawled along the top of the back-rest of the divan and attacked— Why, what's the matter?"

Dr. Ragland had become deathly pale, his face broken out in sweat. He sat staring at Stoke in a fascinated manner, as if hypnotized, horror depicted on his countenance. As Stoke paused, he started, passed his hand across his forehead, got up rather unsteadily, and poured out another glass of wine, which he gulped hastily.

"Nothing, nothing," he gasped, "the picture you paint is so vivid and so horrible that it has affected my nerves a little."

The doctor sat down again and seemed calmer.

"Proceed; exciting as it is, the story is also interesting," he said.

"The murderer," continued Stoke placidly, though his listener winced as he spoke, "had probably departed half an hour or more before death actually took place. In addition to her other troubles I believe Miss Sigurda also had a weak heart. Fright may have contributed to her sudden demise."

"What a fiendish method to bring about the death of an inoffensive person!" commented the doctor, mopping his brow with a silk handkerchief.

"I think that the culprit may have had in mind returning after his live weapon," went on Stoke, "and he may actually have done so. It is possible that the gardener was also an accomplice. I am sure that he knew more about the whole affair than he ever revealed before he became the unfortunate second victim of the fer-de-lance."

"It seems to me," remarked the doctor, as if with an effort, "that there was a flaw in the plans which would indicate not quite so much intelligence in the—ah—murderer as you would give him."

"Ah, but you forget that while we may have solved the mystery as to the cause of death," Stoke answered, "we are still considerably, if not completely, in the dark as to who conceived this idea. We know the how, but not the who."

"That is true," agreed Dr. Ragland, who now seemed himself again. "What progress are you making in that direction?"

"There again the mosaic is incomplete, but not without some stones," said Stoke. "A crime such as this must, as I have suggested, have a motive. As soon as we secure fairly complete facts about the past history and current life of the dead girl, we shall have more parts to fit into those which the facts at hand give us for our mosaic pattern. But we already have sufficient, haven't we, to deduce the personality of the man who might have consummated a crime such as this?"

"From the psychological point of view, yes, you probably have," was the reply.

"Let us assume," said Stoke, "that the person who was responsible for the death of Beatrice Sigurda was actually present this evening when I put on what Yates is pleased to call my show."

"Perhaps he was," murmured the doctor.

"Perhaps," said Stoke laconically.

"Despite the theories I have advanced regarding my colleague Dr. Rollin and your friend the professor," the psychiatrist continued, "I would not eliminate either of them completely. Such a brief test is not conclusive, and both, being men of some inherent ability, may have been prepared for any exigency. Knowing you, they must have suspected and expected something of a revelatory nature."

"Agreed," said Stoke, "but for the moment let us assume that neither is guilty, but that the real murderer was there with us. Just how would he have reacted, in your professional opinion, to the disclosure that the police and their assistants had found some damning evidence and were, or may have been, getting hot on the trail?"

The doctor paused a few moments before he gave his opinion. In those brief seconds there flashed through my mind the scene in the garden of the Serpentine Club, and with it came a query, a foolish thought. Why had Dr. Ragland refused to go to the scene of the murder, a much more important matter than the tantrum of some relatively insignificant neurotic female patient? And yet he had been the one to suggest to Commissioner Selden that Stoke be invited to participate in the investigation.

Then through my mind passed the incident concerning the psychiatrist's text-book on ophiology, the science of reptiles. And then his agitation a few minutes ago while Stoke was describing the *modus operandi* of the crime. Why should I meditate on such matters? What had Dr. Ragland, leader of the local medical profession, to do with the death of a woman like Miss Sigurda? The idea was preposterous, but it would not down. When I came out of my reverie, the doctor was speaking.

"I think that the murderer in this case," he said impressively and with no trace of his former perturbation, "would have listened to your narrative with an attitude of disdainful contempt. Although psychasthenic, he is not the type to show emotional stress or excitement in the face of danger. Instead, he has a superiority complex. He would have been outwardly calm, unmoved by your recital, though mentally alert. He would have given no indication of his guilt. You will have to get iron-clad facts, evidence such as only a court of law will accept, not psychological reactions, to convict this person."

The doctor's voice had risen as he discoursed. When he finished, he leaned back in his chair and smiled. Stoke had been listening intently.

"From my meager knowledge of psychiatry," he stated, "I should have come to the same conclusion."

"One other thing," said the doctor a little ominously; "this kind of man will stop at nothing to make this crime an unsolved mystery. If I were you, I should be constantly on my guard."

"I am," replied Stoke, a grim look on his face.

"If I were you," continued the doctor, "I should go armed, or else drop this case and leave it in the hands of the police, whose real job it is."

"I appreciate the warning," said Stoke.

CHAPTER XVII
RUNY TURNS UP RAGGED

A light drizzle was falling as we left Dr. Ragland's house. The night was dark and somber, not unlike that midnight when we had gone to the house on Q Street the day following the crime. As we hurried through the deserted streets, the scene in the garden, with the sudden flash of pistol-fire from the wall, came back to me. Stoke must have read my thoughts.

"Yes," he muttered, "it's another nice night for a murder."

"Do you take the doctor's warning seriously?" I panted.

"Enough to be on the alert," was the reply. "He is correct in saying that we are dealing with a dangerous, a sinister force, a man who would stop at nothing to prove himself master of the situation. If we begin to find out too much, if we get too obtrusive, nothing would be more natural to this egoist than to remove us—if he could."

The last words were spoken with a trace of a challenge. Stoke was becoming imbued with the zest of the combat. We went on for a block or two in silence.

"Someone has been following us ever since we came out of Ragland's," my companion whispered suddenly.

I started to look back, but my friend laid his hand quietly on my arm.

"Pay no attention," he said; "follow me."

We were near the corner of Fifteenth and Q streets when Stoke steered me quickly into one of the alleys. Before I knew it, we were round another corner and ensconced in the recess made by a stable door. Although there was a street light near the entrance to the alley, its beams did not reach to our hiding-place. For a few moments we stood in silence. After a short interval shuffling footsteps could be heard. They sounded as if someone were coming cautiously over the uneven bricks of the alley. Near our corner the footsteps stopped. In my mind's eye I could see a man peering about.

"Let's grab him," said Stoke in such a faint whisper that I hardly heard him, although his lips were close to my ear.

The footsteps went the other way, however. For another five minutes we waited; then the footsteps returned. At the corner another pause. Then a tall figure came past us. I waited for the signal.

"Good evening, officer," said Stoke as he stepped toward the figure, who wheeled sharply in our direction. In his hand I could see dimly a shining object. The man stood still and said nothing.

"This is Mr. Stoke," called the owner of that name quickly.

"Walk out to the light," commanded the voice.

"Come on, Jim," said Stoke nonchalantly, as he led me toward the corner.

When we were near the light, our follower peered at us quizzically.

"Well, you gave me the slip, all right," he said in a grieved tone. "The sergeant said not to let you out of me sight."

"The sergeant neglected to inform me of the bodyguard," replied Stoke, "but if he wants to have me seen home, all right. I appreciate his solicitude. Will you walk with us?"

"No, go ahead," said the plain-clothes man, who did not seem to enjoy his assignment, "I'll follow."

The pursuing footsteps accompanied us to the door of Stoke's apartment. When we had arrived there, Stoke paused, and the officer came up.

"Are you stuck with this job the rest of the night?" asked Stoke.

"Well, er, no," was the reply, "the chief said to watch you goin' home. He didn't say nothin' about hanging round. Are you goin' in now, huh?"

"We are about to retire after a hard day's work," replied Stoke.

"Well, I'll hang about for a while and then beat it and report," remarked the policeman.

As it happened, we did not retire for some time. Events moved fast from that moment.

Stoke was thoughtful as we went up in the elevator. At the door of the apartment he paused. Then he looked at me and grinned.

"Little by little the net is closing around someone," he said. "Perhaps the precautions are well taken."

"Closing around whom?" I asked as he opened the door and I followed him in, shutting it behind me. Stoke was groping for the light-switch, which was in the wall about four feet from the door.

"Around—" he began, but the sentence was never finished.

The word was hardly out of his mouth when I was flung violently against the door. A heavy body had collided with me with such impact that for a moment I was stunned.

Half-dazed, I became aware of a struggle going on in the pitch-black room. Two men were grappling. I could hear their panting breaths as they exerted themselves, and yet they must have been standing in one place, as there was no sound of overturning furniture. It was uncanny, hearing this almost silent struggle there in the dark.

"Lights!" came a hoarse voice out of the gloom.

It was Stoke. Arousing myself, I felt for the switch, found it, and snapped it. Instead of a welcome flood of light, there was nothing, only the same weird darkness. Outside, the rain was pouring now.

"Flashlight," gasped Stoke.

Before I could get or use my flashlight, there was a crash as if a small stand of some kind had been knocked over. Then a thud. Footsteps on the fire-escape outside the window, which was open. Where was the screen, I wondered?

In my awkwardness several minutes must have elapsed before the beam of the flashlight showed me a prostrate figure on the floor. Warily I approached. It was Stoke. His face was livid and his breathing stertorous. His eyes were closed. I rushed for the bathroom to get water, but when I tried the door, it was locked. By the time I had returned to Stoke, his eyes were open and he was looking at me more or less in his usual manner.

"Don't be alarmed," he said as he got up, rather shakily, and sank into a chair. "Try screwing up the electric-light bulbs."

I did as he suggested, and in a moment the room was filled with a pleasing glow of light.

"Are you hurt?" I asked.

"No, are you?" he replied.

"Only shaken up," was my answer, "but tell me what hit me?"

"I hit you," he said.

"You?"

"I jumped back," answered Stoke, "because whoever was in here, stabbed at me. You will find the knife in the corner by the desk."

Exactly where Stoke had designated was a flat knife. On its shiny steel blade were engraved figures. They looked like the hieroglyphics one sees on ancient monuments. Near the end was a coiled serpent, the fangs extended so that they formed the point. The handle of the knife was carved from bone, and it, too, had a snake along the entire edge, the head protruding to make a grip for the fingers.

"I am sorry that I hit you like a ton of bricks, as I did," continued Stoke, "but this knife"—he was turning it over and over—"came so close that it literally blistered me. Look."

In his shirt there was a clean vertical cut about three inches long.

"What a swing that fellow had, and what a grip!" Stoke ruminated. "He was trying to choke me after I wrested the knife from him. He was strong, but clumsy. Well, we have one more clue. Let's wash up."

"The bathroom door is locked," I said, remembering that fact with a sudden shock.

"I never lock it," countered Stoke, rising with some alacrity.

That was something I also knew.

Stoke, apparently now himself again, strode to the door and tried it. There was no question that it was fastened.

"Hadn't I better phone Yates or headquarters?" I said, picking up the instrument.

"Yes, but you can't do it from here," he replied quietly.

"Why not?" I retorted, beginning to think that my friend's reason had been affected by his struggle.

"Because," he continued blandly, "the cord is cut. Probably with this quaint Aztec dirk," he added.

"Shall I go outside and phone, or help you get the door open?" I inquired, and then, a second thought coming into my head, I suggested: "Perhaps I had better telephone and ask Yates to scour the neighborhood for the man."

"Don't do that," replied Stoke, "he won't be in the neighborhood. Besides, I think I know where I can find him whenever I so desire. Don't raise your eyebrows like that. Give me that bunch of keys you weigh yourself down with."

Completely nonplussed I handed him my keys. He had often made fun of my old-maidish proclivities in carrying a bunch of miscellaneous keys, some active and some inactive, but now the practice proved of some value, for one of them unlocked the door.

The first thing we saw when we opened it was a pair of feet. They were facing us. On the floor was the form of Lieutenant Runy O'Mara, neatly bound and gagged.

Stoke still had the knife in his hand, as he seemed reluctant to let go of this piece of evidence. With a few deft strokes he severed the thongs and cut the gag; together we helped Runy to the couch. Stoke rubbed his arms and legs where the rawhide had cut into them.

"Thanks," murmured Runy. "So he got away, did he? I heard you boys battling. What a mess I was all during the festivities."

"Now that you are unbound, Prometheus-like," said Stoke with a smile, "you might explain your intrusion into my apartment."

"With pleasure," returned Runy, his jaunty self once again, though with a little admixture of ruefulness. "I spent the morning following up the snake leads. Say, I ought to see snakes tonight. Have you, by the way, any snake-bite medicine handy? If so, I feign would sip of it."

"Do you mean anti-venin?" asked Stoke artlessly.

"No, I do not," replied Runy with some asperity.

Stoke, apparently considering that Runy's nerves and disposition required a little stimulant, produced from a hidden recess the necessary "medicine," which Runy imbibed with a sigh of relief.

"Now I feel better," he admitted. "In the course of my inquiries I discovered that the Washington Zoo has no such reptile as a fer-de-lance. It seems, however, that this zoo handled two of these slimy things, one for the Boston snake house and one for the Bronx Zoo in New York. They were ordered from a professional animal-dealer in Buenos Aires and shipped to Washington with some other living curiosities by a tramp steamer which called at Norfolk. Following up this lead, I found that the Bronx Zoo still has its fer-de-lance safely caged in its reptile house, but that the Bostonian one caught pneumonia or something and up and died. It was either fed to the python or buried with due obsequies."

"Where does that get us?" asked Stoke politely.

"Listen and you shall hear," countered Runy. "Further discreet inquiries elicited the information that the tramp steamer in question, which, strangely enough, is named the *Beatrice*, was due to arrive in Norfolk this or last evening."

"In other words," said Stoke, "you think that the captain of this vessel might be interrogated to advantage."

"You steal the very words from my innocent lips," answered Runy. "I even went so far as to induce one of my aviating colleagues to pilot me to Norfolk this afternoon, or, since it is now tomorrow, yesterday afternoon. The boat had not arrived up to the time we departed, about an hour and a half before sunset. The plane had to be back in its garage by nightfall, so we returned. On the way back from the naval air station, I regret to say that we were in such a hurry that an unfeeling and obstinate cop got us on the highway bridge and detained us for some time. I couldn't reach Yates to get us off and we had to go to the precinct station, be lectured by a dirty-faced desk sergeant, the big martinet! He got angry just because I sassed him some, and there was more delay, not to mention a deposit of ten dollars collateral."

"It is barely possible that Yates can recover it for you," suggested Stoke.

"He'd better," said Runy grimly. "I reported at the club, but you had vanished. Then I met a friend and had dinner with her. About eleven thirty I returned to the club, but you were still absent, and there was no message, so I wandered over here. It must have been midnight when I arrived."

"And then?" said Stoke with a trace of excitement.

"I came to your door and pressed the buzzer. There was no reply to the first ring, so I pressed it once more. Again there was no reply and I was about to leave when the door opened. Thinking you had been asleep, I walked in. There was no light and the room was pitch-dark. I made some remark, asking where were you, when something hit me a fierce wallop on the head and down I went. The blow wasn't too bad, though, because I came to fairly quickly, to find myself lying on my stomach on your couch with a gag in my mouth. There was a knee in the middle of my back and someone was just finishing tying me up. I struggled a bit, but it was no use."

"Did you see this person?" asked Stoke.

"No," answered Runy regretfully, "it was as black as the ace of spades. He did his job by feel, I guess."

"Did he say anything?"

"Yes, when I twisted a little, he put his face close to mine and hissed out the words: 'This will teach you to mind your own damn business.'"

"Was the voice at all familiar?" was Stoke's next question.

"Nothing that I could recognize," Runy replied. "The words were spoken in good English, with no foreign accent. They were hissed in a low tone, as if the speaker were gloating at my predicament."

"Was that all?" asked Stoke.

"Not quite. Then he lifted me up with very little effort and deposited me on a cool floor, shutting and locking a door on me. There I stayed until you found me, an extremely unpleasant couple of hours, if it was that. It seemed like a year. I had ample time to consider all my sins and curse this whole fool business. We'll get him yet, though."

"We will," agreed Stoke, and there was a quiet determination to his tone. "This is not the first time an attempt has been made to intimidate me when I have had a duty to perform. The attempts have invariably been unsuccessful."

"Lying there in the dark on your bathroom floor made my senses acute, and I heard things while I waited," continued Runy. "The first procedure of your unwelcome visitor was to remove a screen from the window."

"He must have entered by the door, then," suggested Stoke. "Jim, make a note to make some inquiries as to whether anyone saw a man come in about midnight tonight."

I made a note.

"Then he prowled round the room," Runy went on. "His footsteps made no noise, but I could hear him opening drawers and looking into things. After a while there was silence, and I presume he was waiting. At one time there was a noise as if he were honing a razor."

"Sharpening the knife, perhaps," said Stoke, as I shuddered.

"Finally I heard you two come in and Jim say something about 'closing around.' Next came thuds and a struggle. And me, a fighting Irishman, trussed up like a market hen. What a life!"

"Who could this visitor have been?" I asked.

"Undoubtedly the murderer of Miss Sigurda," was Stoke's immediate answer. "The trail is getting a little too warm, and he took a desperate chance. And yet not so desperate for him. The mental attributes of this man are most interesting," my friend went on confidentially. "He is obviously a profound egoist, a person who derives satisfaction from an assumed mastery of the whole situation. Not only did he get a certain pleasure out of the crime—"

"Two crimes," interrupted Runy.

"No," Stoke corrected him, "only one, at least this time, as the death of San Remo was an accident, a fortunate one for the murderer, perhaps, but not premeditated. Killing Miss Sigurda was probably a pleasure to him, gruesome as is that idea; but equally inspiring to this brilliant but perverted mentality was the working out of the method and the deliberate combat with the organized forces of law and order. Keen as is the intellect of this man, he makes one fatal mistake."

"And that is?" asked Runy.

"He overrates himself," was the answer, "and thus he plays into our hands. Coming here tonight was courageous, but foolhardy, because unnecessary. His coming has only resulted, aside from some physical discomfort to all three of us, in leaving more parts to fit into the mosaic."

"You mean the knife, of course," said Runy.

"Compare this dagger with the one left in the door of the Serpentine Club on the night of the murder," suggested Stoke, opening a drawer to get the other.

It was gone.

"Right," said Runy, "I remember the other, and they are similar, except that this one is less worn and apparently newer than the other."

"The knife, yes, is a most significant clue," remarked Stoke, "but so is the stuff that he used for tying you up. Take a good look at it."

Runy was up in an instant and returned with the rope-like substance that had bound him. It was not rope, however, but a thin strip of leather, such as is used by cowboys.

"That is a lariat," explained Stoke, "and I have a sneaking suspicion that it was used much further south than the Rio Grande. It looks, in fact, like the kind of lasso that sees service on the Argentine pampas. Moreover, it has not been used for a long time. See, there is still dust on parts of it. Do not handle this evidence any more than you can help. Even the dust may give us a clue. This lariat had either been hanging on a wall or had been in a closet for a long time before it was employed for its purpose tonight. Our intruder brought it with him for a purpose."

"Well, you have a couple of good clues to add to your collection, then," remarked Runy.

"There was a third that was better than either," continued Stoke quietly. "As you know, I have a delicate touch. In my brief struggle with our ex-ranchero—" he paused, smiling.

"Yes, yes?" cried Runy. "I'm all agog."

"—my hands," said Stoke, "touched him in many places."

CHAPTER XVIII
A TRIP TO THE WATERFRONT

"Contact."

In response to the pilot's order a mechanic gave the propeller a whirl, and the motor started with a roar. I was nearly blown out of the ship by the sudden rush of wind. Stoke sat beside me calmly watching the proceedings, for he was as much a veteran in the air as I was a novice. When he had been in charge of anti-malaria measures at several posts during the war, he had made flights all over Louisiana in order to inspect his drainage ditches and oiling-operations. It was he, in fact, who first suggested dusting mosquito-breeding pools from an aeroplane, and he had devised a chemical which remained on the surface of the water, forming a film which prevented the mosquito larva from coming to the surface to breathe.

Runy sat beside the pilot, one of his friends, who was prosaically named Jones. After warming up the engine for a few moments, the sea-plane was turned round and headed down the river into the wind. The pilot gave it the gun and we skimmed across the water, finally leaving it for the air. We were *en route* to Norfolk to follow up Runy's seafaring lead.

All of us wore old clothes and none of us had shaved that morning. A more disreputable-looking trio would have been hard to find. In addition I had a discolored eye where the back of Stoke's head had collided so vigorously with me the previous night, and Runy's eye was still black. Before leaving, Stoke had called up Yates and reported on the events of the night and had also informed him of our destination and its purpose. The detective had promised to prevent any more raids on the apartment.

It was to be hoped that he would, for in checking up in the morning, we discovered only one thing missing besides the dagger, but a very important item. The intruder had broken into a locked drawer in Stoke's desk and taken the bullet which had been found in the garden of the house on Q Street the morning after Stoke had been the target for the silenced gun. Stoke shrugged his shoulders at his loss and remarked that he had exchanged an indifferent clue for a better one—the second knife. Most of the other objects which he considered as potential evidence were now safe at police headquarters.

After the rain of the night before, the morning was clear and beautiful, the country lying below us in all the splendor of early summer. In a few minutes we were over Mount Vernon, looking down on the well-ordered green box hedges and the noble white mansion where George Washington had lived. Only a little farther, or so it seemed, although the distance was nearly twenty miles, and we were over the marine camp at Quantico. From there the pilot did not follow the bend of the Potomac, but cut across country, rejoining the river at Lower Cedar Point. To me it seemed like a needless risk flying a seaplane over dry land.

Eventually we left the river, passing Point Lookout, with its trim lighthouse, and turned south over Chesapeake Bay. Along the coast we sailed, past the mouth of the Rappahannock and Mobjack Bay. In the distance we could see Cape Charles on the Maryland shore, and beyond it the broad reaches of the Atlantic.

In Hampton Roads several ships of the fleet were at anchor, and Runy waved them an affectionate salute as we soared overhead. The pilot headed past Old Point Comfort, with its big, rambling hotel, and directly into the Elizabeth River, which cuts through Norfolk like a canal in Venice. After some jockeying about, he found a quiet spot, descended to the water, taxied into the wind, and finally came to rest opposite the naval air station.

Runy knew Norfolk well, and so we put ourselves in his hands, as I had been there but once, and Stoke had merely visited this attractive Virginia city without, as he put it, "snooping about." It was early in the afternoon when we reached the wharf district. By means of much astute questioning the day before, Runy had ascertained approximately where among the hundred and fifty wharves of Norfolk the *Beatrice* might be expected to dock.

It was a tough neighborhood. On one side of the street were rows of ramshackle brick and wooden buildings, with shops on the street level. Some of them were devoted to nautical wares, while others, with their opaque windows and swinging doors, were unquestionably given over to dispensing liquid cheer to longshoremen and the other denizens of this disreputable district. Across from these blind tigers, brothels, and a few more or less respectable stores were the docks.

A motley collection of steamers and colliers was before us. On some of them there were signs of activity, with Negro stevedores busily at work, at least as ardently as is the Ethiopian custom. Trucks laden with barrels and boxes passed us in the street. Everywhere were the noises and confusion, the smell and the color of the busy waterfront.

For a while we sauntered along, like three seamen looking for a job. For once Runy, with a decrepit cap over his usually immaculately parted hair, and clothed in an old suit of Stoke's, which was somewhat too large for him, looked like a tramp, rather than the debonair friend of the debutantes. Stoke had the appearance of a fairly decent purser, while I might have passed as a galley slave on a windjammer.

At one of the docks was a shabby gray steamer with a black funnel, upon which a red "B" was painted. Alongside the once elaborate but now faded figurehead at the bow was the name *Beatrice* in dirty black letters. The ship was tied up at the dock, but the only activity was the process of taking on coal from a lighter fast to the riverside.

Stoke and I stood looking at the uninviting craft as Runy shambled aimlessly along until he came up to a hatchet-faced man whose only object in life seemed to loaf in as comfortable a manner as possible while he expectorated into the oily water.

"Morning," said Runy as he sauntered along. "See the old tub got in."

To which the only answer was "Yep."

"Who might be master of her now?" asked Runy innocently.

The man spat with his customary delicacy.

"Captain Tracy was last night," he replied, "but who in hell is now, God only knows." He paused for effect.

"How's that?" Runy prompted him.

Punctuating his conversation copiously with profanity of a superior order, the loafer explained that half the crew had deserted and the ship was due to sail at sundown. He characterized the boat as a scow, alleged that it was haunted, the captain incompetent, the first mate crazy, and the owner a weasel. Except for these few drawbacks, he seemed to think well of the *Beatrice*. Runy finally disengaged himself from his pleasant friend and went on. We joined him.

"As the most respectable-looking member of the gang, I will go on board in quest of the captain," said Stoke, "while you wait here."

"And catch you when you are thrown down the gangplank," suggested Runy. "Let me go. I know a poop deck from a forecastle, even if I am in the Bureau of Engineering of the Navy."

"My dear sir," replied Stoke, "I make no claim to naval knowledge, I am merely a lawyer's clerk looking up some information for an insurance-placing client."

With that he walked in a business-like manner up the gangplank. In a few minutes he had returned.

"A considerably inebriated gentleman, whom I take to be the ship's cook, informs me that the captain is at Sweeney's. Do you happen to know where that particular night-club is?" he asked Runy.

"I regret to disappoint you in that regard," answered Runy.

"All right," said Stoke. "Pie-eyed Pete back there tried to direct me, so we will set off in search of the Sweeney hostelry."

We went on for three blocks, then turned into a side street, turned again along a street which paralleled the waterfront and into another lane at right angles to it. The environment was one of the most unsavory I had ever seen. Stoke had his directions properly, however, for ahead of us on the left was a yellow wooden building, somewhat less decrepit than the others along the way. It was adorned with a bleary sign reading "Sweeney's" in blue letters.

"Seen Captain Tracy around?" Runy inquired of another loiterer, who merely pointed toward the door of the dive.

"What a choice dump!" muttered Runy as we entered.

At one end of the room was a bar. Between it and the door were half a dozen or more wooden tables. The floor was sprinkled with sawdust and decorated here and there with cracked cuspidors. On the walls were lurid prints, which might have been taken from the *Police Gazette* of the late nineties.

A couple of men were standing at the bar, while another sat at one of the tables, evidently asleep, as his head lay across one arm on the table. In a corner at another table sat a large, florid, domineering-looking man, with a napkin tucked under his chin. Before him was a dish of stew and beside it a huge beaker of what might have been beer, judging solely from the froth. Hovering over this man stood the proprietor or bar-tender or waiter, whichever he was. He was clad in an apron, much soiled, and was leaning familiarly over the other's shoulder, talking earnestly to him.

As we entered, the proprietor straightened up as if caught in a reprehensible act. Without a glance at him Stoke led the way to the bar, and the man resumed his conversation for a moment and then hurried to serve us. Stoke gave an order and while the soiled gentleman was preparing it, leaned idly against the bar and casually surveyed the room.

"Say," he remarked to the bar-tender, "ain't that Captain Tracy over there?"

"Do youse know him?" was the suspicious reply.

"Sure," answered Stoke, "why my company done business with his owners for years."

"Jarvis and Leake," grunted Runy.

"Old man Jarvis run that ship for years," continued Stoke confidentially. "Right after Leake died, in 1910, the boss says to me: 'Go down and see Captain Tracy in Baltimore and inspect the *Beatrice* so's we can write that policy over,' and he gives me the wink, see, and I never even left Philadelphia, where we was then, and they gives her a Class A rating."

After this amazing revelation Stoke burst into loud guffaws, in which we all joined. The proprietor beamed. Chicanery was a language which he evidently understood well.

"Do youse guys want a nice berth on that boat?" he inquired ingratiatingly, "because if you does, I can fix it. Captain Tracy is looking for two or three guys to take the place of some of the crew what got sick and went to the horspital."

"I ain't following the water now," replied Stoke, "but I must go speak to the captain."

With that he edged over and greeted the florid gentleman who was shoveling the stew in with must gusto.

Runy and I sat down at one of the tables.

"When no one is looking, spill that sulphuric acid out of your glass, or you'll wake up on board the *Beatrice*, shanghaied," cautioned Runy.

Stoke told the captain the same general story he had related to Mr. Sweeney, and the captain, desiring to be affable, recalled the incident perfectly.

"What are you doing now, Mr. Brown?" he asked after some further conversation.

Mr. Brown, otherwise Trevor Stoke, leaned toward the captain.

"I've got a swell job now," he said, "I'm a keeper in the zoo in Washington."

"Is that so?" remarked Captain Tracy with much interest. "Sweeney, bring a couple of set-ups. You know, me, I handle animals for that place every now and then. Have regular business with Señor Cortez in Buenos. Why, I brought a dozen young monkeys up this here trip. You didn't happen to come down after them, did you?"

"No, I'm on a vacation. Came down to visit my Cousin Joe, that fellah over there," replied Stoke waving toward me.

"Is that Joe? Come on over here," shouted the captain to us.

We joined Stoke and the captain, who had already consumed several glasses of the fiery liquor and was gradually becoming more and more loquacious. The two bums at the bar had left and Sweeney was busy elsewhere, so we had the place to ourselves, except for the sleeping beauty at the near-by table. He was snoring with disgusting regularity, but no one paid any attention to him.

"I don't work in the monkey house," continued Stoke, as Runy coughed decorously, keeping a straight face with some difficulty, "I'm in with the hippopotamus. Also have the snakes. Say, we've got some swell rattlesnakes now."

"Is that so?" boomed the captain. "Why, you old son of a sea cook, I brought you one of them rattlers, right from Señor Cortez. Had a hell of a time caring for them. There was four of them and one got loose on the voyage up. Poisonous, too. The cook climbed the rigging when he heard of it and wouldn't come down. 'Mr. Wiggs,' I says, 'you come down outer there.' 'Please don't make me,' he says."

There was much more of this, the climax having occurred, according to the captain's narrative, when he took a couple of shots at the cowardly Mr. Wiggs, who promptly descended. The captain drank a health to Mr. Wiggs.

"But we only got one of them South American snakes," Stoke went on. "We sent one to Boston. Did you say there was four?"

"Sure, four. The two for the zoo, and two for that guy in Washington," was the captain's answer. "I only give him one, 'cause it was one of his'n that escaped."

The captain smote the table with a ham-like hand and took another drink, Runy's, as it happened, having been deftly substituted for his empty glass.

"Jeez, but he was sore when he and that Indian comes to the dock to get them," continued Mr. Tracy. "They was waiting for the boat to tie up, they was so anxious, and the first thing he says is: 'Have you got Mr. Remo's order?' 'What t'ell is that?' I says."

Another long explanation followed. From it we gathered that a man who answered the description of San Remo, Miss Sigurda's half-breed gardener, and another man had met his steamer on his last call at Norfolk in order to receive a consignment of two snakes from a professional animal-dealer in Buenos Aires.

Stoke professed great interest in the episode and by much skillful if apparently artless questioning endeavored to obtain a complete description of San Remo's companion. In this he was partially successful, although the captain was gradually getting more and more befuddled, both mentally and physically. One thing he could not tell, and that was any name except Remo.

Finally the captain rose unsteadily.

"Must get back to ship," he muttered. "Come on, Brownie. Hey, Sweeney."

Stoke insisted upon paying, with very little protest from the captain.

"Be sure'n get those men on board," Captain Tracy admonished the leering proprietor, as he reeled out. As we were leaving, I noticed that the sleeper had roused and was also preparing to depart. On the way I managed to detach myself from the party. Stoke and Runy had more difficulty in taking leave of the now maudlin sea-captain. What excuse they gave or subterfuge they used I do not know, but they deposited their cargo on his own gangplank. His attention was eventually diverted to the manner in which the coal was being placed in the hold, and with a string of picturesque oaths he charged the lighter, to rebuke, politely, the gentleman who was supervising this performance.

The three of us then made our escape. We had the information we wanted. Stoke had a working description of San Remo's companion, which, he confided, fitted into his mosaic.

"The blue glasses were a disguise, of course," he said; "also the slouch hat pulled down, but the size of him and the facial characteristics all agree with what I already know. It was undoubtedly the murderer and we can get Yates to check up on his movements at the time when he was supposed to be here with San Remo."

"You must be about ready to put him in the jug," commented Runy.

"Not quite," admitted Stoke. "There are two or three pieces yet to be supplied and then the evidence is complete."

Within an hour or so we were back at St. Helena, ready for our return trip. After some little delay Runy located his friend Lieutenant Jones, who had regaled himself in a movie during our absence.

"By the way," said Jones in a matter-of-fact tone as he was about to climb into the cockpit, "there's a telegram for you, Runy."

He handed the message to Runy, who tore it open impatiently. He uttered an exclamation of surprise as he read it.

"This upsets the apple-cart," he said as he passed the telegram to Stoke.

The latter took it and read it calmly.

"Just what I expected," he remarked.

"But it changes the whole aspect of the thing," expostulated Runy. "They both couldn't have done it."

"They didn't," answered Stoke. "Rollin is deluded, that's all."

I was overcome with curiosity at this repartee and was much relieved when Stoke finally handed the telegram to me.

This is what I read:

DOCTOR ROLLIN HAS MADE COMPLETE CONFESSION OF THE MURDER STOP RETURN AT ONCE. YATES.

CHAPTER XIX
MORE THAN ONE CONFESSION

A thousand questions surged through my mind on the return flight, although the noise of the motor prevented conversation. Had this confession finally cleared the mystery? Yet Stoke had said something about a delusion on the part of Dr. Rollin. The situation was, if anything, more complicated, but Yates would provide the answer in an hour or two.

Lieutenant Jones finally brought the plane to a graceful landing on the Potomac in the vicinity of Anacostia. We disembarked, shook hands with our pilot, and proceeded directly to a telephone booth at the flying-field, where Stoke endeavored to reach the detective. It was then about five o'clock in the afternoon.

"Yates was not sure when we would reach Washington," Stoke informed us when he emerged, "and so he has set seven o'clock for us to meet him at the house on Q Street. We can get dinner first and see him later. He was not in his office, but left this message."

"I could eat if urged," agreed Runy, who generally could. "Jones's bumpy flying would give anyone an appetite."

As luck would have it, one of Runy's numerous female friends happened to be visiting the field, and after a little palaver he succeeded in getting a ride back to the city for the rest of us. Stoke and I rode in the rumble seat of a red car, which went so fast that we barely noticed how intimately the driver and Runy seemed to be conversing, if nothing else. In a relatively brief space of time we were delivered at Runy's residence. He invited us in while he changed his clothes and also looked to see if any important communications had arrived. One had. There was a long cablegram, of which more will be said later.

From Runy's place we walked hurriedly to Stoke's apartment, where we found everything intact. There were no notes on the door, and nothing was disturbed inside.

"I don't expect any more intrusions," Stoke assured us. "Besides, Yates has a man in the yard on the look-out, and another in the street. If the murderer has any sense, and we know he has, he won't repeat his call."

At the apartment we shaved and resumed our respectable garments and then betook ourselves to the Serpentine Club for sustenance.

"If we only had old Bushy, Dr. Ragland, and his nibs, the commissioner, here now," remarked Runy, "we could hold another council of war."

"Speak of the devil and he appears," said Stoke with a smile.

In the doorway of the garden stood Starr-Smith, glancing nonchalantly about. He caught sight of us, waved, and as Runy beckoned, strolled in our direction.

"If I intrude on any recondite discussions of criminology, expel me without compunction," was his greeting.

"Sit down, sit down," exclaimed Runy, "and come off of your high horse. Have you evolved any bright ideas as to who or what murdered Beatrice Sigurda."

"I gathered from the performance the other night that the what had been determined," the architect replied with faint sarcasm. "The who seems yet to be solved."

"It is solved," said Stoke calmly.

"Indeed!" answered Starr-Smith archly. "And the culprit is arrested, no doubt?"

"No doubt," was Stoke's answer; "at least he has confessed."

"But I thought you said—" I began, only to receive a glance from my friend which caused me to lapse into silence.

Starr-Smith looked at me inquiringly and then turned to Stoke.

"Your remarks are cryptic, as usual," he said.

There seemed to be an almost imperceptible antagonism between these two. The famous architect was said by some to have a jealous disposition and I presumed that he resented the leading part that

Stoke had taken and was taking in the solution of this crime, while he more or less sat on the side lines. I had the feeling from his attitude that he would have enjoyed being more completely in our confidence, although Runy or others had kept him reasonably well-informed of developments.

"If you would care to accompany us to the house on Q Street in half an hour," Stoke told him, "you will have the pleasure of hearing this confession."

"It may be more of a disappointment than a pleasure," replied the architect. "Has the third degree finally worked on one of your suspects?"

"That remains to be seen," was the answer. "I am as hazy as to the details as you are."

"I take it, then," returned Starr-Smith blandly, "that your professional friend has beaten you to it in solving the crime."

"That also remains to be seen," said Stoke.

Twenty minutes later we were on the way to the house on Q Street, Starr-Smith waxing ironical on the necessity of dramatizing all these events by holding them at the scene, or supposed scene, of the crime.

In the living-room we found Commissioner Selden, Yates, one or two policemen, and an abject figure which turned out to be Dr. Rollin.

"Can't you ever join us without bringing a gang with you?" was Mr. Selden's rather petulant greeting.

"Their presence may be more useful than you think," replied Stoke, as Runy jauntily took a chair, and Starr-Smith glared at the commissioner. I slunk into the room as unobtrusively as possible.

"Dr. Rollin," announced the commissioner in a businesslike way, which caused that person to cringe a little, "has told us that his actions were responsible for the death of Miss Sigurda. Since you have been concerned, semiofficially, in the solution of this crime, we thought it desirable to inform you of his explanation. Detective Yates will read the confession."

Yates rustled some papers and cleared his throat.

"If the commissioner will permit me," he said unctuously, "I might explain first that while you gents were chasing round Norfolk, I got hold of this here secretary of the doctor's and—"

"Gave her the third degree," murmured Starr-Smith.

"—interrogated her," continued Yates, not noticing the interruption. "Blondy spilt enough beans so that I got hold of her boss and finally got out of him what actually happened. He was warned that what he said might be used against him, and this is it."

The detective took up the paper, as Dr. Rollin, haggard and unkempt, seemed to shrivel in his chair. Starr-Smith shot him a contemptuous glance.

"On the evening of June 10 I called on Miss Beatrice Sigurda, who was one of my patients and also a friend. I arrived at her house about half past six. I found Miss Sigurda mentally depressed. At her request for a palliative, I gave her a hypodermic injection of morphia.

"Question. Then you lied when you told us that you had never given her narcotics by means of hypodermics.

"Yes, I lied, as I often gave her relief in that way. Then we went out to dinner at the Sevilla. We returned directly to the house, and again Miss Sigurda complained of mental and physical distress. She refused to explain what was troubling her and we had a slight disagreement about the matter.

"Question. Why were you so interested in her affairs?

"To be perfectly frank, Miss Sigurda and I had planned to be married. She told me, however, that all her money was gone, but that was not what was troubling her. It seems, oh my God, that another man was involved.

"Question. Who?

"I don't know. She would not tell me. At any rate, I finally consented to give her another hypodermic, so I mixed up some morphia in my syringe. Purposely I made the dose unusually strong, although I knew she had a weak heart. I gave it to her and there was an immediate reaction. I feared anaphylactic shock, but she came out of it. The whole procedure was foolish and I knew it, but I was distraught. Then, as I had to visit another patient in Georgetown, I left. That must have been about ten o'clock or a little later.

"I returned to my office for a while, talked with my secretary, who was working late, told her about Miss Sigurda, and then drove to Georgetown. Before leaving I telephoned to Dr. Ragland to ask him to join me in consultation with respect to this patient, a violent mental case. He was out, but I left a message.

"The opiate I had given to Miss Sigurda was on my mind, so when I left Mrs. Carpenter, I went into a store and called up her house. The maid answered and I asked for Beatrice. After a while she told me that there was a light in her room, but that she must be asleep, as she could not rouse her. I was frantic, for I felt sure that the drug had killed her, as I am sure now that it did.

"In my excitement I then did another foolish thing. I called up the medical examiner and sent him out to Tenleytown on a useless errand. I thought that if I delayed examination of the body, the drug would be dispersed.

"Ever since this affair life has been hell for me. I have been in practice only a few years, and a case such as this, which looks like malpractice, would ruin me. My office girl has blackmailed me as her price to keep still about it. I am sure that Dr. Ragland suspected me all along. He found traces of the drug in the body, but attributed the death to an obscure poison. It is no longer fair for him to try to shield me as his protégé.

"I swear to you it was an accident. I had no cause to kill Beatrice Sigurda, whom I loved. I would not kill her for a petty quarrel. I tell you it was all a mistake."

Here followed the customary verification and oath, stating that the confession was made without duress and with full knowledge of its import and implications. When Yates had finished, Stoke leaned forward.

"May I ask one supplementary question?" he said.

"Certainly," assented Mr. Selden.

"On what part of the body was the hypodermic administered?" asked Stoke of Dr. Rollin, to whom the question had to be repeated before he seemed able to collect his distracted mind to answer.

Finally he stammered: "On the leg."

"That is all," said Stoke.

"Does anyone else want to contribute anything?" demanded Mr. Selden in a manner that implied that no one had better do so, and no one did.

"Dr. Rollin is under arrest and will undoubtedly be indicted for manslaughter," announced the commissioner, as the doctor slumped back again.

"He'll be lucky if it's no worse than that," commented Runy as we moved to take our departure.

"Are you satisfied with this confession?" asked Starr-Smith, as we stood on the steps.

"I will drop in at your studio tomorrow evening and talk it over with you, if you have no objections," replied Stoke.

"Delighted," said the architect cordially. "I have been anxious to entertain you there. Bring your companion," indicating me, "and we will have another council of war. Until then adieu, and take care of yourself."

As we were about to walk away, the plain-clothes man on duty hailed Stoke.

"Pardon me, cap, but the old guy next door is very anxious that you should see him right away," he informed us. "Says he has something important to tell you."

"Another confession probably," remarked Starr-Smith with undisguised sarcasm. "I'll wait to hear about that one later," he added as he walked away.

As we were turning toward Professor Kent's, Yates and another officer emerged from the Sigurda house with Dr. Rollin between them. His knees sagged so that the two literally had to support him. They placed him in a police car and drove away as Mr. Selden appeared on the doorstep.

"Well, Stoke, the crime seems to be solved," remarked the commissioner as he joined us. "Too bad you have had all your efforts in vain, but I suppose they amused you."

"Are you sure it is all over?" asked Stoke.

"Certainly," answered Mr. Selden, "no jury would fail to convict on the strength of that confession. I told you Yates would get the culprit sooner or later. Your help has been very valuable, though, Mr. Stoke, and we all appreciate it."

"Thanks," said Stoke a little wearily.

"See you at the trial," called the commissioner as he departed.

"Sooner, perhaps," murmured my companion as we turned toward the professor's house.

Inside we found Kent pacing up and down in his study. He seemed less apathetic than formerly; he possibly was even a little excited. Stoke shook hands with him cordially and we sat down.

"When these police"—and the professor shuddered as he spoke—"so thoroughly searched my house in my absence, the morning you kept me waiting next door, they found what seemed like an effective clue, but they missed a really good one."

He paused for effect. When Stoke expressed surprise, he beamed childishly.

"These wise police never thought to look at my books," continued Kent.

"Books?" queried Stoke.

"Right here on this shelf," indicated the professor, "were several albums. The topmost of them is of importance to this case."

"What is it, a diary?" asked my friend.

"Not a written diary, no," resumed the professor, "but something just as good. It is a collection of photographs and snapshots taken mostly in the Argentine. The album belonged to Miss Sigurda, who gave it or loaned it to me several months ago."

Stoke's eyes sparkled.

"Why did you not turn this over to me at the beginning of the case?" he inquired.

"Honestly," answered Professor Kent, "it never occurred to me. My mind hasn't seemed to work well lately and I had completely forgotten about it. Lately, however, I got to thinking about the case, and it seemed to me that the early or earlier history of Beatrice might have some bearing on who could have done this horrible deed. This morning I was looking for a paper by Professor Singleton on reptilian life in the subtropics, and in moving some books came across this album. To tell you the truth, my first impulse was to destroy it. To tell you another truth, I did destroy one picture in it."

"You shouldn't have done that." Stoke reproved him as he would a naughty boy.

The professor blushed.

"The picture I burned was of no importance to the investigation," he said excusingly. "It was not even pasted in. It showed Beatrice and me on a bench at Great Falls. There was nothing compromising about it, as our relations were always honorable. You believe that, don't you, Trevor?"

"Certainly," answered Stoke promptly.

"But it was best not to permit it to be found," continued the professor. "I have troubles enough. The remainder of the album is just as she gave it to me."

"Give it to me, then," suggested Stoke.

The professor took from his bookcase a rather dilapidated photograph album and handed it to my friend, who opened it with obvious curiosity. It contained about twenty-five photographs, some a little discolored by age. Under most of them titles and comments had been written in a woman's hand. These phrases were in Spanish, and most of them bore dates.

"This is most valuable," commented Stoke. "It is almost the last piece for the mosaic."

The pictures at the beginning of the book depicted various scenes at a ranch. Some showed Miss Sigurda on horseback, and one was a view of her in riding-costume beside a rather ferocious man with a black mustache. He was short, but broad-shouldered. Under this picture was the caption: "*Mio hombre.*"

"Her husband!" ejaculated Stoke in surprise. "So she had a spouse back in the old country. I wonder what became of him."

A later picture showed the exterior of a large church.

"Look," said Stoke, "a funeral procession, and below it is a statement that it was taken at the obsequies of Don Caspar Derqui."

Somewhat further Stoke found several pictures which drew from him an expression of triumph. He called my attention to one under which there was simply the caption: "Ricardo."

"It is he," exclaimed my friend.

"Who?" I asked in excitement.

Examining the photograph, I saw a tall man, clean-shaven, wearing a sombrero. In his hand was a coiled lasso, and on his feet were highly ornamented spurs. There were several other poses of this man, two of them in company with Miss Sigurda. One of these showed him in profile, sitting opposite Miss Sigurda on the veranda of the ranch house. Under it was a quotation from Cervantes to the effect that love was the first child of happiness.

"We shall put this in a safe place," declared Stoke.

"Then you don't consider the case closed as yet?" I asked.

"Not quite yet," replied Stoke.

We returned to the apartment, picking up a late evening paper on the way. The coast was clear. Stoke locked the album in a cabinet.

"Let's turn in early," he suggested, as he glanced idly over the paper. Then he sat up suddenly.

"Here's an interesting item," he remarked quietly, and handed the newspaper to me.

In a corner of the second page I read the small headline:

"Sea-captain Drowned in Port."

The story went on to say that Captain Marvin W. Tracy of the steam trawler *Beatrice* had been drowned at Norfolk late that afternoon. He had apparently accidentally fallen from his ship, but there were no witnesses to the calamity. His body was found floating in the river.

That was all.

"It's lucky we saw him when we did," I remarked.

"Lucky?" said Stoke. "Not for him."

CHAPTER XX
SWAN SONG OF THE NIGHTINGALE

The next morning the newspapers all blossomed forth with a lurid story of the capture (*sic*) and arrest of young Dr. Rollin. The accounts were rife with references to the able work of Detective Stephen Yates, premier investigator of the metropolitan police force. Mr. Selden's capable part also came in for copious mention. There were even editorials commending the efficiency of the local police department.

Stoke threw down the paper with a gesture of disgust.

"What rot all this is!" he exclaimed. "Anything satisfies the deluded Fourth Estate. All that any newspaper wants is a sensation. Truth is secondary. 'Garble all the news that's fit, or unfit, to print,' seems to be the customary slogan."

"Then you definitely doubt that Dr. Rollin did what he said?"

"No, he told the truth," was the reply.

"Well, then," I countered, "that settles it."

"He told the truth," repeated Stoke patiently, "but mis-interpreted the meaning and effect of his actions."

I took up the newspaper. It was decorated with pictures, somewhat blurred, of the house and street, of Beatrice Sigurda, and even one of Miguel San Remo. Another paper, a tabloid, had a photograph of a shrouded figure on a stretcher, labeled: "Second Victim of Doctor. The Body of San Remo Borne to Morgue." The picture might have been—probably was—faked.

"See if there is anything more about the drowning of the sea-captain," suggested Stoke. "That is really important news. It probably is not even mentioned."

I looked for the item in vain.

Stoke swept the newspaper to the floor with a contemptuous movement and went to his desk, where he began to study his notes. He had reduced his scribblings to an ordered outline. As he was perusing them, the telephone rang. I hastened to answer it. On the other end was the still jocund voice of Runy O'Mara.

"Is Mr. Max Carridos, the celebrated detective, there?" he inquired flippantly. "Tell him Philo Vance would feign converse with him. And tell him quick, Jim, old dear."

I summoned Stoke, whose scowl evaporated as he listened to the excited tones of his friend.

"We will be right over," he said, as he hung up the receiver.

"Where?" I demanded.

"That Runy man really missed his calling," he told me. "About all he did when we were at Tech together was study like a grind and play chess for recreation. He even commuted to Natick, or some such outlandish place, and never played poker once on the way. And now look at him: not only a brilliant inventor of aeronautical devices, but a social light of parts, and a better detective than the impulsive Yates."

"What has he accomplished this time?" I asked as we prepared to depart.

"With rare intelligence, he went to Rollin's office, waited for the office secretary, and attempted to get her reaction to the arrest of her employer."

"Did he get it?"

"He did," was the reply. "Let's go."

On the street the newsboys were yelling in raucous tones that the slayer was caught. Probably similar cries about the capital murder case were being shouted in many cities.

"What a shock it would be to Selden and Yates," I suggested, "if they turned out to be mistaken!"

"You can't shock a policeman," commented Stoke. "Nor his boss," he added.

In a few moments we had arrived at the physicians' building on Vermont Avenue. Inside we proceeded at once to the office of Dr. Rollin and knocked on the door marked "Private." Runy appeared at once and invited us in.

His blonde friend was sitting at the doctor's desk nervously smoking a cigarette, an action not so profusely indulged in by women at that time as has since become the custom. She had a pout on her rather handsome face, but her eyes were red as if she had been crying. I suspected that Runy might have been sympathizing with her, as his uniform, in the neighborhood of the upper chest, had powder marks upon it, and also one or two stains which may have been tear-drops.

The girl looked at us without interest as Stoke and I took chairs by the desk. Runy sat upon it, idly dangling one leg.

"Miss Mannheim has some matters of importance to communicate," said Runy.

"Ought we to have Yates here?" asked Stoke. "I don't like to go into important matters without him."

"I phoned him, but he can't come over right away," was the reply, "and he said to go ahead with the investigation. He did not seem greatly impressed with its significance."

"These police are damn fools," exclaimed the girl bitterly.

"Maybe so, maybe so," Runy soothed her. "Anyway, tell it all to your friend Mr. Stoke. Begin at the beginning, Peggy. It's great stuff, and he wants to hear it all."

"Why should he bring this other person with him?" she demanded, waving her cigarette toward me.

"That, oh, that's no person," replied Runy, with more than a trace of pleasantry. "Don't mind him, he's the official stenographer and assistant. He never bites and is well-behaved."

"If you're going to be fresh, I won't say a word to anyone," said Miss Mannheim petulantly.

Runy thereupon brought into play those wiles and blandishments which had made him the favorite of Capital society. The lady yielded, as do all ladies when Runy entreats, begs, pleads, asks, requests. She lit another cigarette first.

"Dr. Rollin didn't do it," she began, "I did it."

Miss Mannheim paused to note the effect. Stoke rose to the occasion.

"This is most serious news," he said, "serious for you. Lucky for the doctor."

"The fool police have no right to hold him," continued Miss Mannheim. "I alone am to blame. That Sigurda slut got what she deserved, and I am glad she did, glad that I had a hand in it."

"Begin at the beginning," Runy urged her once more.

"All right," she said, "I will. My father and Beatrice's mother were cousins. They both went to the Argentine from Germany many years ago. They were both poor. My family stayed poor—had nothing—but Cousin Luisa made a fortunate marriage with Don José Sigurda. He wasn't so much himself, but the family amounted to something and knew the right people. My mother had to work, as a servant, and she married a poor good-for-nothing peon. Yes, that is what my father was, a peon. What do I care?"

She jabbed the cigarette butt on the glass top of the desk defiantly.

"My father drove a truck," said Runy. "He did it so well that the people later sent him to the Massachusetts legislature. Go on, it doesn't matter what our fathers were."

"Yes, it does," replied Miss Mannheim, with increasing bitterness, "because when I was a young girl, I wasn't good enough to associate with my cousin Beatrice. Finally my father had the decency to die. Mother became housekeeper in one of the best families, supervised lots of other servants, sent me to school, and planned to marry me off to a head butler or something like that. Then Beatrice went and eloped with this Derqui. He was a hard-living rascal, handsome and very rich, but a real Don Juan with the women. He took her out to his ranch at Cavorita. They did let me go out there once, probably to lord it over the poor relation. I wasn't so gawky, either, and the foreman made love to me. I didn't mind that, because he was a regular guy, but when Don Derqui tried it, I slapped his nasty face and went home. Yes, I made a scene and told Beatrice what I thought of her husband."

"Who was this foreman?" asked Stoke.

"An Americano named Ricardo," answered Miss Mercedes Mannheim, with a strange fire in her eyes.

"I shall want you to identify a picture of him later," said Stoke.

"If it is him, I'll recognize it, all right," she replied with a sigh, and a disregard for rhetoric.

"Never mind him," interrupted Runy, with apparent jealousy, "proceed with the story."

Before she continued, Miss Mannheim patted Runy's hand reassuringly.

"Not long after that I had a chance to go to America as companion to a rich woman. I had studied English, and grabbed the opportunity, although the old woman was a shrew. I never went back. After a couple of years in New York, I came to Washington, where I had various jobs. Finally I got this place with Dr. Rollin."

"How did you happen upon it?" asked Stoke.

"To tell you the truth," she replied, "Beatrice got it for me. I heard from Mother after I came here that Derqui had died and that Beatrice was traveling all over Europe, while I, of the same flesh and blood, slaved in an office here. How I hated that girl!"

She paused, a venomous light in her eyes. I gathered that she could be an ardent hater, as most Latins can.

"Finally she came here. Several months after, I went to see her. I had made up my mind to ignore her presence, but curiosity drove me to go. I wanted to see what she was like since I had seen her last in the Argentine. She was the same haughty creature, cold and highbrow. She insulted me by offering me a position as her personal maid. I almost took it, thinking I might spy on her and find some opportunity to do her harm."

"Why didn't you take the position?" asked Stoke.

"I was afraid," was the answer.

"Afraid?" asked Stoke.

"Yes, afraid that I would kill her in cold blood if I had to be in her presence every day. So I refused and went back to work in the store. Then I found out that she was interested in a young doctor who had become her physician. I went to her, was sweet, got into her good graces, explained that I was dissatisfied with my work, asked her to help me to get something else. She spoke to Dr. Rollin about me and had me over to her house on Q Street one night when he was there. I did not like him at first, but when he said he wanted a secretary in the new office which Beatrice was helping set up, I took the position."

"Why did you do that?" prompted Stoke.

"Because," she blazed, "I wanted to get her man away from her. I wanted revenge. I was circumspect with the doctor at first, but we became more and more friendly. In spite of all I did, however, and I went a long way with him," she declared brazenly, "he would not give up Beatrice for me. I could have torn her eyes out. I lay awake nights planning ways to lure him from her. I told him gossip about her, but he laughed it off. When I saw that my methods were unsuccessful, I wanted to kill my cousin. I would have done so with pleasure if the chance had arisen."

"And it never did?" asked Stoke.

"Not for a long time. Finally an opportunity came. Beatrice called up one night about a week ago. Said she was nervous and wanted Roger to treat her. The doctor was not in when she called, but I assured her I would give him the message. When he came in, I did so. He asked me to put some morphia in his bag. That was my chance."

She was speaking now with a quiet virulence. What a magnificent blonde tigress that woman was! Runy was watching her with undisguised admiration.

"I saw my chance and I took it. While he was telephoning, I busied myself with the medicine vials. I filled them partly with morphia and partly with hyoscine."

"Hyoscine!" exclaimed Stoke.

"Yes, the deadly poison, hyoscine," was the ready reply. "I hoped he would inject it and kill her. I even suggested that he give her a heavy dose of the stuff. I watched him go with eagerness and I gloated after he went. My chance had come."

She clenched her hands, then reached suddenly for another cigarette.

"What time was this?" asked Stoke.

"Rollin left the office about six or a little after," she answered. "I went to dinner and returned to the office. Rollin came in about ten, seemed surprised to see me, but sat down and told me he had given Beatrice the hypodermic. I was delighted. Revenge at last! Rollin had to go out to Georgetown. He telephoned to his friend Dr. Ragland and went."

"Then what did you do?" asked Stoke.

"At first I was going to go home and gloat some more. On an impulse I decided to visit the house on Q Street and see what condition that woman was in. I put on one of the doctor's old caps and one of his dark coats and went directly to the house. In order not to be seen, I sneaked up the alley and went in through the garden."

"Was the door unlocked?"

"No, but I took one of Rollin's pass-keys. He had a way of getting in through the alley."

"She must have been the figure Kent saw entering the garden that night," exclaimed Runy excitedly.

"You forget," Stoke reminded him, "that Kent described the visitor as a tall man. Miss Mannheim is gracefully petite. By no stretch of the imagination would anyone class her as even moderately tall. Did you see anyone else during your visit?"

"Not a soul," was the answer. "I got into the garden all right, but, to tell the truth, my courage failed right there, and I turned round and made my escape. I didn't dare to face what was upstairs. I went home then."

"You didn't come to the Serpentine Club, did you?"

"No."

"Not to the office?"

"No. Home. The next day when Rollin came in, he was all flustered. He thought the hypodermic he had given to Beatrice had killed her. It had, but he thought it was only morphine. I knew different. I rather made life miserable for him. He raised my salary to keep me quiet about it. He was so afraid his patients would find out and he would lose all the practice he was beginning to build up."

"What did he do about it, besides commiserate himself?" asked Runy.

"Several days later he said he couldn't stand it any longer. He declared he would go and make a clean breast of the whole thing to the only medical man who had ever befriended him. Most of them tried to injure him every way they could. Doctors are like that," she declared savagely. "I tried to get him not to do it," she continued, "but he went and told this other man all about it."

"Who was the other physician?" asked Stoke.

"Dr. Ragland," was the reply.

"That probably accounts for his peculiar actions the night we talked to him," I put in.

"Possibly," replied Stoke enigmatically. "What next?"

"That is all. That is enough, isn't it?" she demanded. "Now Rollin has got so scared he has gone and confessed to something he didn't do, and these idiots of police have put him in jail."

"Did you write the note I found on my door one night?" inquired Stoke.

"Yes, I did," she admitted. "There was no sense to it, but I thought I might scare you off the case with a warning."

"It would take more than that to scare me off," said Stoke kindly; "but look at this picture." He took a photograph from his pocket. "Who is it?"

"Why, that is Ricardo, the foreman at Beatrice's ranch," she said as she identified the picture.

"One more question, and only one," continued Stoke pleasantly. "Why do you now reveal your complicity, if it is that, in this unfortunate crime?"

"Because," she said simply, with tears in her eyes, "because I love him."

"What?" demanded Runy.

"Yes, I love him," she declared defiantly. "At first I only tried to get him away from Beatrice, but finally I found that I had another motive. I was jealous, but not so much of her as of him. I hated her, but in hating that loathsome woman I came to love Roger Rollin. And I knew he wanted her and not me, although I gave myself to him."

She covered her face with her hands and cried without shame. Stoke sat gazing at her, as Runy tried to comfort the distraught girl. The scene was interrupted by a knock on the door. It was Yates.

Stoke took the detective into the ante-room, where he explained matters. When they returned, Yates seemed decided about something, but Stoke acted as if he disagreed with it. He was, in fact, expostulating, but subsided as they entered.

"I'm sorry, young woman," said Yates officiously, "but I've got to take you along as a material witness."

Miss Mannheim clapped her hand to her mouth with a gesture of despair and held it there for several moments as if in a daze. With an effort, she removed her hand and sat up. She was smiling.

"Too late, Mr. Detective," she said, "all the while I have been talking, I have had a cyanide capsule in my hand. I have just swallowed it. You may take me to the police station if you want to, but not alive. Nothing else matters, anyway. O Roger, Roger, why couldn't you really love me?"

Her body fell across the desk. Runy rushed excitedly about looking for some object with which to administer first aid.

"I am afraid nothing can be done," said Stoke quietly. "Cyanide acts too fast. She is past human aid now, poor girl."

"Don't that beat hell?" commented Yates.

"What a brave girl!" murmured Runy.

"Bad as this is," said Yates, "it seems to clear up the case completely."

"My dear man," asserted Stoke with some asperity, "this unfortunate death is one more crime to be attributed to the real murderer of Beatrice Sigurda."

"The real murderer?" repeated the detective.

"Yes, the real murderer," said Stoke.

CHAPTER XXI
THE FAVORITE OF CAVORITA

"Cavorita," Stoke was saying, "is a small town in the Argentine, about a hundred and fifty miles west of Buenos Aires. It stands on a broad pampa and is the center of a thriving cattle industry. The town has long been the feudal domain of the Derquis, a family prominent in the history of the nation."

"I am convinced that you are better as a geographer than a detective, Mr. Stoke," amiably remarked Commissioner Selden, in whose office we were sitting as we munched sandwiches and drank chocolate malted milk.

Stoke had spent part of the morning with Runy, poring over the album and reading cablegrams received from Buenos Aires. Runy had been having an expensive cable correspondence with the naval attaché there, who was a close personal friend, being the brother of one of the leading contenders for the attractive, if somewhat fickle, lieutenant's heart. With this material, supplemented by the album, by the files of numerous Buenos Aires and other Argentine newspapers which Runy had consulted at the Congressional Library, and by various other sources, Stoke and Runy had laboriously reconstructed the past life of Beatrice Sigurda.

At noon he had insisted upon reporting the facts to Commissioner Selden, and that official, who was less busy than usual and feeling quite complacent, had invited us to a buffet lunch in his office. There we found Detective Yates. In response to Stoke's inquiry, he announced that Dr. Rollin had spent the night in the District jail and that he did not yet know of the tragedy in his office.

"You'll have doc convicted and hanged before you get the real facts," Runy informed him.

Yates grunted, but refused to commit himself. Mr. Selden was more outspoken.

"All this poppycock about that Argentine rattlesnake seems to have gone by the board," he had told us.

"What killed the gardener, then?" demanded Runy.

To this the commissioner was evasive, but he seemed convinced that Miss Sigurda had departed her life as the result of a deliberate overdose of a dangerous drug, administered with malice by Dr. Rollin.

"Let me recount the interesting and suggestive events in the immediate past of this beauty," said Stoke, "and see if that alters your views."

"Go ahead," replied the commissioner pleasantly. "You have a good reputation as an able raconteur, even if none as a sleuth."

What Stoke told him indeed proved revelatory.

"About the time our Civil War was beginning," Stoke continued, "a Derqui became president of the Argentine, but he resigned soon after and migrated to Montevideo. Caspar Derqui, who figures in my story, was a collateral descendant, whose family remained in the Argentine, but left Buenos Aires for political reasons and took up life on the pampas. For years the family were caudillos, or chiefs, in the vicinity of Cavorita. They became immensely wealthy and maintained a huge ranch house, to which many gauchos were attached.

"Young Caspar Derqui was a typical country magnate. He journeyed to Buenos Aires frequently and on one of his trips met a most attractive girl, blonde, unlike most of his beautiful countrywomen. She was Beatrice Sigurda, daughter of a prominent Argentinian citizen who had married a German immigrant of good family but no fortune. Señor Sigurda was able to introduce his daughter into society, but his own lack of resources prevented much of a splurge on behalf of his only child.

"Señorita Sigurda was literally swept off her feet by the dashing, dark-eyed caballero. He danced the tango with her, strummed a guitar to her in a moonlit garden, and otherwise displayed amorous intentions."

Stoke's discourse was interrupted by a deep sigh from Runy. With a smile the narrator went on.

"Chaperoned by a somewhat comatose aunt, Beatrice visited Don Derqui at his plantation at Cavorita. There the two pledged their troth under the stars of the Southern Cross. The consent of Don Pedro Sigurda was necessary and Derqui told his loved one that he would come to seek it.

"He came one night after she had returned home, but instead of going to her father, he climbed the balcony and summoned her to him. Together they rode off in the moonlight, sought out a convenient priest, and were married. At first Don Pedro was furious, but the fact that Derqui was a very rich man may have assuaged his anger. At any rate, he forgave his impetuous daughter and his fiery son-in-law."

"This is all interesting," commented Mr. Selden, "but it seems a bit extraneous."

"Don't stop him," begged Runy, "this part is really inspiring."

"The newly married pair took up residence on the plantation at Cavorita," Stoke went on. "At first the novel life intrigued Beatrice. She rode over the wide pampas with her husband, watched the hardy gauchos rope their cattle, and lolled listlessly of an evening while Don Caspar played his guitar. For a year or so the life was a happy one.

"The master assigned to his wife a young manservant named Miguel San Remo, a half-breed Indian. He was devoted to her, as were all of the servants and all of the men on the ranch. She was vivacious, she brought new life to the range. In the town some miles from the ranch she was equally popular, for her rare blond beauty excited all the men, even if it aroused jealousies among the women. Beatrice Sigurda reigned as the favorite of Cavorita.

"On a visit to a neighboring ranch one day she caught sight of a tall man whose complexion was fair like her own. She inquired of her host who was this man who rode so well and seemed so dexterous with the rope. He replied, with a shrug, that it was only Ricardo, the Americana a handsome ne'er-do-well who had drifted to the pampas probably because the States were too hot for him. He was a gambler, a drinker, a nobody here, though some said he came of good family back in Philadelphia.

"This Ricardo was a dare-devil. On one of the numerous occasions when the Derquis were visiting the plantation where he was employed, having come at the urging of Señorita Beatrice, he had killed a fer-de-lance as it was about to attack Don Caspar.

"For this service Caspar bought the man from his neighbor, acting on a suggestion of his wife's, and installed him on his own ranchero. Henceforth the visits to the neighbor became few. Soon Ricardo made himself so useful that he was promoted to be overseer of the plantation. There was some grumbling among the gauchos that a gringo should be put over them, but one or two of the most raucous complainers disappeared and soon the situation was accepted. Ricardo ruled. He liked power and he used it, despotically perhaps, but Don Caspar saw the revenues come in regularly and cared little for details of administration.

"Señorita Sigurda had been accustomed to accompany her husband on his occasional trips to Buenos Aires. She was city-bred and often longed for the glamours of the urban drawing-room in place of the comparative loneliness of the pampas. Although she was surrounded by every luxury at the ranch, the life had sometimes palled upon her."

"Until Ricardo came," blurted the irrepressible Runy.

"Until Ricardo came," assented Stoke. "Then, strangely enough, Buenos Aires possessed no magnetism for her. On one pretext or another she excused herself from joining her husband on these excursions. She seemed strangely contented with the pampas."

"Was her regard for her environment strictly Platonic?" chuckled Mr. Selden, now much interested in the narrative.

"Probably not," murmured Runy.

Yates merely looked puzzled, and a little bored.

"Our researches have not revealed that point at this stage of the proceedings, but later on their relations were unquestionably not," resumed Stoke. "During the course of almost another year the interest of the dashing blonde became greater and greater in the masterful Ricardo.

"On one of her husband's absences the overseer came to her, as was his wont. This time he told her a fact which he had just discovered. The boy San Remo was the son of her husband by a native Indian woman. It seems there were other children in the vicinity whose paternity could be traced to a similar source. Beatrice had had no offspring.

"From this time there was an even greater change in her attitude toward her husband—a change accentuated by an experience report-ed by her cousin Mercedes, who asserted that Derqui made energetic love to her during a visit. Finally she succumbed completely to the wiles of Ricardo, gave herself to him. The two of them discussed ways and means of getting rid of Don Caspar. Ricardo recalled the time he had saved his employer from death by the fer-de-lance.

"They laid their plans carefully. Ricardo rode the pampas and practiced snake-catching. He risked his own life, yes, but he became proficient with the forked stick and in the capture of deadly reptiles. He even shipped one or two to Señor Cortez, the animal-dealer in Buenos Aires, who sold them to zoos in various parts of the world.

"Then one day in September, when it is spring in the Argentine, he rode out with the master to inspect a distant part of the ranch. Señorita Beatrice and San Remo accompanied them. They rode most of the morning, for they were as much at home in the saddle as on the porch of the hacienda.

"About noon they came to a rocky plateau whither Ricardo had led them. They dismounted and San Remo set about preparing lunch. Ricardo suggested that he and Don Caspar stroll toward a promonto-ry. To reach it they had to pass through a hollow place between two rocks. The ground was covered with leaves and brush. Ricardo drew back deferentially to let Don Caspar precede him. The Señor strode ahead. Nothing happened. Ricardo followed, very, very warily. Lucki-ly for him, nothing happened. The plan had failed, so far.

"After their inspection, during which Ricardo pointed out the pos-sibilities of a range at this point, they returned the same way. Beatrice was waiting just beyond the slight declivity, rather impatiently.

"Once again Ricardo drew back. Don Caspar plunged into the hol-low. There was a sudden hiss, the whir of a darting body, and a fer-de-lance had sunk its deadly fangs into the side of the señor's leg, just above the leather puttees. The plan had worked.

"It was all over in half an hour. Don Caspar died in his wife's arms, with his friend—his false friend—and his bastard son doing all they could for him. Before they departed for home with the body, Ricardo slipped into the hollow and killed the snake. Then he cut the thong that bound the viper to a convenient bough. He probably used a certain knife which I now possess. San Remo saw this action. He told me so.

"A physician was called, and certified that death was caused by the accidental bite of a poisonous snake. There was no doubt as to the cause, and only San Remo doubted the accident. Beatrice Sigurda had no doubts. San Remo was intelligent and he knew enough to keep his mouth shut. He feared Ricardo as much as he worshipped his mistress.

"They gave Don Caspar a splendid funeral in the cathedral in Cavorita. A bishop came out from Buenos Aires and officiated. Beatrice inherited most of the estate, although several collateral heirs got some. She was rich, she had a lover, but she was troubled.

"Another year on the plantation was enough. With the spirit which characterized her, she suddenly left Ricardo there and went to her father in Buenos Aires, who was slowly dying of cancer. Within two or three months he had expired. Ricardo came to her, but she was undergoing a revulsion of feeling. After a scene he went back, and she sailed for Paris. Another two years were spent in Europe.

"In the meantime the ranch was mismanaged. Ricardo seemed to lack his former fervor. Finally he, too, left suddenly after a slight fracas with the neighbor, his former employer, who was found with a knife sticking between his ribs. It was never definitely proved who killed him.

"Ricardo went back to the United States. His movements for the next year and a half are not wholly clear, but eventually he came to Washington and set up in the profession he had followed before he migrated to the Argentine, by way of the West Indies. This man's past life would make an interesting story, I am sure, but I haven't been able to trace it yet."

"Where is this Ricardo now?" asked Mr. Selden.

"Let me tell it logically," said Stoke. "Señora Derqui finally wearied of Europe and came to America, accompanied by the faithful San Remo. Eventually she drifted to Washington. Her income was curtailed, but she still had enough to live on comfortably. She rented a house on Q Street and set up her establishment there. Soon she was as much a favorite in the society of the capital as she had been in Cavorita or Buenos Aires or Paris. Such beauty is rare. Runy will testify that it is appreciated."

"I will," said Runy.

"Imagine the surprise of Miss Sigurda, who had resumed her maiden name, when one day at a social function she met a tall, distinguished man. His appearance was different, and his name was changed, but she immediately recognized Ricardo.

"The meeting was a shock to her, for she thought she had left this part of her life safely behind her. Ricardo came next day to her house. He demanded money, as his resources, embezzled from her own estate, were nearly at an end and the profession at which he worked brought him but little revenue. She gave him what she could.

"For the next year he bled her of her slender resources. They resumed their former relations, at his insistence, although against her will. Her health suffered. She consulted a young physician, who was sympathetic as well as therapeutic. They fell in love, but she dared not inform him of her liaison with Ricardo."

"Who in the devil is this Ricardo?" demanded Mr. Selden.

"Yes, who is he?" echoed Yates.

"Wait," said Stoke. "Finally she came almost to the end of her resources. Ricardo could get nothing more from her, as there was nothing more to get. He, too, was tired of the relationship. In her desire to escape from this bondage she threatened him. He determined to get rid of her.

"Now, this Ricardo, whose name was really Richard, was a domineering sort of person. He had a pathological mind, could hate intensely; and his love for the fair Beatrice had long since turned to hate. He decided to avenge himself on her. He determined to bring about her death in the same manner that he and she had plotted the death of her husband. Such a vengeance would be sweet indeed. It was!

"The problem was to get the fer-de-lance, which is indigenous to South America and is never found in this country. He remembered his friend Señor Cortez, in Buenos Aires. He wrote and told him to ship two of these dangerous snakes. Runy's friend in Buenos Aires has interviewed Mr. Cortez and has cabled us a copy of the letter, the original of which he secured. It is now on the way to us.

"The reptiles came on board a tramp steamer, which was ironically named the *Beatrice*, captained by our late florid friend Captain Tracy. Ricardo and San Remo met the boat in Norfolk and returned with one fer-de-lance, the other having escaped during the voyage."

"It probably took a look at the captain and jumped overboard in despair," commented Runy.

Mr. Selden glared at this impertinent interruption.

"With this instrument of death the crime was committed," Stoke continued.

"Well, I'll be damned," ejaculated Yates.

"An interesting tale," commented the commissioner, "but what about Dr. Rollin's confession?"

"Everything that the doctor has said is probably true," said Stoke. "He was an unwitting accomplice. The narcotic which he administered did not kill Miss Sigurda, but it left her in a semi-daze, so that she was an ideal prey for the fer-de-lance. Her body and mind were sufficiently deadened so that she had no opportunity to escape, but she roused up sufficiently to realize the horror of the situation. She uttered one scream and then lapsed into unconsciousness. The snake probably crawled out the open window into the tree and then into the yard. It finally got into the cellar and killed San Remo a day or two later."

"Why should Rollin confess, then?" asked Mr. Selden.

"A delusion, pure and simple," replied Stoke. "Check up with Ragland on this and he will give you the psychiatric explanation. Dr. Rollin believes he was actually the instrument of the crime, although he really did not do it. He looks upon it as an unfortunate but culpable accident. His conscience has worried him and finally drove him to confess."

"Why should Miss Mannheim confess also?" demanded the commissioner.

"Another delusion," answered Stoke. "She only thought she mixed hyoscine with the morphine. It was distilled water in an old hyoscine tube. There was some left and I have had it analyzed."

"Your story rings true, but I certainly want some better evidence before I let Rollin go free," Mr. Selden asserted.

"So do I," agreed Yates. "You can't convict a man on a story."

"Some have been," commented Runy.

"Who is this Ricardo, anyway?" demanded the commissioner. "Is he still in Washington? If so where? Why not arrest him at once?"

Stoke shot a meaning glance at Yates, who I suddenly suspected might be more in Stoke's confidence than I had realized.

"In less than twenty-four hours I will have your man," he said quietly, "and I will have conclusive evidence for you. In the meantime I want to consult with a friend—and rival."

CHAPTER XXII
STARR-SMITH ENTERTAINS

"Take some anti-venin serum along, by all means."

The speaker was Runy. The three of us had dined in Stoke's apartment and now over the coffee and cigars had been recapitulating the tangled skein of events which had culminated in the murder of Beatrice Sigurda.

"Why?" asked Stoke in response to Runy's rather flippant remark.

"For use," returned the lieutenant in a sprightly manner, "in case he makes any venomous remarks. Take a quart of the stuff," he added.

Stoke laughed. We were about to pay our deferred visit to the studio of Starr-Smith, the eminent architect who had been our confidant in the attempt to solve this mystery.

"In these dangerous days of attacks in the streets and alleys, and even in one's own apartment, I am carrying something more offensive than anti-venin," he said, as he filled the magazine of his automatic. "I also have the knife which slit my coat the other night. I want to get Starr-Smith's opinion on it."

It was about eight o'clock when we started out for the studio. We left Runy, who was not invited, poring over his notes on the case, and proceeded through the still sunlit streets to the alley upon which this bizarre workshop was located. It was about half-way between the Serpentine Club and the house on Q Street.

This combination studio and residence had once been a stable and later a tea-room. One side of it abutted on the alley and still had a large black double door on the street level, where the coaches of some departed senator or cabinet officer had formerly passed through. Over this door was a lattice window built in the opening where once the hay and straw had been taken into the upper floor of the old stable. In its tea-room days this had been a favorite spot for the debutantes who took up one passing fad after another.

The entrance to the studio was at the side of the building and was approached through the garden, which was surrounded by the high brick walls which hid most of these back yards. The house to which the stable had once belonged had been joined with another building to form a fashionable restaurant. The lower windows had been bricked up, and the yard next door was utilized for deliveries and other necessary commercial purposes, so that the garden now went with the studio.

Starr-Smith lived here in solitude. He had no housekeeper and took most of his meals out. He used the lower portion of the converted stable as a sitting-room and workshop, occupying the quarters above as a bedroom, where it was rumored he occasionally entertained visitors. In my opinion, no one but an eccentric bewhiskered bohemian would have lived in such a place, although I suppose the privacy of it had some advantages for a professional man.

The heavy door leading from the alley into the garden was ajar as we approached, no untoward incidents having occurred on the way. As we entered, Stoke fumbled with the lock and then we stepped along a rather crooked flagstone walk bordered by flower-beds to the plain doorway in the farther end of the brick building. It had all of the unprepossessing appearance of a side door to a stable. It was flanked by open windows adorned with somewhat garish draperies.

Starr-Smith greeted us on the threshold. He wore a white sport-shirt, open at the neck, covered by a dilapidated smoking-jacket, but he had on riding-breeches and boots as if he had just returned from a canter in Potomac Park. His costume went with his stable. He shook hands with us cordially and conducted us into his living-room.

The interior of this studio was far more attractive than the exterior. It had a distinct air of comfort and at the same time of efficiency. The room was a large one, covered with handsome rugs. At one end was a drafting-table, with an assortment of T-squares, triangles, rulers, and other paraphernalia such as would be found in an architect's office. Opposite the table was a massive black walnut desk with a portable typewriter on it.

In the middle of the room was a large fireplace, dark, of course, at this time of the year, and above it was a huge mantel, adorned with vases and various other objects. Above it were the horns of a longhorn steer. The walls were adorned with numerous prints and trophies, and in a cabinet in one corner was a collection of rifles and other firearms. It was the room of a man who had traveled, had hunted, had collected, and was a connoisseur of art. It was, in fact, a very interesting place.

The architect waved me into an easy chair, while Stoke took a seat on a davenport which was placed diagonally near the fireplace. On one end of it was a guitar. As Starr-Smith brought some wine out of a cabinet, Stoke picked up the musical instrument.

"This must have been the diabolical thing you were playing one night as we passed by," he said.

"No doubt," replied Starr-Smith. "I often make the night hideous with its tinkling. Only today one of the neighbors complained because I played the thing night before last after midnight. It's a citternino, which I picked up some years ago in South America."

"I thought it might have come from there," answered Stoke, "because San Remo, the late Miss Sigurda's late gardener, had one quite like it."

"How is progress in the *cause célèbre*, anyway?" inquired Starr-Smith as we sipped the wine, an ambrosial liquid of obvious antiquity.

"You heard Dr. Rollin's confession last night," said Stoke. "That would seem to settle it. At any rate, my work is practically over. Even if it were not, I should have to stop sleuthing, as I received orders today sending me to the Virgin Islands to fight hookworms instead of murderers. I sail within ten days."

"That is unfortunate," commented our host politely, "although perhaps, as you say, the case is closed. Rollin's confession seems like a good way out."

"I understand from Runy that you also contemplate a trip," continued Stoke.

"While you are receiving a warm reception from your virginal hookworms, I hope to be on the way to Alaska," was the reply. "I prefer cool climates to places where they make it hot for a man."

"What do you really think about this so-called confession, though?" asked Stoke.

The architect shrugged his shoulders with a deprecatory gesture.

"As I said, it is a good way out, but," and he paused as he sipped his wine pensively, "if you are willing to accept it as a solution, you are not so clever as I think you are. A cringing bungler like that," and his voice was full of contempt, "lacks the capacity to plan or commit a crime. The death of Miss Sigurda showed real finesse. It was no accident, but a carefully conceived piece of work, perfectly executed."

"Perfectly, did you say?" asked Stoke.

"Perfectly," assented Starr-Smith. "You know as well as I do that whether Rollin gave that girl a dose of narcotic or not, it did not cause her death. Improbable as your dramatic disclosures have been, I agree that death was caused by the jararaca you found."

"The what?" exclaimed Stoke.

"Jararaca is the name given to most of these venomous snakes by the native South Americans," answered the architect.

"There is a snake called the jararaca in the Argentine," replied Stoke, "but this was a fer-de-lance, of the same general family, which is a bad one."

"Even if you do know what caused the death of Beatrice Sigurda," continued Starr-Smith, ignoring the correction, "the man who did it was too clever for you. Do you know how he got the reptile there or anything at all about the actual technique of the crime?"

"I do know that this viper, one of two that the murderer ordered from Señor Cortez in Buenos Aires, arrived about a month before the crime was committed and was delivered to this man in person in Norfolk by the late lamented Captain Tracy of the good, more or less, ship *Beatrice*," replied Stoke.

"You have done pretty well," agreed Starr-Smith, although there was a peculiar inflection to his voice, of envy possibly. "What then?"

"These snakes have to be kept carefully," Stoke went on. "They feed on rats. They also have an affinity for certain native woods, similar to those found on the Argentine pampas. A box or receptacle made of such native wood makes an ideal cage."

"All very interesting," laughed his hearer, "but how do you explain the manner in which the snake reached its prey. Did your friend—I am speaking figuratively of course—train it and send it over to Q Street by itself?"

"Hardly that," replied Stoke with a smile. "On the night of the crime he chilled the fer-de-lance just enough to make it torpid, without doing it harm, put it in a paper bag, such as might be found in any ash-barrel near a store or similar establishment, and took it to Q Street himself."

"And handed it in person to the lady?" exclaimed Starr-Smith. "I am afraid you tax my credence."

"Oh no," replied Stoke; "he entered the Sigurda house from the alley, walked through the arbor, where no one could distinguish him, entered the house, and said: '*Buenos noches*' to San Remo, who recognized him, for, you see, this man had been a regular caller for a year or so."

"Yes? Go on."

"He went up the cellar stairs, bearing his deadly burden, but paused at the door, as Dr. Rollin was just leaving by the front entrance. With the doctor out of the way, he went upstairs and directly to the empty sitting-room, where he placed the bag under a pillow on the divan. Then he went into Miss Sigurda's bedroom. After a few minutes the two were disturbed by a knock on the door. The man returned to the sitting-room, passing through the door between the two rooms just before Miss Sigurda admitted Professor Kent, the deluded lover, from the hall."

"Lover, you say?" commented Starr-Smith. "I wouldn't think that old Mayan could rate so high."

"Then the man departed by the same way he came in and went to his club," Stoke resumed. "Beatrice finally got rid of the professor and went to her sitting-room to read. By this time the morphine Rollin had administered was beginning to work and she sat half-dazed on the divan. By this time, also, the snake was thawed out. It emerged from the paper bag, crawled out from under the pillows, and attacked the horrified woman."

"Horrible!" said the architect.

"All the worse for her when one considers that she had aided in the murder of her own husband by a similar method in the Argentine a few years previously."

With rising sarcasm Starr-Smith said: "Since you are so familiar with the intimate details of this crime—"

"The perfect crime," interrupted Stoke suavely.

"—perhaps you are also aware of the exact time when these episodes happened."

"I am," replied my friend. "It was approximately half past ten when the dangerous visitor paid his call. The death of Miss Sigurda occurred about an hour later."

"No doubt all of this is correct," agreed his listener, "but I would still be so impertinent as to ask what of it?"

"By that time," continued Stoke, "the murderer could easily join some group of persons who would testify in good faith that he was with them at the precise moment when the crime occurred."

"A perfect alibi," murmured the architect.

It was Stoke's turn to be cynical.

"About as perfect as the rest of the arrangements," he said scornfully.

"How would you prove all this in a court of law?" asked Starr-Smith blandly. "It is one thing to have these beautiful theories, which, I grant you, ring true, and possibly are true—"

"You know they are," said Stoke.

"—but evidence is essential to support them."

"The evidence will be forthcoming at the trial," Stoke assured his hearer.

"Apparently I have misjudged your abilities as a detective," remarked Starr-Smith. "Only one further item is needed to convince me, and that is the name and a description of this culprit."

"His name," Stoke replied, "was Richard Smithers."

"Was?" asked the architect in apparent surprise. "Is he dead?"

"In Cavorita he was generally known as Ricardo," continued Stoke, "but when he came to Washington after mismanaging the estate of his mistress—and I use that word in a double sense—he had assumed another name."

The room was getting darker with the coming dusk.

Starr-Smith rose and turned on a floor lamp beside the davenport where Stoke sat. He also put on another light on the desk, so that the room was diffused with the glow of soft light. Instead of sitting down, however, he lit a cigarette and stood leaning idly over the back of the chair in the corner by the cabinet. The light barely reached his tall form, and his face, with its black beard, was almost merged with the gathering darkness.

"This is a most interesting and, I might say, suggestive narrative," he said in his resonant voice. "And what is the name now used by this murderer?"

"Can't you guess?" replied Stoke. "I understand that you once lived in the Argentine."

"That is true," was the answer, "and I once knew a certain Ricardo, too. If it is the same man you have in mind, and I can well visualize that it is, I think it best to warn you that he is a desperate person, a man who permits no one to get the best of him, a man who, having killed once, never hesitates to kill again if necessary."

The words were spoken with a quiet intensity. There was something decidedly ominous about them.

"I realize full well the danger," answered Stoke, "and yet it is the quarry that counts. The risk is worth the opportunity to apprehend him. In fact, the arrest will be made tonight. Whether I survive to go to the Virgin Islands or not, the culprit will be taken."

"Don't be too sure of that," said Starr-Smith quietly. "Enough of this palaver. Put your cards on the table, Stoke. Who do you think is this celebrated Ricardo who murders women with such finesse?"

"Who also, incidentally, murdered Don Caspar Derqui with equal subtlety," said Stoke.

"You are a long time coming to the point," answered the architect sharply. "Name your man!"

Stoke crossed one leg over the other and leaned back comfortably before he replied. Starr-Smith never moved, one hand resting on the back of the chair, the other invisible in the gloom by the cabinet. His eyes gleamed in the reflected glow of the lights.

"The murderer of Beatrice Sigurda," said Stoke quietly, "is now known as Lance Starr-Smith."

For a moment there was complete silence. It was broken only by a low laugh, a sinister laugh, more like a chuckle, but absolutely devoid of merriment. Starr-Smith was showing his teeth.

"So," the word was drawn out, "you think you have solved the perfect crime, do you? You are a smart man, Trevor Stoke, a clever man, but you are also something of a fool. Sit still, damn you."

The architect was standing straight now. In his hand was a steel-blue automatic, a heavy weapon.

"Yes, I killed that blonde slut, Beatrice Sigurda," he almost snarled, "and now I am going to kill you, you and that nincompoop toady of yours."

Ignoring this flattering reference to myself, I looked at Stoke. He sat quietly, a contemptuous look on his face.

"Behind me is a staircase leading to freedom," continued Starr-Smith. "I suppose you have some of those half-witted police posted outside. They will never hear me kill you, as this gun is equipped with a silencer; nor will the clodhoppers get me. So you thought you were a better man than Ricardo, did you? No man has bested him yet, you fool. I missed you once, but not this time."

He raised his arm. As I stood up intending to do something, I am not now sure what, a shot rang out, with what seemed like an echo with it. For a moment everything went confused in my mind

When I came out of my momentary daze, Detective Yates and Runy were standing beside me. I saw nothing of my companion.

"Where's Stoke?" I blurted. "My God, is he shot?"

"No, you idiot," said Runy pleasantly, "he's over looking at the body."

"Body, what body?" I murmured.

"A clean hit," said Stoke, moving the light nearer the chair. Sprawled over it was the form of Lance Starr-Smith. He was dead. On the floor beside him was that ugly revolver.

Yates pushed his hat back on his head, using the barrel of the gun he still held in his hand. Runy had put his weapon back in his pocket.

"Guess we both fired at once," said the detective. "Wonder who hit him?"

"There are two holes in his carcass," Stoke told him, "one through the chest, the other through the head. I congratulate you both on your marksmanship. You also had the pleasure of saving my life."

"An honor, I am sure," said Runy, more debonair than ever. "What an egotistical, insulting, supercilious, insolent, blatant specimen he was! And to think how neatly he took me in early in the game! I reported every detail to him. Anyway, I avenged the roping incident in your apartment."

"Sure, he's all you said he is," assented Yates. "The big boob thought us officers is half-witted, huh?"

"Not to mention my lack of intellectual powers and Jim's even less favorable attributes," remarked Stoke.

"I'll call the coroner," announced Yates.

"Well, gentlemen," said Stoke, "the Capital murder case is over. Let's go home."

As we went out, past the bluecoat at the door, I looked back for one fleeting glance at the room which had so nearly been the sepulcher of Stoke and me. Yates, hat tilted back, cigar in mouth, was telephoning, one leg thrown nonchalantly over a chair.

Across that other chair was that limp figure. It was crumpled, and yet—on the face there was still a faintly sardonic smile. Ricardo was beaten by a better man, but he died as he would have wished.

CHAPTER XXIII
THE METHODS OF TREVOR STOKE

"Let me be the first to congratulate you," said Commissioner Selden impressively and rather effusively. "I was convinced from the beginning that you were on the right track."

"Thank you," replied Stoke, as Runy and I exchanged significant glances, remembering what the commissioner had so conveniently forgotten, his lack of faith in our friend's methods, which he had expressed only a few days previously.

The five of us were dining once again in the garden of the Serpentine Club. Three days had elapsed since our harrowing experience in Starr-Smith's studio, and this time Mr. Selden was our host. In addition to Stoke, Runy, Dr. Ragland, and me, Detective Yates was also with us, which was certainly where he belonged. The story of the crime had finally departed from the front pages of the daily press, though it still got an inch or two on the inside pages of the newspapers.

"I am sorry you are sailing so soon for the Virgin Islands," continued the commissioner, "because you missed your calling. You can have Yates's job any time you want," he went on with a wink.

"Sure," put in Runy, "give Stoke's job to Yates. That would be a fair exchange. The chief knows all about germs now. He could disinfect a place by shooting them right off the wall. What ho, Yates, old boy?"

"That's right, admiral," grinned Yates, who was thoroughly enjoying banter which would have jarred his professional dignity ten days before.

"Well, anyway," blurted Runy, "I certainly am grateful to you for getting that last traffic charge dismissed."

"Shh!" warned Yates in alarm, but Selden ignored the remark. Even a sedate commissioner can be tactful among friends.

"Do you remember," said Dr. Ragland, "how we sat in this same garden on the night of the murder and discussed crime with the murderer, whom none of us suspected?"

"He was a cool specimen," commented Runy.

"But an arrogant one," remarked Stoke. "You will also recall that after Mr. Selden had reported the crime to us, Richard Smithers, alias Ricardo, alias Lance Starr-Smith, deliberately called our attention to the fact that all of us, including himself, had been sitting here in the garden at the time the crime was committed, or apparently committed. Thus he produced an alibi, an excellent one, which ought to have kept suspicion from himself."

"When did you begin to suspect him?" asked Dr. Ragland.

"That is difficult to say," replied Stoke. "After analyzing the crime, it was evident that it had been performed by someone with a superior, if unbalanced, intellect. Further analysis pointed to an individual with a mind that was not only superior, but inflicted with a superiority complex. Early in the game I found myself saying that a man such as Starr-Smith was the type who could plan and execute a crime like this. And yet I had no grounds for suspicion, nor did I actually suspect him for a long time, although eventually I did."

"He certainly suspected you, all right," said Runy. "He showed it first by taking a pot-shot at you in the Sigurda garden that night you and Jim were prowling about."

"Yes, he must have followed us from his studio that night," assented Stoke, "watched us enter the garden, then sneaked into the adjoining backyard and waited for an opportunity to shoot. As I look back on it, I admire his suavity the next day when we discussed the event with him."

"The trouble was," went on Runy, "that he was always discussing the lurid details with some one of us. What a fool I was to reveal everything to him as we went along! Why, he began the very night of the crime itself when he joined Mr. Selden and me in a ride out to Cleveland Park in the commissioner's car and got me to walk back afterwards."

"Walking back yourself must have been a new experience for you," commented Dr. Ragland archly.

"I trust you do not insinuate that I ever caused anyone else to walk back from an auto ride," protested Runy, "but, be that as it may, this bewhiskered slayer pumped me every chance he got. He also managed to insinuate himself into every one of our important conferences."

"Do you remember," said Mr. Selden, who seemed in a reminiscent mood, "how, at our council of war here, he made some remark about Dr. Rollin's trying to throw suspicion on another? Why, that was just what he was doing all the time. He deliberately set up Rollin as a straw man. Not content with murdering this poor girl, whom he had ruined, he threw suspicion on an innocent man, probably taking pride in making him suffer."

"That is explainable by his mental make-up," interposed Dr. Ragland. "He was an intense egotist, the type of person who wants to dominate and who partially expresses his desires in the commission of a crime. He looked upon that episode as an exciting game with the police, an encounter in which he would unquestionably be the winner."

"It was this over-confidence which eventually ruined him," said Stoke.

"He ran up against a better man," asserted Yates admiringly.

"A combination of men," replied Stoke with modesty. "If you look back upon our first session in this very garden, you will recall that Starr-Smith himself pointed out how deluded each of us was to think that his own system was the only efficacious method for solving a crime. He was quite correct, since in the solution of this one it was necessary to apply the deft analytical science of Runy, the engineer; the keen insight into morbid personalities of Dr. Ragland, the psychiatrist; the practical experience of Mr. Yates, the well-trained detective; the official support of Mr. Selden; and the correlative influence and mosaic-building proclivities of Jim and myself. It was all of these together that brought about the solution of the Sigurda mystery."

"What were the various parts of this very gratifying mosaic of yours?" asked Selden.

"The circumstances were confusing at first," replied Stoke. "Suspicion actually pointed toward Dr. Rollin, and then veered somewhat in the direction of Professor Kent. In Rollin's case, it was much too obvious to be compelling. Neither Rollin nor Kent possessed the kind of behavioristic personality for this crime and I had discarded both of them early in the proceedings. Frankly, I suspected Rollin's office secretary more than anyone else, as soon as it seemed evident that she had put the warning note on my door."

"As it turned out," interrupted Ragland, "she would have been entirely capable of committing the crime, and, in fact, she did attempt to murder her cousin."

"When did you get a clue as to the instrument of the crime?" catechized Mr. Selden.

"Snake bite was one of the first possibilities that occurred to me as soon as I had seen those punctures on the neck of Miss Sigurda. The similar death of San Remo strengthened the suspicion, which was further accentuated by the peculiar death of the rat in the Sigurda garden. Autopsy revealed symptoms of poisoning by a reptilian source. I read up on ophiology, the science of reptiles, and then Jim and I went on a hunt for that dangerous game. Fortunately, we were successful, as I got my quarry, the fer-de-lance. Did it ever occur to you that Richard Smithers may have had some unconscious impulse to assume the pseudonym 'Lance'?"

"A throw-back to a dramatic experience earlier in his career," exclaimed Dr. Ragland. "It was an atavistic impulse."

"On the night that Yates and I staged the rather theatrical scene in the Sigurda house, I definitely suspected Lance Starr-Smith, but it was a suspicion only. It was he I wanted to test, and only incidentally Rollin and Kent. Their actions were what we expected. So were those of Starr-Smith. A man of his caliber, if he had done the crime, would behave exactly as he did. He was outwardly unaffected, except that he showed his scorn a little too boldly. If he had been a really consummate artist, he would have pretended, in a mild way, to admire the finesse of the test. Instead, he was patently contemptuous. That attitude strengthened my suspicion."

"Probably another complicating factor was my own agitation when we discussed this test," remarked Dr. Ragland. "I will explain the reason for it. You see, Rollin had recently come to me and made a clean breast of his part, or supposed part, in the affair. Now, it happens, strangely enough, that I have always liked the boy, despite the defects of character he displays. I did not believe that he was the real agent of the crime, but I was not sure, and I was much disturbed. The mistake I made was in not telling you the whole story."

"That is quite explicable under the circumstances," Stoke went on. "The next mistake that Starr-Smith made was to lie in wait in my apartment. Here again his supercilious nature got the best of him. He probably figured that he would have no difficulty in ripping me to pieces. Instead he failed and left me several excellent clues which filled in the mosaic."

"After leaving me on the mosaic tiles of the bathroom floor," sighed Runy.

"The knife and the lariat would both have been excellent pieces of evidence," continued Stoke. "That knife, decorated with reptilian forms, was a unique psychological clue to the trend of the man's thoughts; but better than that was the fact that in our struggle my hand touched his face. It was a bearded visage. Beards are not especially common these days."

"They are even less so now," interjected Runy.

"That in itself was not positive evidence," said Stoke, "even if Starr-Smith was the possessor of a luxuriant beard. You cannot convict a man on a passing touch in the dark. The sea-captain in Norfolk gave us the next part of the mosaic. His description of the man who accompanied San Remo to the dock to receive the shipment of the fer-de-lance pointed to a man having the physical characteristics of Starr-Smith, although he was more or less disguised at the time."

"Who," I asked, "pushed the captain overboard immediately after our interview, and why?"

"Was it an accomplice of Starr-Smith's?" inquired Mr. Selden.

"This man had no confederates," answered Stoke, "he played a lone game. San Remo could not be classed as an accomplice. Instead he was a dupe, the tool of a superior intellect. If the poor mulatto had not accidentally lost his life, I think it probable that Starr-Smith would have made way with him sooner or later. The half-breed knew too much."

"Was it San Remo," asked Dr. Ragland, "who came to this garden on the night of the murder and disturbed us by knocking on the door with his knife, by shrieking, and then running away?"

"Despite Mr. Selden's rash promise to have the police solve that problem," answered Stoke, "they have never done so. Neither have I. It is my theory, however, that it was San Remo, and that he knew that Starr-Smith was here. He probably realized that his beloved mistress was in serious trouble and came to get Ricardo or Starr-Smith to help him. Perhaps it was a warning or even a report. The knife he left is quite similar to the one Starr-Smith tried to use on me."

"But how explain the untimely death of the handsome and attractive Captain Tracy of the worm-eaten tub *Beatrice?*" asked Runy.

"Yates got the story from the Norfolk police," replied Stoke. "It was revenge for an entirely different matter. A seaman with a grudge took advantage of the opportunity to push him off his own boat."

"I'll bet it was the sleeping beauty we saw in Sweeny's beautiful saloon," suggested Runy.

"That's just who it was," Yates contributed.

"Starr-Smith can be absolved of that one crime, but he was responsible for the three other recent deaths, and God knows how many more in the past," Stoke went on, "although the only direct murder was that of Beatrice Sigurda, his former lover; the deaths of San Remo and Miss Mannheim, who went by her mother's maiden name and not that of her peon father, can be considered as direct results of the first crime."

"Poor Peggy," sighed Runy.

"The finishing touches to the mosaic were furnished by the album produced by Professor Kent," Stoke continued. "The likeness was undeniable, even though the pictures in the album showed a clean-shaven person. The profile was unmistakable, as were also the eyes and brow. Then I was sure of my man."

"Was Yates aware of your suspicions?" demanded Mr. Selden.

"You bet I was, commissioner," explained the detective. "Mr. Stoke didn't keep nothing from me, except," he added cautiously, "the professor's pipe, but that didn't count. It was only an oversight."

"Thanks largely to Runy's labors," said Stoke, "we were able to reconstruct the past history of Miss Sigurda, which I related to you in Mr. Selden's office."

"And how vividly!" commented Runy, having in mind, no doubt, certain of the amorous details.

"That past history revealed much that helps to explain the psychology of the crime," commented Dr. Ragland. "Having already killed Beatrice's husband, Don Derqui, by a plot employing a deadly reptile, what more natural than that Starr-Smith, or Ricardo, should employ the same scheme for his discarded lover, who had known of the subtle method of her husband's demise?"

"Yes, it revealed the motive. All that remained was to gather sufficient evidence to identify Starr-Smith as Ricardo and show his role as the culprit. I must confess," Stoke added, "that I was none too certain when I decided to call on him—"

"To beard him in his den, as it were," murmured Runy.

"—that I had all the evidence needed to convict him. With Jim as witness, I hoped to jar the man into some kind of an incriminating statement."

"You certainly showed real courage," exclaimed Mr. Selden. "You took your life in your hands, all right."

"I had two factors of safety in Runy and Detective Yates," Stoke acknowledged. "They were both invited to the festivities and both came armed. Fortunately, both are marksmen of real ability. Otherwise, I might not be discussing the matter with you now."

"We heard old Bushy confess," exclaimed Runy, "and could have testified to it in any court, except," he added ruefully, "a traffic court."

"You keep out of traffic courts from now on, young man," warned Mr. Selden, though with a twinkle in his eye; "your immunity is over, or practically so."

Behind the commissioner's back Detective Yates gave Runy a broad wink. I surmised that the jaunty lieutenant would have no more difficulties with the police department.

"It has been an exciting game and a worth-while one," said Stoke in conclusion. "You can fight crime as you can fight disease."

"Crime is a disease," murmured Dr. Ragland, "but primarily a mental disorder."

"Crime is really a phase of engineering," said Runy, "but engineering is no crime," he added hastily. "You solve crime by applied science."

"Crime is a civic defect," asserted Mr. Selden. "You can never correct it without the forces of law and order, as exemplified by such splendid men as Detective Yates."

"You sure need some practical experience," assented Yates. "Mr. Stoke was just like one of us."

"All of you are right," I put in, "and Stoke used all of your methods, as well as his own, didn't you, Stoke?"

"Yes," answered Trevor Stoke, "my methods were simply the methods of each of you adapted to the particular circumstances."

"I guess there won't be any more crimes around here for a while," said Mr. Selden complacently.

Hardly had he finished the words when Sam, the colored steward, approached.

"Urgent message for Mr. Selden," he announced.

"What the devil has happened now?" said the commissioner as he hurried out. He was back in a few moments.

"Gentlemen," he declared, "while we have been dining here, discussing the methods of Mr. Stoke, the body of Congressman Bramhurst has been found crammed in a locker of a leading golf club in the District of Columbia. It seems to be murder. You can't go to the Virgin Islands, Stoke, you've got to stay and help us with this case."

Stoke did not go to the Virgin Islands.

AFTERWORD

AFTERWORD
THE COLOR LINE IN *THE CAPITAL MURDER*

Curtis Evans

During the years between the First and Second World Wars, known to fans of classic crime writing as the Golden Age of detective fiction, white reviewers of mysteries appear to have devoted very little thought (in print anyway) to the questions of racial and gender prejudice that so preoccupy cultural commentators today. To be sure, depictions of "sinister Chinamen" were frowned upon by aestheticians of detective fiction like England's Father Ronald Knox, yet this view did not arise from some kindly compunction about avoiding racism in crime writing. Rather, it was due to the fact that such over-the-top characters, with their outlandish white slavery gangs and opium drug dens, were deemed the province of the sort of "cheap shockers" which were produced in great profusion in the 1920s and 1930s, allegedly solely for the consumption of credulous house servants, office clerks and shop girls, by such hugely popular authors as Edgar Wallace and Sax Rohmer. Thus while monstrous "Oriental" criminal masterminds like Sax Rohmer's Dr. Fu Manchu may have been exiled from the pages of true detective fiction by the Thirties, throughout the Golden Age of detective fiction in both the United Kingdom and the United States there still paraded through purportedly higher-browed tales of ratiocination no end of demeaning and disparaging depictions of myriad non-white peoples, be their ancestral origins Asian, African, or Indigenous American. Nor were Jews, Arabs, Irish Catholics, Slavs, or people of southern European origins (Italian, Spanish, Greek) spared from portrayals which ranged from mildly condescending to cruelly caricatured. Such regrettable renderings are found in the works of the period's most renowned writers of detective fiction (Agatha Christie, Dorothy L. Sayers, Mary Roberts Rinehart, Ellery Queen), as well as those which were produced by the vastly larger legion of the forgotten; and they appear in mysteries written by authors of both conservative and liberal persuasions.

To borrow from black American social reformers Frederick Douglass and W. E. B. Du Bois, a kind of color line—an often invisible yet all too palpable divide among races and ethnicities—permeated Anglo-American crime fiction in the two decades that fell between the World Wars. In the United States, where African-Americans accounted for close to 12 million of the country's population of nearly 123 million, black characters were a common enough presence in American mysteries, including tales with both urban and rural southern settings; yet these individuals belonged almost entirely to the menial and petty criminal classes (and even the latter were not bosses but rather henchmen). As Frankie Y. Bailey put it in her pioneering study *Out of the Woodpile: Black Characters in Crime and Detective Fiction* (1991), when explaining the dearth of black detectives in Golden Age crime fiction: "Clearly, in real life, black males who were acceptable to whites did not possess (or at least did not display overtly) such masculine qualities as courage and resourcefulness. Black females who were acceptable to whites were 'mammies,' not adventurous females pursuing careers as journalists, actresses, or nurses." Black characters in Golden Age American detective fiction typically speak in clumsily exaggerated dialect (like cockney characters in British detective fiction) and are surpassingly superstitious and credulous. Ultimately they contribute to the era's mysteries not anything resembling ratiocination but rather local color (no pun intended) and putative comic relief.

Defenders of Golden Age detective fiction argue that all this merely reflects the unfortunate temper of the times. While this assertion is a simplification of a complex issue (some writers from the period are much worse than others) and has been dismissed by detractors of Golden Age detective fiction as nothing more than special pleading by indulgent mystery fans, there is some truth to it. In the modern era publishers reprinting vintage crime fiction have evinced a tendency to scrub from it any vestige of offensive renderings of non-white peoples, yet in their doing so we, the readers, lose a valuable and fascinating—if sometimes rather eye-flinching—record of American and British literary and social history before World War II.

The Washington, D. C. of Dr. James Alner Tobey's *The Capital Murder* (1932) historically has been (and is more so today) a city with a significant concentration of black residents. In 1930, over 132,000 black Americans lived in the District of Columbia, comprising more than a quarter of the population. Although the Washington of this era was dubbed "the Negroes Heaven," during the 1910s and 1920s there were, as was the case throughout the country, considerable stresses and strains in the relations between blacks and whites in the city.

The 1912 election as President of the United States of native Virginian Progressive Democrat Woodrow Wilson, the first Southerner since the Civil War elected to the highest office in the land, saw the implementation of racist policies which negatively impacted the black citizens of the District of Columbia and were never fully withdrawn by successive Republican administrations in the 1920s. The period of Wilson's presidency (1913-1921), explain the authors of *Chocolate City: A History of Race and Democracy in the Nation's Capital* (2017), was a time not only of a promised "New Freedom"—"Wilson's Progressive vision of an ordery society"—but of what outraged black Washingtonians derisively dubbed the "New Slavery"—"the imposition of Jim Crow across the city." Under Wilson, blacks in Federal civil service positions suffered demeaning treatment and even demotions and dismissals. Throughout federal buildings in Washington work spaces, dining areas, locker rooms and toilet facilities were segregated by color and objecting black employees saw their employment imperiled. Emboldened by the imposition of this noxious new racial regimen in the nation's capital, resurgent southern Democrats in Congress, notes *Chocolate City*, "attacked residual integrated customs" in the District of Columbia by "reintroducing bills to segregate streetcars and prohibit interracial marriage in D.C." For his part, Nevada Senator Francis Newlands, a Natchez, Mississippi native and an avowed white supremacist who at the 1912 Democratic national convention had attempted to insert a plank into the platform calling for the repeal of the 15th Amendment (which prohibited states from denying the right to vote to citizens on racial grounds), "proposed sending all black people out of the United States, while the National Democratic Fair Play Association lobbied hard against the appointment of black people to federal positions."

President Wilson defended his administration's Jim Crow policies as actually helping blacks by avoiding what he termed racial "friction." "Segregation is not a humiliation but a benefit, and ought to be so regarded . . . ," he lectured black Americans. Meanwhile, D. W. Griffith's *The Birth of a Nation* (1915), the film version of *The Clansman: A Historical Romance of the Ku Klux Klan* (1905), a novel which glorified white southern resistance to Reconstruction after the Civil War and was written by Wilson's friend and former classmate Thomas Dixon, was given a private White House screening before Wilson, members of his Cabinet and their families, much to the consternation of the recently formed NAACP (National Association for the Advancement of Colored Peoples) and other civil rights organizations.

Protests notwithstanding, *The Birth of a Nation* enjoyed tremendous box office success in 1915. That same year the film helped inspire the reconstitution of the Ku Klux Klan in a ceremony held at Stone Mountain, Georgia. This second Klan quickly grew into a powerful political organization, with branches ("klaverns") in states all over the country, all of them dedicated to limiting the influence in the U.S. of racial, ethnic, and religious minorities. Both in 1925 and 1926 more than 30,000 Klan members converged on Washington, D. C. to demonstrate the power of the group by parading in full regalia down Pennsylvania Avenue.

Although the D.C. branch of the Klan remained largely inactive, Washington was shaken, like other American cities that year, by racial rioting that erupted in 1919, as black veterans returned from service in the Great War and talk arose of the rise of the "New Negro"—i.e., a more confident and assertive black populace that was less willing to acquiesce in the inequities of the prevailing racial social order. Increased anxiety over a series of sexual attacks committed by a black man in June and July of that year sparked assaults and armed combat between blacks and whites over four successive days which left six people dead and scores injured. *"Service Men Beat Negroes at Race Riot at Capital; Civilians Join to Avenge Attacks on White Women"* and *"Armed and Defiant Negroes Roam About Shooting at Whites"* screamed headlines in the *New York Times*, which editorialized nostalgically that before the Great War the "majority of the negroes in Washington" had been "well behaved. . . . Most of them admitted the superiority of the white race, and troubles between the two races were undreamed of."

Despite the new assertiveness of Washington blacks, disparate treatment of the races continued in the city during the administrations of the three Republican presidents who followed Woodrow Wilson in the 1920s. "Black people could sit on streetcars, read in the public library, and watch the Washington Senators play at Griffith stadium, but they could not go to concerts, sit next to white people at movies, or watch the Fourth of July fireworks from the Capitol steps," notes *Chocolate City*. "Black shoppers could shop at Garfinckels and other department stores downtown, but they could not try anything on. . . . Even U Street, the signature street of black Washington, included white-run cafes, ice cream parlors, and stores that operated on a segregated basis." With manifest irony organizers of the May 1922 dedication of the Lincoln Memorial, a shrine dedicated to the memory of the nation's Great Emancipator, "forced black ticket-holders to sit in a segregated area far from the stage" and censored the speech of the lone black speaker, leaving him only to mouth platitudes about American racial progress. At this same time restrictive racial covenants increasingly were devised to exclude D.C. blacks from moving into white enclaves, such as Chevy Chase, Maryland, founded by none other than the notorious Senator Newlands.

It was during these years and in this environment that Dr. James Alner Tobey—author of, among many other works, "The Death Rate Among Negroes" (*Current History*, November 1926)—resided in the District of Columbia. Dr. Tobey's sole detective novel, *The Capital Murder*, reflects the patronizing attitudes prevalent at the time among many white Americans, even those who proudly marched within the ranks of the Progressive movement. The novel opens in the garden at the Serpentine Club on N Street ("An old brick building . . . where Secretary Seward had once lived"), where some elite white clubmen are enjoying a nice discussion about murder. When the gentlemen hear "a faint wailing sound" resembling "a woman's scream, prolonged in terrible agony," one of their band, a naval lieutenant and all-round Lothario by the name of Runy O'Mara, snidely dismisses the eerie sound as "nothing but one of the [public service] commissioner's black wagons, probably out after some errant colored gentry." Soon, the butler Sam—whom Jim, the white narrator and "Watson" of the story, dubs "the club's colored factotum"—approaches the group and announces, "with typical Ethiopian unctuousness," that "there am a most important and urgent communication for you-all." Not much later, after returning with another message, Sam lingers, "with the darky's curiosity to see what it was all about." Jim does not let up with this condescension, later referring to his seeing a group of "Negro stevedores" in Norfolk, Virginia "busily at work, at least as ardently as is the Ethiopian custom." Nor does Jim confine his invidious stereotyping to "Ethiopians," later observing of an Argentine woman, "I gathered that she could be an ardent hater, as most Latins can."

Worse yet is Detective Yates of the D. C. police, who refers a couple of times to Pansy Thedford, the black maid of the murdered Argentine woman, Beatrice Sigurda, as a "nigger." When Thedford answers "brazenly" to the policeman's questions and declares "I'm going to get my lawyer, I am," Yates reduces the maid to cowering fear when he rises up before her and threatens, "You're going to answer my questions or go to jail." Later, when confronted with Miguel San Remo, Sigurda's "surly" gardener of Mestizo extraction (or a "half-breed," as the characters in the novel typically say), Detective Yates vows, "I'll break every bone in his nigger body if I have to do it to make him tell. . . . Someone who had a key and who knew this place came in here last night." At another point Yates refers to San Remo as "that dago" and promises to "third-degree him if necessary and he'll tell us or he'll sweat blood." Not one of the elite white characters in the novel ever finds fault with Yates for his pervasively brutish behavior. To the contrary, the detective receives praise for his diligent performance as a policeman—though of course it is amateur sleuth Trevor Stokes who does all the real brain work.

Only Detective Yates threatens minorities with outright physical violence, yet other characters in The Capital Murder share the hateful cop's bigoted attitudes, despite their having, one presumes, rather higher educations. The police medical examiner, upon his tardy arrival at the murder scene, complains, in reference to his lateness, "I've been off on as . . . wild a goose chase as it has ever been my hard luck to run up against. Here I get a hurry call to Taneytown [Maryland] to look at a coon who has been stabbed to death and find what? A trivial flesh wound in a buck who, mind you, didn't even get it in the District of Columbia. The whole festival took place across the line in Maryland. What a life!" Indeed. One can only sympathize with this man's unfortunate patients.

In addition to the D. C. medical examiner, there is that prominent and respected psychiatrist and Serpentine Club member, Dr. Basil Ragland, who gives his colleagues this dispiriting discourse, soaked with the scientific racism of the era, on the question of racial capacities and capital crime: "You can practically rule out the maid . . . the psychology does not fit. This crime was carefully planned. A Negro does not do that. When a Negro commits murder, as unfortunately does happen, it is either in a drunken frenzy or in an impulsive brawl. A mulatto might plan a homicide, but more likely against one of his own race. . . ."

In Twenties America there took place among black people a profound cultural awakening known as the "New Negro Renaissance" (it was associated most prominently with Harlem, New York); yet this vibrancy and wonder is utterly absent from *The Capital Murder*, where blacks appear exclusively as improbably simpleminded servants and, off stage, as cheap criminals. Happily the same year that saw the publication of Dr. Tobey's sole detective novel also saw that of Dr. Rudolph John Chauncey Fisher's sole detective novel, *The Conjure Man Dies*, which is set in Harlem among black characters. Like Dr. Tobey, Rudolph Fisher, an African American who was born in the nation's capital in 1897, was highly educated and knew science, having graduated with a Masters in biology from Brown University and summa cum laude from the Medical School at Howard University, a historically black college chartered in the District of Columbia in 1867, shortly after the end of the Civil War. Readers of *The Capital Murder* are urged to get a glimpse of black life though rather more discerning eyes than those of Dr. Tobey in Dr. Fisher's *The Conjure Man Dies*.

COACHWHIP PUBLICATIONS
COACHWHIPBOOKS.COM

COACHWHIP PUBLICATIONS
COACHWHIPBOOKS.COM

A
Matter of
Iodine

David Keith

COACHWHIP PUBLICATIONS
CoachwhipBooks.com

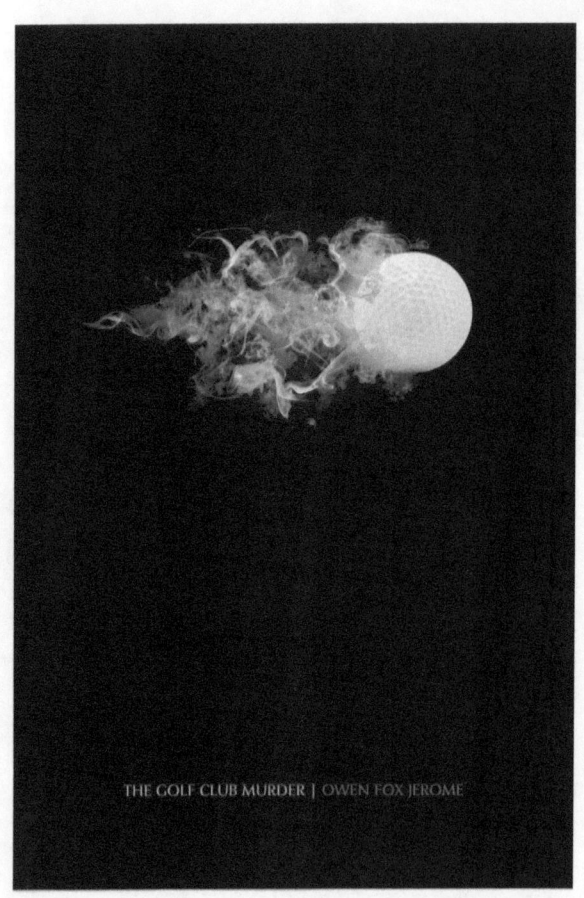

THE GOLF CLUB MURDER | OWEN FOX JEROME

COACHWHIP PUBLICATIONS
CoachwhipBooks.com

THE HEX MURDER

Alexander Williams